One Weekend

By

Shelley Banks

For the Grace Girls

Chapter 1

Evie looked down at the mountain of used tissues on the bedroom floor as if each one represented a tear. She would have to pick them up before she left, but she didn't have the energy yet. Nick's words from the night before kept repeating over and over in her head.

"Can't you do anything right," he'd said. "It was a simple task I asked you to do."

It was minor, at least to her, and certainly nothing to argue about. She'd forgotten to pick up one of the ingredients for the meal Nick was cooking. It wasn't even a main ingredient, just a garnish to sprinkle on top.

"You've ruined dinner," he'd continued. "I should have gone to the supermarket myself."

When Evie had pointed out that he was supposed to stop at the shops on the way home but had rung her during the day and said he wouldn't have time, it had made him angrier.

"It's all right for you. You don't have a stressful job like mine. You don't know what it's like to be under constant pressure."

Her job as a social worker wasn't exactly stress-free, and most days, she came home feeling exhausted, although it hadn't been the right time to point that out. Instead, she'd watched as he'd turned away from her and poured himself a glass of wine.

"I wouldn't mind a glass," she'd said.

"You know where the wine glasses are. Can't you see I'm busy?"

Considering Evie still had two loads of washing and a basket of ironing to get through before bed, Nick wasn't the only one who was busy. There was no point in offering to help with the cooking, though, because it was the one thing he insisted on doing by himself. He said it relaxed him, and he liked creating something from nothing that would turn out exactly as he wanted. Evie sometimes wondered if that's how he thought about her. She actually enjoyed cooking but only ever did it when Nick was away, travelling as part of his job as an IT consultant.

"While you're getting yourself a glass, can you get the chilli oil as well?"

"The chilli oil isn't anywhere near the wine glasses."

"I know that. But I told you I was busy. You can't just stand there and expect me to do all the work."

"Apart from cooking, you don't do any other work around the house."

"You are so ungrateful. I do so much for you, more than most men would. You're just too immature to see it. Sometimes I wonder how I've put up with you for so long."

He'd turned away from her before the first tear fell. Evie had got the chilli oil and then walked out of the kitchen. When they'd eventually sat down to eat dinner, he'd acted like nothing had happened.

As she continued to stare down at the tissues on the bedroom floor, she thought back to when they'd first started dating. Nick had been charming and adoring, and she felt like she'd been placed on a pedestal. It was after they'd moved in together that things started to change. Even though it was now nine years later, she kept hoping that he would return to the way he was in those first twelve months. A time when she didn't feel like she was walking on eggshells. At least for this weekend, she wouldn't need to worry about tiptoeing around anyone. Outside, she heard a car pull up on the driveway and called out to Nick.

"That'll be Gaby. Can you let her in while I finish packing?"

Her eyes were still puffy from the night before, and Evie didn't want Gaby to see she'd been crying, so she needed a few more minutes to hide the evidence.

From the bedroom, she could hear Nick open the front door. "She's still getting ready. I don't know what's taking her so long."

"That's fine," Gaby said. "I'm early. Do you mind if I make myself a coffee? It's been a hectic morning, and I need another one."

"Help yourself," Nick said. "I'm sure you know where the coffee and cups are."

Evie, still hiding in the bedroom, called out. "Was your morning the usual kind of hectic or more than that?"

"More than usual. Grace and Lucas had sport this morning, and they were misbehaving to the point where Oliver had to ask for my help to get them ready before I left. And Daisy and I had a fight. She's more argumentative than I was at eighteen."

Gaby hadn't had the time to be argumentative between study, a part-time job, and a house to look after. Yet, all these years later, Evie still remembered the weekly schedule Gaby used to pin to the board in her bedroom so she could keep track of everything. She'd been so determined to make a better life for herself. That determination had led her away from a house where a father had never been present and a mother who was always preoccupied with the latest boyfriend to a loving and, more importantly, stable home of her own.

"What was the fight with Daisy about?"

Daisy was Evie's goddaughter, and she'd spent a lot of time with her over the years, so she knew how stubborn she could be.

"She's not sure if she wants to continue on at university. She thinks she might want to try something else."

Evie smiled to herself as she finished packing. As a professor, Gaby found it hard to believe that people didn't want to do tertiary study. She'd met Oliver at the same university where she now lectured, and Evie knew how important education was to Oliver as well.

"It could just be that university is a lot different to high school, and she just needs more time to settle in."

"Maybe. I would hate to see Daisy throw away her degree and regret it later."

The concern in Gaby's voice was evident, even though Evie was listening from another room.

"Are you almost ready, Evie?" Nick asked. "Gaby's been waiting for a while."

"I'll be there in a minute."

Evie walked into the ensuite, closed the door behind her and checked one more time that she didn't look like she'd been crying. She'd done an excellent job with the concealer, but as she stared at her reflection in the mirror, she couldn't help wonder who it was looking back at her. The woman in the mirror had the same blonde hair, the same blue eyes and was still only as tall as the hook that had been fixed three-quarters of the way up on the back of the door. But there was no joy in the face that looked back. She pulled the small alfoil wrapped package out of her pocket and swallowed a quarter of the contents. She knew she shouldn't be doing it so close to leaving, but in the absence of natural joy, an artificial one would have to do. When she thought back, she couldn't pinpoint the moment she stopped recognising herself. She knew it began before she met Nick, although over the years she'd been with him, she seemed to be disappearing at a faster rate. Through the alfoil, she could feel them—three left—each the same size and shape. They were so small yet contained so much inner peace, and Evie didn't know what she'd do without them.

Before leaving the room, she checked that everything was where it was supposed to be and saw a magazine sticking up out of the bin. It was the one she'd read in the bath the other night. She didn't read magazines very often, but an article mentioned on the cover caught her eye. It was about a group of friends who thought they'd known all there was to know about each other. However, it turned out they'd all been keeping secrets, not just from their friends, but from everyone. She'd read the article several times and was still thinking about it days later. She rolled the magazine up and put it in her bag.

"Ready," Evie said as she walked into the lounge room.

"You look rushed," Gaby said. "Busy morning?"

"Not busy, just left everything until the last minute as usual," Nick said.

"No, I didn't," Evie said. "I had other things to do this morning besides pack. Anna rang, and we chatted for a while. She couldn't make her mind up about what to pack."

Gaby laughed. "Why does that not surprise me? It took me about 10 minutes to pack. A few clothes and my running shoes, and I was done."

Gaby had turned up in her usual attire of long pants and a t-shirt, with the addition of a cardigan to protect her from the winter chill. Her shoulder-length brown hair was up in a ponytail as always, and she wore no make-up. The only thing on her face were her glasses, which she rarely took off. It had been a long time since Evie had seen Gaby's hazel eyes without looking through glass.

"Did you ask Anna about her date last night?" Gaby asked.

"Of course I did. She said it was good."

"So in Anna speak, that means it went very well."

Evie had still been thinking about the fight with Nick when her phone had rung earlier that morning. She hadn't been in the right frame of mind to answer but changed her mind in case Anna had a question about the weekend. When she'd answered, Evie had been greeted with a yawn.

"Not enough sleep last night," Anna had said.

"So the date went well?"

"Yes, but not for the reason you're thinking. I had a meeting at the nursery association first, and it ran over, so I didn't get to dinner until late."

Evie could almost feel Anna blushing down the phone line, so she changed the subject. "Who has a meeting that goes into Friday night?"

"I know, but I found it useful, and there were some new people that were worth meeting."

"So, did you speak to them?"

"It took me most of the meeting to work up the courage, but if I want to expand the business, I need as much information and contacts as I can get. Are you packed and ready to go?"

"Almost."

"Me too. I was just ringing to check if we needed to bring our own linen. I tried ringing Laura, but she didn't answer. I forgot to ask her when we caught up on Wednesday night."

"No, we don't need to bring anything like that."

"Great, almost finished packing then. Just need a few more clothes, and I'm done. I'll see you later this morning."

After she'd hung up, Evie thought about how happy Anna had sounded. It had been a long time since Anna had been in a relationship, and Evie was glad that it was going well for her. If only Evie could say the same thing.

"I'll have to ask Anna for more details when we see her," Gaby said. "Are you ready to go?"

"Yes, let's get this weekend started."

"Do you want a hand to carry your things out to the car?" Nick asked.

"No, it's fine. I'll see you Sunday night."

Evie looked out the window as the car moved slowly through the suburban streets. It was still early, and the streets were quiet. No children playing in yards, no vehicles backing out of driveways to reach the first of Saturday's sports commitments on time, no one walking dogs or riding bicycles. The only sign others had been down these streets before them was the newspapers, rolled up in plastic, sitting on front lawns. The quietness helped her relax. She'd been looking forward to the weekend because spending time with her closest friends was just what she needed.

"How's work been this week?" Gaby asked.

"Really busy. I had one client who came in four times. Without going into details, she's a lovely person who's had some terrible things happen over the past two years, and she turned to alcohol and pot to help her cope. I've been helping her organise sessions with a psychologist and appointments with a not-for-profit group that helps people get back into the workforce. It's rewarding to see that she's making progress, but it's draining at the same time."

"I don't know how you do it. I wouldn't have the patience or the tact. And I think it's so dangerous to self-medicate. I wouldn't be able to stop myself from saying no."

Evie sat up straighter in the seat and cursed under her breath for mentioning that particular client. That was not a topic of conversation she wanted to be having.

"What about you? How's work been this week?"

"The usual lectures and tutorials, although I did chair a symposium this week about the expansion of digital media and how it has changed the way we collate and present information."

It's so like Gaby to casually mention something like chairing a symposium. Evie wanted to ask her more about it, but her phone rang.

"Morning," Laura said down the phone line. "Are you on your way?"

"Yes, what about you?"

"We just left. Sebastian was late to pick up Max. I guess I should be grateful that he turned up at all."

Sebastian was Laura's ex-husband, and he wasn't the most reliable person. He was more interested in himself than being there for other people, which sometimes included their son. Much to Laura's dismay.

"I'm glad he turned up, and Max gets to spend time with his dad. And I'm glad you're getting a weekend to yourself."

Laura sighed. "I really need it. This week has been so busy between the gallery and Max. As much as I love him, I can't wait to get there and have some me-time. Did I tell you I'm having another exhibition at the gallery?"

"No, that's exciting."

"I'm so happy about it. I keep teasing my boss, though, saying she only lets me hold an exhibition because I work there."

"You know that's not true. You're such a talented painter. I will definitely be there, and Gaby is nodding, so she'll be there too."

Laura laughed. "My biggest fans. We'll see you when we get there."

"I'm so glad we still go away on these weekends," Evie said.

"Me too," Laura said before hanging up.

Going away for the weekend was a tradition the four of them had started many years before. When they'd first started, it was a frequent occurrence, but as the years went on and their lives got busy with careers and husbands and children, it became once a year. After all this time, it was hard to imagine not being in each other's lives.

They'd clicked straight away when they first met in grade eight, and together they'd navigated their way through their teenage years and discovered make-up, music, clothes and boys. Now in their late thirties, they were still navigating, and it helped to have people to share the journey with. She knew she could always rely on her friends to be there for her. She could ring any of them at three in the morning, and they would come over if she needed them to. Picking up the phone was not something she was good at though.

"Do you ever wish you could go back to when we were teenagers?" Evie said.

"No. It was fun, but I prefer being older and wiser. I like that we've had experiences and that we've grown into ourselves."

"I wonder if I went back in time, knowing what I do now, would I make different decisions."

"What sort of decisions?"

"I don't know. It was just a random thought."

Evie liked the idea of a different life from the one she had now, but it wasn't something she wanted to talk about with Gaby. If Gaby wanted something different, she would make it happen, so her first question to Evie would be, why haven't you done something about it? And Evie wouldn't know what to say in response, so she left the thought unsaid.

"Are you cold?" Gaby said. "You look like you're shivering. I can turn up the heater."

Evie wasn't cold, just a little jittery, and she hadn't realised it was noticeable. It was hard to hide sometimes, and she couldn't bear the thought of Gaby realising what she'd done before she left the house.

"A little. Don't worry about turning the heater up though. I'll put my jacket on, and I'll be fine. Would you mind stopping at the next service station? I should have gone to the bathroom before I left."

As Evie stood in the grimy service station bathroom, she wondered for the second time that day how she had got here and who this person was looking back at her. She hated herself for not resisting the contents of the alfoil package before she left and for lying to Gaby, but she needed to get out of the car. She couldn't let Gaby find out. Or Anna or Laura. She reached into her pocket and pulled out the package. It should have gone to the bottom of her bag, but she'd wanted it close by. If it wasn't for the effects of the first tablet still in her system, she would be crying now, alone in a service station bathroom, trying to figure out how her life had strayed so far from where she wanted to be.

Chapter 2

"I think I can see Anna's car," Evie said. "Three behind us."

Gaby looked in the rear-view mirror. "Yes, that's them. Give Laura a call and see if they want to stop for a coffee somewhere."

Caffeine was the last thing Evie needed, but she called anyway. Laura said she'd seen a sign for a café and antique store in the next town, so they made plans to stop there.

As the car pulled into the café, Evie wound down her window and felt the drop in temperature. She'd always loved that time in autumn when the days were still warm, but there was a slight chill in the air. She closed her eyes for a minute, letting the cool air settle around her and thought back to a childhood holiday visiting relatives in Canberra. It had been autumn, and the leaves on the trees had started changing colour to vivid reds and oranges. She remembered how much fun she'd had playing in the thick piles of coloured leaves that had fallen on the ground, throwing them in the air and jumping around in them. Until her parents told her to stop because she was getting dirty. When she opened her eyes all she could see, apart from the café and shop, was a pub and a general store surrounded by hills that were sparsely covered with trees and a few cows grazing in paddocks. It was so quiet, and she liked it. So different from where she and Nick lived in Albion, with neighbours all around, cars driving by continuously and trains thundering down the track on the nearby train line.

Evie turned down the radio. "Listen to that."

"What?" Gaby said. "I can't hear anything."

"That's what I mean. There's no noise. Doesn't it seem strange?"

"You get used to it, I suppose," Gaby said. "It wouldn't suit me. I know it's peaceful, but I don't have much free time, and I like things to be close by. I have a short attention span; I need lots of different things to stimulate me."

Evie laughed. "I know. Remember Chris, the English backpacker. He was certainly different and talented if I remember rightly."

"That's not what I meant, and that was years ago. I'd rather forget that. Let's go meet the others."

Evie didn't have any experiences like that in her past. She'd moved out of home and in with her first serious boyfriend when she was nineteen. When they broke up four years later, it was only a few months before she met Matthew, who eventually became her first husband. It turned out that while he liked the idea of being in a committed relationship, after seven years together, he decided he wanted a different life and joined Médecins Sans Frontières and headed to Africa, leaving Evie behind. There had been a lot of jokes about a seven-year itch, but Evie hadn't found any of them funny. It wasn't long after that when she met Nick.

"I thought you'd be ahead of us," Gaby said as she gave Anna a hug.

"Laura forgot her sketchpad," Anna said. "We had to go back and get it."

Laura tumbled out of the car, her bag falling out behind her. "Nobody make me feel bad, please. I've had a rough morning, and Meg came over for a visit last night and didn't leave until late."

Evie smiled and gave her a hug. "So you're up for a big night tonight."

"I'll be fine. It's not the first time, and I'm sure it won't be the last."

Evie watched as Laura picked up her bag, tucked her long red curls behind her ears and pulled her sunglasses down from the top of her head, covering her green eyes. She straightened her cream jumper, so it sat over the band of her jeans, then checked if anything else needed adjusting. There was something different about her this morning, but Evie couldn't put her finger on it. She looked drained, as if she'd been up late and had a bad morning.

Anna leaned down and picked up the lip balm that had fallen out of Laura's bag. "Are you sorted now?"

Laura poked her tongue out in reply. "You know it's your job to help keep me organised."

Anna laughed. "And has been since high school."

"How long since you've seen Meg?" Evie asked.

"Three weeks ago, when she called in to drop off some hand-me-downs for Max."

Meg was Sebastian's sister and was the opposite of her brother. While Sebastian was the black sheep of the family, Meg and their parents were very family-oriented. It was important to them that Max spent time with his relatives. They were the opposite of Nick's family. The thought of catching up with any of them on her own didn't appeal to Evie at all.

"Can we sit at the table under the awning?" Anna asked after they'd ordered their coffee. "I've left my hat in the car."

As they sat down, Evie made sure she was on the side of the table looking out so she could keep her sunglasses on.

"This is such a luxury," Laura said. "Just to sit still and not have anyone calling out for you every five minutes."

Gaby smiled. "Couldn't agree more."

"This weekend, it's Sebastian who'll have to deal with that," Anna said.

"That's what I'm worried about. He's not the most hands-on dad in the world, but he needs to spend time with Max."

Gaby reached over and grabbed Laura's hand. "He'll be fine. For all his faults, he would never let anything happen to Max."

"I know, it's just hard not to worry. But if I'm going to relax at all this weekend, I have to stop thinking about it. And I can't think of a better place to relax than the top of a mountain. That's why I chose it."

Each year they took turns choosing where they would go. The previous year, Evie had arranged a penthouse overlooking the beach at Mooloolaba. The year before that, Gaby had booked a beach house on Stradbroke Island. When it had been Anna's turn, she organised a cabin in the Bunya Mountains. She had initally suggested they try camping for something different, but that idea was immediately dismissed. None of the others were enthusiastic campers. They liked electricity, running water and flushing toilets too much. Evie had only been camping once, on Fraser Island while she was in high school. She'd gone with the neighbours and their kids. She'd enjoyed it, except for having to squat behind a tree to go to the toilet and getting bitten on the backside by insects. If she'd gone a few more times when she was younger, she might still enjoy it. She'd never slept as well as she had then with the sound of the ocean to sing her to sleep and wake her gently in the morning.

"What time can we get into the house, Laura?" Gaby asked.

"Not till 2pm. That's when the neighbour will be home to give us the key. I thought we could have lunch first."

"Always thinking of food," Anna said.

Laura turned to look at Anna with a pouty look on her face. "I don't always think of food. I'm just very hungry today."

Anna laughed. "You know I'm teasing you."

"Anyone else want to have a look in that antique shop when we've finished our coffees?" Evie asked.

Anna nodded. "I would."

"As long as you don't take too long," Gaby said. "I want to get up to the mountain so I can relax."

There were so many objects crammed into the cool, dark, musty shop that it was hard to walk around without knocking something over. Evie loved old furniture and knick-knacks because she felt they told a story. She stopped and looked at an old Singer sewing machine standing solidly, almost proudly, near the front counter, and she wondered about its original owner. What was she like? Where and when had she lived? Had she been loved? There was nothing like that in the house she shared with Nick. Clutter, he called it, someone else's old junk. Their home was full of modern furniture, clean lines and lots of space. It was a lot like the house she'd grown up in. Her parents didn't see the point of spending money on anything old or anything that didn't have an exact purpose. She couldn't recall them ever buying anything just because they thought it was beautiful.

"Found anything?" Anna asked.

"These earrings are pretty," Evie said. "I wonder how old they are."

"If you buy them, make sure you disinfect them before you wear them," Gaby said.

"The earrings are pretty and would look great on you, Evie. Has anyone else found something they want to buy?" Anna asked.

"There's nothing here that would last more than five minutes in my house before someone broke it," Gaby said.

Evie laughed. "That's because your children are like you and can't sit still."

Every time Evie went to Gaby's house, it was a whirlwind of activity. No matter what time of the day it was, there was always something going on. It was a loud and chaotic house but also a happy one. The sound of laughter would always be heard at some point during her visits. It was also a house brimming with love.

"What about you, Anna," Evie asked. "Seen anything?"

"I love some of this furniture," Anna said as she ran her fingers across the top of a mahogany hall table with carved legs and gold handles gracing its two drawers. Her fingertips left a trail through the thin layer of dust on top. "It's so elegant and graceful. I don't know how I'd get it home though."

Laura walked up to her and playfully took hold of Anna's arm and began to pull her away. "You don't need any more furniture."

Anna turned to look at her and poked her tongue out. "Needing more furniture and wanting more furniture are two very different things."

Images of the rooms in Anna's house popped into Evie's mind, and the hall table would fit in perfectly with the rest of the antiques she had. She always felt like she was stepping back in time when she went to Anna's, and it was so calm and peaceful that she instantly felt relaxed as soon as she walked through the door. She felt immediately welcome too.

Laura laughed. "You shouldn't want any more furniture either."

"I know, I'm not going to buy anything. Are you?"

Laura nodded. "I want some of those knick-knacks over there. I've got a craft piece that I'm working on, and they would work really well with what I've done so far. I might get a pair of those earrings as well. I like the ones Evie's picked up. I'll be quick, so we can go and find somewhere for lunch."

Anna looked at Laura and sighed. "I don't know anyone who eats as much as you. I don't know where you put it either. You're almost the same size you were in high school."

Laura patted her stomach. "Fast metabolism, and now I'm a size ten, not a size eight. I think those days are long gone."

Anna looked down at her own stomach. "I wish I had a fast metabolism."

"What are you worried about," Laura said. "There's nothing of you."

"There's more of me than there is of you."

"You obviously need to buy a new mirror. Come on, we better hurry. Gaby's waiting."

"Ok. Just give me a second. I want to have one more quick look at that chair over there. I won't be far behind you."

Alone in the shop, Anna watched as Laura walked towards the car. She was so beautiful, and for Laura, it was effortless. Anna couldn't remember a time when she wasn't trying to do something to change the way she looked. As soon as Laura mentioned lunch, Anna's stomach started grumbling. The fruit and yoghurt she'd had for breakfast had been delicious, and a large serving she'd thought, but at the first mention of food, she started to feel hungry. It had been the same last night when she'd had dinner with Ethan. She'd ordered a Vietnamese salad, and it had been a large serving too. But as soon as Ethan mentioned ordering dessert, her stomach started making noises. It had been hard not to order dessert and then sit there and watch every mouthful he took of the cheesecake.

Anna paused to look at the chair one more time before she walked out of the shop. As much as she liked it, Laura was right; she didn't need any more furniture. However, buying it would have stopped the thoughts running through her mind. Before getting into the car, she had a quick look at herself in the side mirror. She was glad she'd been to the hairdresser and had the colour re-done. She loved having black hair. It made her sapphire eyes pop. But if she didn't get the colour refreshed regularly, it could look dull.

"Stop looking at yourself in the mirror," Laura said. "You look as beautiful as always."

Laura often told her she was beautiful, but she never believed her. Anna knew what she looked like. She pulled on the baggy jumper she was wearing so it covered as much of her thighs as it could.

"Everyone ready to go?" Gaby asked.

They all nodded and got into the cars.

"Are they new jeans?" Laura asked.

Anna nodded. "I decided to treat myself and get a new pair for this weekend. The boots are new as well."

Laura laughed. "How many pairs of boots do you own now?"

"Not that many, and they suit my life. I can wear them to work and on the weekend."

"I hope you wore high heels on your date last night."

"Yes, I did. I even wore a dress."

"Glad to hear it. So how did the date go?"

Anna spent the next few minutes talking about the date with Ethan.

Laura smiled and reached over and squeezed Anna's hand. "I'm so happy for you. He seems like a really nice guy. I'm glad you're back in the relationship game."

"I wasn't ready before this. And you can't talk. You're not in a hurry to start another relationship."

"I'm still trying to deal with the fallout from the last one. It's a lot harder when there's a child involved. And besides, we're not talking about me."

"Aren't we?"

"No, now we better go, or we'll lose Gaby and Evie," Laura said as she turned to look out the window."

Over in Gaby's car, Evie was also staring out the window, but not at the scenery, when Gaby's phone beeped.

"Can you check that for me just in case it's Oliver or one of the kids?"

She'd been thinking about Nick and their fight again. As much as she didn't want to think about it because she didn't want it to ruin the weekend, it still crept in. Evie picked up Gaby's phone. The entire family was staring back at her from the photo Gaby had as the wallpaper. They were all smiling and had their arms around each other. It took her a moment to stop looking at the photo and open the message.

"It's Oliver. Both kids won their matches this morning."

"That's great. They'll be happy about that."

As they drove on, Evie thought back to when she was a child and wanted to play a sport. Being part of a team was something she craved. Spending time at training or at games with kids her own age, all working together for a common goal, all relying on each other to do their part and not let the team down. Her parents were so busy with their lives—jobs, friends, interests—that they didn't have time to take her to the training sessions or the games. She'd done ballet for a little while only because the neighbour's daughter also attended the same dance school, so more often than not, she got a lift with them. She'd only been going for five months when she lost interest. After her first recital, her parents said to her that maybe ballet was a waste of time and money because she wasn't very good. After that, she didn't try anything else.

"It's peaceful driving up the mountain with trees lining both sides of the road," Gaby said.

"More peaceful than down there," Evie said, pointing to the Gold Coast in the distance.

From the car, they could see the entire Gold Coast and the sparkling Pacific Ocean. Evie hoped the house they were staying in had a view like the one they were looking at. She'd always felt there was something calming about a beautiful view, and ocean views were her favourite. She liked going to the beach. The warm, gritty sand between her toes and the crispness of the cool water when she dived under the waves.

"I'm glad we're up here and not down there," Gaby said. "I really need a break, and going to the Gold Coast isn't relaxing."

"Is that because of this morning's fight with Daisy, or is it more than that?"

"Yes, it's because of Daisy, but not just the fight. She hasn't been acting like herself lately, and this morning isn't the first time we've had a fight. It's been happening a lot lately, and I don't know why."

"Maybe things aren't going as well as she'd like with the new boyfriend. Or maybe something is happening at university. That might be why she's not sure if she wants to continue with her studies."

"I don't know what it is because every time I ask, she says nothing is wrong and tells me to stop asking."

"Is there anything I can do to help?"

Gaby shook her head. "I'm sure everything will be fine. It's just been a tough week. All I want to do this weekend is not argue with anyone. I just want peace and quiet."

Evie reached over and squeezed Gaby's hand. "Ok, but I'm here if you need anything. And you'll have that as soon as we get to the house. I hope the setting there is something like what we're driving through now."

The higher up the mountain they drove, the more beautiful it became. The air was clearer, the grass thicker and greener, there were birds in the trees, and the view expanded so they could see more of the coastline because of the higher vantage point. At that moment, they were driving through a national park that looked like a forest from a fairytale with lots of thick, dark trees and, Evie thought, an underlying hint of menace like all good fairytale forests should have. She liked the changing scenery. The contrast of the brown lifeless grasses, ravaged by the lastest drought, at the base of the mountains, to the deep green undergrowth that flourished beneath the thick canopy of trees as they ascended.

When they finally reached the village at the top of Mt Tamborine, Evie couldn't believe how different it was from what they'd seen on the way up, and she wasn't sure if she liked it. The wide, tree-lined main street was swarming with people wandering up and down, stopping to look in craft shops and art galleries, buying things for their city homes. There was even a cuckoo clock shop for those who felt inclined to add such a thing to their lounge rooms. Evie wondered what it would look like with all the tourists gone and if the people who lived there sometimes wished the tourists would all go back to where they came from. They walked along the main street until they found a café with a menu that looked appetising.

"Everything looks so delicious," Laura said. "I don't know what to get. What are you having, Anna?"

"The salad."

"I don't know why I asked. You always order a salad. What about you, Evie?"

"I don't know. I'm not that hungry."

Laura peered at her over the menu. "Don't tell me you're on a diet or something."

Evie shook her head. It wasn't a diet. It was a side effect of the tablets. Not that she'd tell them that. "No, just not hungry. Maybe I'll get one of the entrees."

"Are you ladies ready to order?"

Evie looked up at the incredibly handsome waiter standing next to their table. She couldn't think of the last time she looked at Nick the way she was looking at the waiter, and she couldn't take her eyes off him the whole time they were ordering. Even though she'd always thought Nick was good looking, it had been a long time since she'd wanted him like she used to.

"If that's everything, I'll go and place your orders and bring your drinks back in a minute. It shouldn't take too long for the food to come out. If you need anything, just give me a shout."

"Thanks," Gaby said.

Laura watched him as he walked away. "I wonder what his definition of anything is."

"Behave yourself," Anna said.

"I am behaving myself. I can look, can't I?"

"That's all you can do. This is a girls-only weekend, remember."

"Spoilsport. Anyway, you know I'm not ready for anything like that."

"So, Anna, how was your date last night?" Gaby asked. "Evie didn't have a lot to tell me."

"That's because I didn't say a lot on the phone. I was in a hurry this morning."

"We've got plenty of time now," Gaby said. "And we're all curious."

"I'm not," Laura said. "I grilled her in the car."

"Then, Evie and I need to catch up."

"I don't understand why you're all so curious."

Evie smiled. "Because we're sticky beaks, and Gaby and I haven't met him yet. And because it's been a while since you've been in a relationship, which is understandable considering how the last one ended, but we'd like to see you with someone again."

Anna's last relationship had ended because her fiancé had cheated on her. She'd been with him for eight years, and it turned out that he'd cheated on her more than once during that time. The experience had put Anna off dating for a few years. And it had taken her a long time to trust again. But Anna was more than capable of being on her own. Unlike Evie.

"I had a great time. Ethan is a really nice guy, and we get along well together. We went to dinner, and then he drove me home. He's taking me out again tomorrow night after we get back."

Gaby smiled. "Very keen. I like that."

Laura smiled too. "Yes, he is very keen. Or so Anna's told me."

Anna blushed. "That's enough for now. Time to change the subject. Guess who I bumped into this week? Rachel Anderson."

Gaby groaned. "I couldn't stand her in high school, and I doubt I'd feel any different now. Was she still the same?"

Anna nodded. "She only stopped for a couple of minutes to tell me about the trip she'd just taken to Paris and the pool they were having put in at home. The home they'd just extensively renovated, she had to add."

Evie hadn't liked Rachel in high school either. They'd been friends in primary school up until grade seven, but then Rachel started to change and began thinking she was better than everyone else. The first day of grade eight, when they were lining up for the bus to go to school camp, she'd walked right by Evie as if she didn't know her. Evie had been upset the whole way to camp, but as soon as she got there, she met Gaby, who was in the same dormitory. She had the bunk under Evie's, and she'd offered to share her packet of sherbet lollies. She also became friends with Anna at the camp, but not until the last day. Anna had been so shy that she'd spent the whole week on her own. Evie couldn't stand anyone being on their own, so on the third day, she marched up and told her that from now on, she would be her and Gaby's friend. Evie had met Laura in homeroom when she sat down next to her. Laura had always been artistic, and she did the most beautiful drawings and paintings. She'd sold quite a few, and even back in high school, was selling them. Laura had always been the most outrageous one. She'd always said it was because of her artistic temperament, but Gaby, Evie, and Anna had always told her she used that as an excuse for how she behaved. Evie remembered her going up to a group of tourists one New Year's Eve and asking them if she could kiss them on the cheek and then proceeded to kiss all five of them before she walked away. Evie knew she was lucky to have such long-lasting friendships, but she wondered what would happen to those friendships if the others found out about the alfoil package and its contents. Thinking of that brought her back to the magazine article she'd read. The more she thought about it, the more she realised she would never be able to do what the women in the article had done—tell a secret that had never been told before. The secret she had was worse than anything the others could possibly have.

Chapter 3

"Look at this place," Evie said. "It's wonderful. How did you find it, Laura?"

"The lady who owns it plays tennis with Mum. She uses it as a weekend retreat, but she's gone overseas for a month and was happy for us to use it."

"Great timing."

"Yes. I was a bit worried before we got here though. Mum said the house was lovely, but you know what her taste is like sometimes."

"Remember that night when your mum picked us up from the school disco?" Evie said, laughing.

Gaby laughed at the memory too. "I will never forget the sight of Laura's mum getting out of the car in her hot pink leopard print pyjamas with matching slippers."

"That's mum," Laura said. "As far she was concerned, it was late, and she couldn't be bothered changing before leaving the house."

Evie hadn't known at the time what had shocked her more –
that Laura's mum had left the house in pyjamas or that she owned
hot pink and leopard print pyjamas. Evie's mum only owned navy
blue or dark grey pyjamas, and if she'd seen the hot pink and leopard
print ones, she would have said they were vulgar.

"It's perfect," Laura said, surveying the view. "I'm glad I
went back to get my sketchpad. I'm going to sit out here tomorrow
morning and draw everything I can see. The light will be better
then."

Anna rested her hand on Laura's shoulder and grinned.
"Does that mean you're getting up early?"

Laura turned to look at her with an expression that Anna had
seen many times before. "Early-ish. I'm going to take a few photos
now so I can paint the scene later. I'll get a couple of the house as
well. I'm sure I'll add it to a painting or drawing at some point."

The house was an old Queenslander, raised on stumps with a
verandah along the front and side. The yard was bigger than Evie's
at home and much greener. Nick was supposed to do the gardening,
but he never spent much time in the yard, and the comments he

made when Evie did it put her off doing any gardening more than a few times a year. *You didn't prune that tree evenly. There are still weeds in that garden. The potted plant you bought doesn't suit our yard. You don't have a green bone in your body.* Nick's words whirled through her mind until she forced herself to focus on what was in front of her. A yard and gardens that had been lovingly tended. She kicked off her shoes so she could feel the thick, soft grass with her bare feet.

"Evie, can you sit on the love seat?" Laura said. "I want to get a photo."

As soon as Evie sat down, she could see why the owners had put the love seat where it was. The house stood on the side of Mt Tamborine that faced the Gold Coast. Evie could see all the way down the mountain, across the flat, farming land, to the suburbs behind the coast and then all the way to the ocean. The way the light glistened on the water was magical. She could see why Laura wanted to take photos and later turn them into paintings.

"Gaby and Anna, can you come and sit down as well," Laura called. "It might be a bit crowded on the chair, but I'd like to get some photos of the three of you."

Laura took a couple of photos and said she'd give them all a copy.

"What about you?" Gaby asked. "We need one of the four of us."

"I'll set the timer then. Move over."

Laura rushed over and jumped onto the end of the seat, bumping into Anna, who bumped into Evie, who bumped into Gaby. Then, all three watched as Gaby fell off the chair and onto the grass. In the background, the camera went off.

"That's going to be a great photo," Laura said, laughing.

"Excuse me if I disagree with you. You're not the one who was on the ground with one leg in the air," Gaby said, although she was smiling as she said it.

Evie couldn't stop laughing. "I bet it's a great photo. You could get it framed."

Gaby looked up at her. "Ha, ha. Now, move over so I can sit back on the seat like a grown-up."

Anna reached over and squeezed Gaby's shoulder. "Are you all right?"

Gaby nodded. "Yes, I'm fine. Although I do have a grass stain on my pants now."

"That'll come out," Laura said. "Now, everyone look towards the camera again. I'm going to reset it."

The four friends squished together on the seat, put their arms around each other and smiled at the camera. Evie was smiling partly for the photo and partly because she was thinking about how nice it was to be with the people she knew so well and cared about so much. She would frame and cherish the copy of the photo she got.

"Smell these flowers," Anna said as she leant down next to the rose garden that had been planted beside the love seat.

The garden was filled with red, white, yellow and apricot roses. Evie loved apricot roses. They were her favourite flower. She'd already smelt them before she sat down but now that Anna had mentioned them, she got up to have another look and to smell them again. She couldn't remember the last time anyone had bought her roses. Evie leaned over and touched the petals. They were soft to touch, and the smell wafted up under her nose. It reminded her that sometimes the simple things were the most amazing. She straightened up, headed over to the house, climbed the timber stairs, crossed the verandah and walked through the front door. Her hand went up to lift her sunglasses off her face when she stopped herself. What if there was something about her eyes that would give away what she'd taken in the bathroom at home? She hoped enough time had passed. The only time she'd taken them off since she'd left home was in the service station bathroom and the antique shop. It had been very dark in the shop, so she felt sure that no one would have noticed anything.

Gaby came and stood beside her. "Who wants what room?"

"Don't care," Evie said.

Laura walked through the door and threw her bags into the first room. "I want this one. I want to look out at the view in the morning."

The room Laura chose was the most beautiful in the house, with a black wrought iron four-post bed with a white lace canopy, two wrought iron tables with oil lamps resting on them, and a timber wardrobe that stood in the corner of the room, the smell of lavender coming from its open doors. In the morning, Laura would be able to open the French doors that led out to the verandah so she could take in the view.

"What do you think?" Laura asked. "Isn't this room amazing? It's so beautiful. I don't feel graceful enough to be in here."

Evie sat down on the bed. "I could always sleep in here instead of you."

"No chance. I'll get over it."

Anna stuck her head in through the open doorway.

"I'm going to take the room opposite if no one else minds."

"Fine by me," Gaby said. "I've already looked in there, and it's almost identical to this room, both of which are too frilly for me. There's a bedroom down the hall that's decorated in a much plainer way, and that suits me."

"Guess that leaves the only remaining room for me," Evie said.

Evie walked further down the hallway, taking in every detail as she went. She loved old Queenslander style homes. She loved their beauty and grace, their sense of warmth and homeliness, and also their history. According to the plaque beside the front door, the house had been built in 1911 and had all the features she loved about old houses – casement windows, VJ walls, polished timber floors, twelve-foot high ceilings, hanging lights, ceiling roses and a long hallway that ran down the middle of the house. The house had character, and it felt like it had been lived in. At the end of the hall, she found her room. When Gaby had said it was decorated in a much plainer style, she was right. There was a timber double bed, a small wardrobe and dressing table and an oval-shaped mirror on the wall next to the window. Through the window, she could see the backyard. The room reminded her of staying at her grandparents' house when she was a child. Her dad's parents' house hadn't been as fancy as this one, but it had felt just as warm and inviting. Across the hall, she could hear Gaby unpacking. Before leaving her room, she pulled the package out of her pocket. She added the tablets to the others in the small plastic zip-lock bag at the very bottom of her overnight bag where no one could accidentally find them. She also hoped it would be less tempting to think about them if they were in another room, so she walked across the hall to see how Gaby was going with her unpacking.

"You must be excited to have a bed to yourself."

Gaby nodded. "I'm tempted to sleep diagonally and take up the whole bed. No one will be snoring, and no one is going to come in while it's still dark and jump on the bed."

Evie pointed to the running shoes on the floor. "You'll be up early anyway for your run."

"Yes, but it won't be as early as I usually go. I'm going to treat myself and sleep in until 6.00am."

Evie laughed. "You do realise that most people wouldn't think of 6.00am as a sleep in."

"It is for me.

"What are all those?" Evie asked, pointing to bottles of expensive cleansers and moisturisers on the dressing table. "You don't normally use that stuff."

"I won it at a raffle at the kids' school, so I thought I may as well use it. No point wasting it."

Evie picked up one of the bottles. "I wonder if any of these would work for me."

"You don't need them, and they're a waste of money," Gaby said. "If I hadn't won them, they wouldn't be here. What's your room like?"

"Much the same as this one but the side wall looks like a more recent addition than yours. I wonder if it used to be a sleepout on a semi-enclosed part of the verandah."

"It's possible. A lot of these old houses had sleepouts."

"My grandparent's house did, and that's where I used to sleep when we visited when I was a kid. James and I would always fight over who got what bed because we both wanted the one under the windows."

"Who used to win?"

"He did. I'm going to finish unpacking."

"Ok. I'll do the same. Then I think we should crack open one of those bottles of wine."

Gaby watched Evie leave her room. She'd already unpacked, but she needed a few minutes before she joined the others. The fight with Daisy that morning was still bothering her. Something had been going on lately, but Daisy wouldn't talk to her about it, and Gaby knew it was more than not being sure if she wanted to continue with her degree. They'd never had any issues with Daisy before. Until now, she'd always been happy and content and had always spoken to her or Oliver if anything was bothering her. She was grateful for Oliver being his usual level headed, calm self over the past few months since Daisy had started acting up. Gaby didn't know what she'd do without him. Ever since that first day when they'd sat on the grass together back at university and talked for their entire break period, Gaby had known that there would never be anyone else for her but Oliver. He brought stability to her chaotic life and had a family like she had never experienced. If she was honest with herself, his family was part of the reason she was attracted to him in the first place. Nothing was more important to them than family. So different to Gaby's own family or what there was of it. And then there was the reason that Gaby would always think of Oliver as the most amazing man in the world. The reason she had never told anyone. Surely there was no way Daisy could have discovered something?

"Almost finished unpacking Gaby?" Evie called out.

Gaby got up off the bed. She didn't want Evie walking in and finding her doing nothing when she said she would be unpacking. Evie would know straight away that something was wrong. Maybe that wasn't such a bad thing though. Gaby had been thinking a lot lately about talking with her friends about the secret she had kept for so many years. She knew she would have to tell Daisy, Grace and Lucas at some point. It was Daisy's reaction she was most worried about. For the first time in a long time, she was nervous about something. If she talked to her friends first, they might be able to give her some advice about how to say the thing she should have said years before but kept putting off because she thought the time wasn't right. Gaby knew there would never be a right time, and she also knew she shouldn't put it off any longer. Before Evie had spoken, Gaby had been sitting on the bed going over the fight and the words Daisy had hurled at her in the lounge room that morning.

"You don't understand me. And you don't listen to me either. I'm not happy being at university."

"Maybe it's just the course you're doing. You should look at some other courses and see if there is something you might like better."

"Why aren't you listening to me? You're so frustrating. You've just ignored what I said. It's not the course. I don't know if I like going to university."

"But it's the best option for you."

"No, it's not. It's the option you want for me. It's my life, and I want to do what makes me happy. Stop trying to turn me into you."

"I'm not. I just don't want you to make the wrong decision."

"I'll make the decision that's right for me. I'm eighteen now. I don't have to listen to what you tell me anymore. It's my choice and my decision, so leave me alone."

Gaby had watched as Daisy stormed out of the lounge room, ran up the stairs to her bedroom and slammed the door. She hadn't responded when Gaby had knocked on her door and said she going. She still hadn't replied to the text message Gaby had sent while they'd been having coffee at the antique shop either.

"Did you hear me, Gaby," Evie called out again

She put her phone down before replying to Evie. "Yes, sorry. One more minute and I'll be done."

"Ok. I just need to take my shoes off and put my slippers on, and then I'll head out to the lounge room. I think Laura is already there. Anna is probably still unpacking. You know she always packs too much."

"I heard that," Anna called out. "And I don't overpack. I just want to make sure I have everything I need and an outfit to suit whatever we might do."

Evie stuck her head through the doorway to Anna's room. "We usually don't do anything on these weekends but sit around, talk and drink wine."

"We've gone out before," Anna said.

"Not very often."

"It doesn't hurt to be prepared," Anna said. "I'll be finished unpacking in a minute."

Chapter 4

Laura listened to her friends bantering from the lounge room, where she was already curled up on a comfy chair. She didn't have the energy to unpack, so she just dumped her bag on the bed and came and sat down. Between the dramas that morning and how she felt, she needed a few moments alone. It had started when she woke up with a bad headache and a queasy stomach, which neither bacon and eggs nor two cups of coffee could fix. Then Sebastian had turned up, looking happy and content with his new life. She'd cried after he'd gone. Even though it had been two years since he'd moved out, it still hurt every time she saw him and saw how easily he'd moved on with his life, as if the years they'd spent together didn't matter at all.

Laura's thoughts were interrupted as Gaby walked into the room. "Can you find some wine glasses? I think they're in that hutch in the corner of the dining room. I'll grab the wine from the fridge."

The thought of wine made Laura's stomach turn, but she got up anyway and found the glasses. In the back of her mind, she could still see the two empty wine bottles sitting on her kitchen floor at home, hidden behind the bin. She'd been so busy getting Max ready to go with his dad and finishing her own packing she hadn't had time to take them to the recycling bin outside. She could still picture the look of excitement on Max's face as he waited for his dad. She'd been happy that Max was spending time with his dad, but at the end of the weekend, she would be the one who would have to deal with the tears after Sebastian left. It was something she'd talked about with Meg last night. Meg had been married for fifteen years and had four children. She couldn't understand why Sebastian had left, and she said that to him every chance she got. She spent more time with Laura than she did with her own brother, although that had more to do with Sebastian than it did Meg. It had been nice to spend some time with Meg, but Laura now wished she'd gone to bed earlier and hadn't drunk any more wine after Meg had left. She thought about getting a headache tablet, but Anna walked in and sat down.

"I'm relaxed already. Are we going to open the wine?"

"Gaby's doing that now, and Evie is putting together a cheese platter," Laura said.

"How can anyone be hungry? We only just had lunch."

"Lunch was hours ago. A nice cheese platter and a chance to sit here by the fire and not move for a while is just what I need."

"I like the sound of that too. I didn't tell you that mum rang after I got home from my date and she wanted to chat. It ended up being after 1am before I got to sleep."

"That's late to be ringing."

"She's as interested in how things are going with Ethan as you all are. She rings a few times a week just to check we're still dating."

Laura laughed. "You know she just wants you to be happy. And you've had enough dates now for it to be classed as a relationship."

"It's only been two months."

"Neither of you is seeing anyone else, and you're spending more and more time together. Sounds like a relationship to me."

"I'm not ready to call it that yet. Ethan is lovely, and we're having a great time together, but I need to take things slowly."

Gaby walked in and put the wine down on the table. "You two look comfy."

Laura smiled. "I figured you had it all under control, so I thought I'd stay where I was."

"Did I hear you say something about your mum Anna?" Evie asked as she put the food on the table next to the wine. "How is she?"

"She's good. She rang really late last night because she went to the local RSL with her ballroom dancing group. They'd had a class earlier in the night, and none of them wanted to go home, so they headed to the club because there is always a band playing on a Friday night."

Evie had an image of Anna's mum on the dance floor. She would be the first one up and the last one to leave, unlike Anna, who would be the first to leave the floor and the last to get up and dance.

"Sounds like she's having a ball," Gaby said as she handed each of them a glass of wine before curling up on a chair. "It's not something I would ever do. You all know I've got two left feet. Being here, though, is something I love. Why do we only do it once a year?"

"Because we're all so busy that it's hard to find a weekend when we're all free," Anna said.

Gaby sighed. "I know you're right. And I know I'm the one that's hardest to pin down for a date and time when I have nothing on. Sometimes I feel like I put things in my diary six months in advance to make sure I can fit it in."

Evie smiled when she thought about all the times they'd texted each other back and forth, trying to find a time when they were both free to catch up. It was hard enough just organising the two of them, let alone all four of them.

"Gaby's not the only one that might need to put things in her diary six months in advance," Anna said. "I have some news, but I wanted to wait until we were all sitting down and weren't going to be interrupted."

All three of them looked at her, wondering what the news could be. Evie went through the possibilities in her head. Marriage? She couldn't picture Anna rushing into that so quickly. Pregnant? No, it couldn't be that either because she was drinking wine.

Moving? Evie didn't think it would be that either because Anna loved her house too much. So that left…

"I'm opening another nursery."

"That's fantastic," Evie said. "When you said this morning you were expanding, I thought you meant the one you already have, not opening a new one. You must be so excited. When did you decide this?"

"I've been thinking about it for a while. This is the first time I've told anyone apart from Laura. It is exciting and also scary."

Laura reached over and squeezed Anna's hand. "I don't think you have anything to worry about. You've done an amazing job with the one you have now. A second one would be just as good."

"And a lot more work," Anna said. "But I love what I do."

Evie thought about her job. Could she say she loved it? Some days she did, and other days she couldn't wait to leave and get away from the stress and the dramas that were an almost everyday occurrence. Not that different from the rest of her life, if she was honest. But she couldn't deny the sense of achievement she felt when she was able to help someone else.

"I think that's great news as well, Anna," Gaby said, "So where is the second nursery?"

Anna spent the next ten minutes talking about the details, including where it was located, how big it was and how she was still in negotiations with the current owners. Even though there was still a lot to do, they could all hear the eagerness in her voice.

"I think we're far enough along, though, that I can talk about it now and feel confident that I'll be able to sign the papers in the next few weeks."

"And we'll have a celebration when you do," Laura said, as Evie and Gaby nodded in agreement. "It's a huge achievement. And we're all here if you need any help or support."

Gaby nodded. "It's definitely something to celebrate. I know how much the nursery means to you."

"Maybe we could help you organise a grand opening," Evie said.

Laura leaned forward in her chair. "Yes! And we could end the day with a cocktail party, and everyone has to get dressed up."

Anna laughed. "I have to sign the papers first but thank you for your support. Once I know the new nursery is officially mine, then we can talk about openings."

Gaby took a sip of her wine then turned to Laura. "I didn't get to hear all the stories you and Anna swapped in the car on the way up, so what's been happening since the last time we spoke."

"Same old—Max, work, painting. The only thing that's out of the ordinary is that Sebastian's rung a few times lately and not just to talk about Max. I get the impression he wants to spend more time with him and is thinking about asking to put a more formal arrangement in place."

"That's a change," Gaby said. "How do you feel about that?"

"As much as it hurt me when Sebastian left, I do want Max to know his father. The only person it will hurt if they don't have a good relationship is Max."

Gaby looked directly at her. "You don't think there's any chance he might want to come back and be a family again?"

Laura shook her head.

"Good," Gaby said. "None of us want to see you get hurt again."

"I don't want to get hurt again either, Gaby. Not everyone is as lucky as you to have a husband like Oliver."

"We have our moments too, like anyone else."

"I can't imagine the moments the two of you have are anything like the ones Sebastian and I had."

"No one else knows what other people are dealing with."

"Maybe not, but until your marriage is falling apart, I don't think you're qualified to say anything about having moments with your husband. Can we change the subject now? Who wants some more wine?"

Evie looked over at Laura as she leaned forward and helped herself to the cheese. She'd never heard her speak like that before. Maybe something was going on that Laura hadn't told them about. Gaby was looking over at Laura too, and Evie could tell she was thinking the same thing.

Anna shook her head. "I'm happy with my glass of wine."

Laura looked at the glass in her hand. "You've hardly had any."

"I'm making it last."

"Ok, but I'm on a weekend away, and I don't have to be responsible for a minor, so I'll have a refill," Laura said, ignoring her headache.

"Well, enjoy every minute of it," Evie said. "I'm going to grab a cardigan. Anybody want anything while I'm up?"

Three heads shook, so Evie got up and headed to her room.

Evie sat on the bed and thought about what Laura had gone through when Sebastian had left and how hard it had been for her. She'd been so strong during that time, and Evie wondered if she could be that strong. There had been so many times in the past six months that she'd wanted to talk to Laura about what it was like to have a marriage end but she'd never found the words.

Evie sighed and lifted her bag onto the bed and began digging through it in search of the cardigan she'd come to find. As usual, she couldn't find what she was looking for. It didn't matter how small her bag was or how little it contained; she always ended up emptying the entire contents before she ever found what she was looking for. And today was no exception. In the pocket, she found a ticket for a party she'd gone to with a friend when Nick had been away for work. As she held the ticket in her hand, memories came flooding back. A crowded club, dark except for the laser lights coming from the stage. The more she thought about it, the more real it became, and she heard the music in her head and started moving to the beat. She'd had such a fantastic night, surrounded by people who enjoyed the same things she did, were feeling the same buzz she was and were as happy with the world as she was at that moment.

"Evie," Gaby called. "Can you grab another bottle of wine while you're up?"

The lights and the music stopped. "Sure."

"You're such a cold frog," Gaby said as Evie walked back into the room. "I was just telling Anna and Laura about work. So, the first-year students have just handed in their end of semester assignments. It's always interesting reading them because some have picked up what they need to do straight away while others still think they're in grade twelve. It takes a long time to go through and mark them all."

Laura laughed. "You say that every year."

"I know. Oliver says the same thing. I'm just lucky he's so good at helping out with the kids and the chores or I wouldn't be able to give as much feedback as I do."

Evie sat down and got comfy again. "You're much more patient than I am. I'd want to get that over and done with as soon as possible."

She couldn't imagine having a job like Gaby's. She'd gone to one of her lectures when she'd been visiting a client who lived near the university where Gaby worked. She'd stayed longer than she had planned because she couldn't stop watching Gaby. She had two hundred students hanging on her every word, and there was no doubt at all who was in control of the lecture theatre. In all the years she'd known Gaby, she'd never seen her at work, and Evie felt so happy for her friend. For all that she'd achieved. Gaby had everything she had ever wanted.

"That's why you do your job, and I do mine. I don't know how you can be a social worker. I'd last about five minutes. The things you have to deal with every day."

"I like helping people. It's a wonderful feeling when you see someone get their life back on track," Evie said.

"Evie was telling me in the car about a lady who had become dependent on drugs and alcohol to cope and how she was getting her life back to normal. Even though it isn't for me, I can see how satisfying that must be at the end of the workday."

Anna shuddered. "There's no way I could do what you do. You have to talk to people all day."

"So do you," Gaby said as she stood up and stoked the fire. "What about your customers?"

"I let my staff deal with them as much as possible."

Laura laughed. "Why does that not surprise me?"

She then turned to Evie and asked what Nick was up to while they were away.

"I think he was planning on going fishing."

Evie had no idea if that's what he was planning to do. It was the first thing that came to mind. Anything to take the focus away from what Gaby had said. She didn't want that to turn into a topic of conversation.

"Can't stand fishing," Laura said. "So boring, and I can't stand touching the bait."

"I hope Nick is planning on taking you out on Sunday night after you get home," Gaby said. "He's been away a lot for work lately, hasn't he?"

"Yes, he has. He didn't mention anything, although he might surprise me when I get home."

Even as she said it, she knew there would be no surprise. The last time he'd surprised her was over a year ago when he'd taken her out for dinner to a restaurant she'd wanted to try for 'date night'. She'd been so touched when they'd got out of the car and realised where he was taking her. Until she got inside and saw that he'd invited his brother Stewart and sister-in-law, Ruth. All the thoughts of a romantic date with her husband flew out of her mind.

"What about Oliver," Evie said. "I'm sure he has something planned."

Gaby smiled. "Probably, and before any of you say anything, yes, I know how lucky I am. Sometimes it feels like we've only just met, and we're still dating. He did catch me off guard the other day though, when he started talking about going to Venice by ourselves and leaving the kids with his parents."

A trip to Venice sounded so romantic. Evie couldn't even get Nick to go to the coast for a weekend. For as long as they'd been together, Evie had been trying to convince Nick to move overseas with her so she could fulfil one of her dreams. But no matter how many times she'd raised the subject, she'd had no luck.

"Wow," Anna said. "How fantastic would that be? And I love that after all these years, you still feel like you've just started dating. I hope I feel like that someday."

Gaby reached over and squeezed her hand. "I'm sure you will."

Evie wondered what it would be like to meet someone new and have that feeling again. She and Nick hadn't been together anywhere near as long as Gaby and Oliver, but that time when you

got butterflies in your stomach whenever you thought about your

partner had long gone.

Chapter 5

"Laura, would you draw a picture of all of us?" Evie asked. "I'd love to have something to take home as a memento of the weekend. I know we'll have the photo you took, but a drawing would be truly special."

"What a great idea," Anna said. "I can't believe I've never asked you to do that."

Laura laughed. "You always ask for a drawing or a painting of a plant."

"I like plants. They're a lot less complicated than people."

"Thanks a lot," Gaby said.

"Except for you three."

"It is a good idea," Laura said. "Why not? But you'll all have to sit still while I'm sketching you."

"We can do that," Evie said. "This is exciting. I've never been in a drawing before."

"I'm only doing the one, though. I want to relax tonight. You'll have to share the picture."

"Or you could do one each year until we each have a drawing," Gaby said.

Evie nodded in agreement. "That's an even better idea."

"All right. One each year, but Evie gets this one because she asked. I'll go and get my sketchpad."

Laura pretended to take longer than she needed to find her sketchpad. The few sips of wine she'd had were not helping her headache. At the time it had been so relaxing, sitting comfortably on her lounge chair after Meg had gone and Max was asleep, a glass of wine in her hand and not having to pretend that everything was ok. She'd cried for a long time over the life that was no longer hers, no matter how much she wanted it to be. The only bright spot was this weekend and a couple of days away from the reality of being almost a single parent. That thought got her off the lounge chair and into her bedroom to finish packing. When she reached up to the top shelf in her wardrobe to grab her slippers, she found they'd been pushed to the back. As she stretched her arms to try and grasp them, she knocked other items off the shelf, including Sebastian's old football jersey, which fell to the floor. She assumed he'd taken that with him as he loved that jersey, but there it was, at Laura's feet. Seeing it brought fresh tears. How dare he break up his family? Laura wasn't sure what upset her more. The fact that he left or the fact that, more than anything, she wanted them to be a family again, and there was nothing she could do to make that happen.

"Have you found your sketchpad yet?" Gaby called out. "We're all excited to get started."

"I'm not," Anna said.

"What are you worried about?" Gaby said. "It's just a drawing."

"Coming," Laura called out.

She pulled a few things out of her bag to reach the sketchpad, the football jersey being one of them. She wasn't sure why she'd packed it. She'd had a random thought about wearing it in bed instead of her pyjamas, but she realised if any of her friends saw it, there would be a lot of questions, and she wasn't in the right frame of mind to answer any, especially not with a hangover. She picked up her sketchpad and headed back to the lounge room.

"No one needs to sit still like a mannequin, but try not to move too much while I draw you," Laura said. "Who wants to go first?"

"Not me," Anna said. "I'm happy to go last. I need to brush my hair first and maybe change my top."

"I'll go first," Gaby said.

"Shouldn't Evie go first, seeing as it was her idea?" Anna said.

"That's ok. Gaby can go first, and then I'll go next."

Evie didn't mind letting Gaby go first. She'd been worried ever since Gaby had said there had been problems with Daisy, so she was happy for Gaby to be distracted. As her godmother, Evie was especially fond of Daisy. She hoped the arguments weren't too serious and that it was just a phase and their family life would go back to the way it usually was. Evie turned her gaze from Gaby to Laura and watched as she drew. She'd been drawing and painting for as long as Evie had known her, and all these years later, Evie thought it was great that Laura still found pleasure in her art. Even though she said she'd only do one drawing because she wanted to relax, she looked very content doing it.

"You can move now, Gaby. Evie, you're next," Laura said. "You can stay where you are, though. You're close enough to Gaby, and I want this to be a natural-looking picture, capturing how we are in this room right now."

Evie was glad enough time had passed that she would be able to sit still, although she was missing the warm, happy feeling the tablets gave her. Except for the one time it hadn't, and as she sat there, the events of that night came flooding back.

"I'm going to Stewart's place," Nick had said.

Evie had turned to look at him. "I thought we were going out to dinner."

"I can't go to dinner. Stewart and Ruth have just broken up. I can't leave him by himself tonight. You only think of yourself, don't you?"

"What do you mean they've broken up?"

"I told you yesterday. You must not have been listening as usual."

Evie didn't need to think back to the day before. She would have remembered if he'd told her. For a moment, she didn't say anything. She couldn't believe Stewart and Ruth had separated. They'd been together for so long and had seemed so happy. She thought they were one of those couples that were in it for the long haul.

"What happened?" Evie asked.

"I don't have time for details now. I want to go soon. Stewart needs some male time."

Evie watched as he headed to the bedroom to get changed. Male time she thought, more like drinking time. And watching some sort of sport. Being there for someone in a time of need was not something anyone in Nick's family did.

After he'd gone, Evie had been watching TV when her phone rang. It was her friend Chelsea who'd recently moved back to Brisbane, calling to see if Evie wanted to go out. As Nick had taken an overnight bag with him, she assumed he wouldn't be back until the following day, so there was no reason for her not to go.

She'd taken a tablet before they'd left Chelsea's, but an hour later, it hadn't done anything, so she took another one in the corner of the club. For thirty minutes, she felt amazing and didn't want the night to end. Then she started to feel disoriented and then hot and then cold. She needed to sit down because suddenly she felt dizzy, but there was nowhere to sit. Chelsea continued to dance and wasn't even looking at Evie. She pushed her way through the crowd to the bathroom, where she splashed water on her face and leant against the washbasin. She put her face under the water streaming from the tap. Her mouth was as dry as the Sahara Desert, and she lapped desperately at the cascading water. A stranger next to her asked if she was alright, and Evie had trouble forming the words to reply. She pushed open a cubicle door, quickly pulled her pants down and couldn't move away from the toilet for the next few minutes while everything that was in her stomach came out. When she was finally able to move, she went and found Chelsea and said she was going home. Chelsea just nodded and kept dancing. By the time she got home, she'd started to feel much better. It had stopped her for a while until the next fight with Nick.

"You're done now," Laura said, bringing Evie back to the present. She pulled her cardigan closer around her shoulders and sat further back in the chair, closing her eyes and willing the memory out of her mind.

Chapter 6

"Lucky last, Anna. It's your turn," Laura said.

"But I'm not ready."

"Of course you are. You look fine. Now sit down."

"I'll just go and brush my hair first."

Anna walked into her room, shut the door, stared at herself in the mirror and sighed before turning away, not liking what she saw. The last person she'd listened to when it came to the way she looked had been her dad. He'd always told her that she was beautiful, intelligent, and talented. And he'd always told her she could do anything she wanted. She'd been thinking about him a lot lately, ever since she'd first thought of opening another nursery. It was his voice telling her she could do it that made it easier for her to have the discussions that were leading her closer to owning her second nursery. Both her parents loved gardening, but it was her dad who instilled that love in her. It happened the day they'd gone to the nursery to buy her mum a plant.

"Do you think she'd like this one," her dad said as he held up an African violet, the purple flowers holding Anna's attention.

"It's very pretty. I think she'd like it," Anna had said with all the confidence a twelve-year-old could possess.

"I think she will too," her dad had said. "Let's check the other aisles and see if there is another plant we can get. It's her birthday, after all, so I think we should definitely get two plants."

"And a necklace," Anna had said.

Her dad had laughed. "Yes, your mum does like her jewellery. Ok then, two plants and a necklace."

As they'd wandered up and down the aisles, Anna had been fixated by the colours, smells, and the different varieties of plants. Each time they came to a plant Anna had liked, he'd stop and tell her what it was and where and when it should be planted. The next day, on her mum's birthday, Anna had joined her dad in the garden in the early morning before her mum woke up and planted what they'd bought. It wasn't long after that when he became sick. The visit to the nursery and the following morning in the garden were some of her last happy memories of him, and she hoped they would never fade.

"Come on, Anna," Gaby called. "It's your turn."

Anna changed her jumper to one that covered more than the one she'd been wearing, brushed her hair and put on some lipstick.

Gaby looked at Anna as she walked back into the room. "What's wrong with what you had on? And did you put lipstick on?"

"I want to look good in the picture."

Laura laughed. "You do realise this is a black and white drawing, not a colour painting."

"It doesn't matter. Just make me look good."

Laura smiled. "That will be the easiest thing about this drawing."

Anna sat in the seat on the other side of Gaby and immediately felt uncomfortable. She'd never even liked having her photo taken. Of all the photos of her friends from the past twenty-five years, Anna was the one who appeared the least. If it was a group shot it was not uncommon for her to be hiding at the back. Even in high school, she was always hiding behind her long hair when they had class photos.

"Anna, you're not at the dentist," Laura said. "Relax."

"I'm trying. And don't tell me to relax. That will make it worse."

"Can I see?" Gaby asked.

Laura shook her head. "You can look when it's done. I've still got to add myself in when I've finished drawing Anna. What's Oliver up to this weekend?"

"Running the kids around to all their activities," Gaby said.

"How are the kids?" Anna asked.

"Grace and Lucas are great. They're doing really well at school, and they love their sport. Daisy seems to be struggling a little bit at the moment. We're thinking of getting her a tutor because her university grades have dropped. They're usually very good."

"That's not like Daisy," Anna said. "Is everything ok?"

"Yes, she's fine. Just going through a phase of thinking she wants to quit her degree. It's common in first-year students, but she'll be fine. Would anyone like a top-up?"

Evie and Anna held up their empty wine glasses, but Laura shook her head.

Anna smiled. "That's unlike you to say no to a refill Laura. You're usually the first one to get a top-up."

"Just pacing myself. The day is still young."

Anna turned back to Gaby. "Are you sure that's all that's wrong with Daisy?'

Gaby sighed. "Whenever I ask her what's wrong, she says nothing and then walks off in a huff. I can only assume that's what it is. I've seen it a lot before."

"I can have a talk to her if you like," Evie said. "She might tell me."

Gaby nodded. "It can't hurt. But for now, I don't want to think about anything other than being here with all of you."

"In that case, what's the plan for tonight?" Evie asked. "Are we staying in as usual, or does anyone want to go out for something different?"

"We have enough food to stay here if everyone is happy to do that," Anna said. Gaby and Laura nodded in response.

"Fine by me," Evie said. "I feel like being lazy."

Gaby reached forward and picked up a magazine from under the coffee table. "This looks interesting. Has anyone seen this story?"

In big letters on the front cover were the words *How well do you know your friends?*

The wine went down Evie's throat the wrong way, and she started coughing. It was the same magazine that was rolled up at the bottom of her overnight bag.

Laura shook her head. "What's it about?"

Gaby turned to the page where the article started. "It's about a group of friends who got together one night and had a few drinks, and the conversation turned to secrets. Not little secrets like someone stole a pencil from a newsagent when they were nine. These were big secrets that had never been shared with anyone before. It says here that they were all scared to do it, but they were such good friends that they felt safe enough to try it and that afterwards, they felt like a weight had been lifted. Maybe we could do that tonight. What do you think?"

They all looked at each other, trying to decide if they were brave enough to do it. Evie didn't mention that she'd seen the article and how scared she'd been whenever she thought about it. Evie wasn't a big believer in fate, but surely this had to mean something. What were the chances of the same magazine being here in the house they were staying in and then Gaby picking it up and reading the exact same article?

"I don't know," Anna said. "It sounds terrifying."

Gaby shook her head. "I don't think it will be that bad. If we can't talk to each other about our secrets, then what does that say about our friendship?"

"Gaby's right," Laura said. "We've known each other for twenty-five years. We should be able to talk about anything. If we do it, I think we need some ground rules. Pass me the magazine, and I'll see if there's anything about rules mentioned."

Evie watched as Gaby got up and handed Laura the magazine. She still couldn't believe it was the same magazine and that Gaby had turned to the exact article that Evie hadn't been able to stop thinking about.

Laura scanned the article for a minute before finding what she was looking for. "Ok, rule number one, what is said in this room can never be repeated. After tonight we can't bring up these stories again unless the person who told the secret wants to. Rule number two. No one is allowed to talk while the stories are being told, and no one can say anything when the stories are finished. The person telling the story gets the opportunity to say something that they've been too scared to say without the fear of being judged. Rule number three. The stories need to be at the same level of seriousness or as close as possible. I know everyone mightn't have a story of the same significance, but I think it needs to be as even as possible. I don't think someone should pour their heart out, and then the next person only says something minor. It wouldn't be fair."

Gaby nodded. "They sound ok to me, but I'll add rule number four, which is unless we all do it, none of us does it."

"I'll do it if everyone else will," Laura said. "Someone who often comes into the gallery mentioned doing something similar with her friends. She said she was glad they did it and that they all got something out of it that helped each of them. And I'm assuming that because you suggested it, you'd do it too, Gaby."

"Yes, so that makes two of us. Two more to go."

Neither Evie nor Anna spoke, and from the look Anna was giving her, Evie knew she wasn't as open to the idea as Gaby and Laura were.

After a few moments, Anna got up and put another log on the fire. "I don't know if I could. What sort of thing would I say?"

"Whatever you're comfortable with," Gaby said.

Evie watched Anna again as she thought about whether she could participate in something like Gaby had just suggested. She'd sat down but couldn't sit still in the chair, moving around as if she was trying to get comfortable and swapping her wine glass from one hand to the other.

"I don't know what I'm comfortable with. And I really don't know if it's something I could actually do."

Evie moved and sat beside Anna. "I feel the same. I don't think I'm that brave."

Gaby looked at both of them. "There's no pressure. If we can't all agree, then we won't do it, but I think it's worth doing."

Laura nodded in agreement. "I think it would be good for us."

Evie and Anna looked at each other again. All Evie could think about was what she would say. She knew what she should say. This was the perfect opportunity to ask for help. Maybe if she went last and heard what the others shared, she'd know whether or not to take the gamble.

"I need to think about it for a bit longer before I make a decision," Evie said.

Anna nodded. "Me too."

Evie stood up and headed for the kitchen. "I'll just grab another wine. It will give me some time to think."

Evie walked into the kitchen, leant against the bench top and looked out the window. The Poinciana tree in the corner of the backyard made her think again about the similarities between this house and her grandparents'. Every time she'd visited when she was a child, she'd jump out of the car and run straight into the backyard and climb their Poinciana tree. She'd done it for years until she turned thirteen when her parents said she was too old for that now. Her grandmother had disagreed and said she would never be too old to climb a tree if that's what she wanted to do. As with most disagreements, Evie's parents had won and that had been the end of the subject. Looking at the tree now, Evie had a sudden, strong desire to run outside and climb to the top, where she could stay hidden among the branches. Because it was winter, the vibrant red flowers this particular tree was known for weren't in bloom, but there was enough green foliage she could hide in, which was precisely what she wanted to do at that moment. Even though she'd been thinking about the article ever since she'd read it, now that she had an opportunity to make the words on the page become a reality, she just didn't know if she could do it.

Looking at the tree again, she wished her grandmother was there. It had been seven years since she'd passed away, and Evie missed her all the time. If she'd been there, she'd tell Evie to march back into the lounge room, stop being scared and take part, just like she had when Evie had spoken to her about Matthew. She could still clearly picture the day she'd sat in her grandmother's kitchen with a cup of tea and talked about how unhappy she was. It had shocked her at the time, but her grandmother had said that while no one was permanently content, you need to be happy most of the time or why are you with that person. Your grandfather and I have been together for sixty-three years, and I can't imagine spending any of that time with anyone else, she'd said. That's how you should feel. And it's what you deserve, so stop being scared and do what you need to do, she'd finished with. Evie hadn't taken her advice, and in the end, it was Matthew who'd ended their relationship. As she turned away from the window and towards the fridge, she knew it was time to take that advice and stop being scared.

Evie walked back into the room and looked at her friends. "I'll do it. There's something that's been weighing me down, and talking about it might help me see it more clearly. And help me figure out what I need to do to change things."

"It's never a good thing to carry around something that weighs you down," Gaby said. "I feel the same, that's why I agreed to take part.

Laura nodded. "So do I. That just leaves you, Anna."

The three of them looked at Anna, but she didn't speak for a few moments. She got up and walked over to the window and pushed the curtains open so she could look outside. "It's beautiful out there. And so peaceful. Will it still be peaceful in here if we go ahead?"

"I don't see why not," Gaby said. "What are you worried about?"

"That one of us will say something that changes things between us."

Evie watched Anna as she stared out the window and absentmindedly twirled a few strands of her hair with her fingers. She hadn't thought about the possibility of things changing between them. Only that she needed help. And that hadn't changed.

"We've been friends for so long, I think we'll be ok. I can't imagine we'd say anything that would change things so much that we couldn't change them back."

Even as she said it, Evie knew she didn't believe it. If she said everything she needed to say, there was no way things would stay exactly as they were now. Anna was still staring out the window, and out of the corner of her eye, Evie saw Laura get up and walk over to her.

"I'm scared to do this too, but I think we should."

Evie watched them as they looked at each other, and she knew then that Anna would take part.

"Ok, I'll do it. I'm still scared though. I just don't know if I could open up like that."

"You won't be doing it on your own," Gaby said. "We'll all do it."

"Should we start now or wait until after we eat?" Evie said.

"I'd like to do it now before I chicken out," Anna said.

Laura looked up from the drawing. "Good idea. All we have to decide is who's going first."

"I should probably go first," Gaby said. "I'm the one who suggested it."

"Can we wait five minutes?" Laura asked. "I've almost finished drawing myself into the picture."

During those five minutes, Evie started to panic. She should never have agreed to do this. It was too much, too hard, too terrifying. She couldn't back out now, though. Maybe she didn't have to tell her secret. Perhaps she could make something up, or maybe leave some things out. At least if Gaby went first, she'd have time to come up with a different story if she needed to.

"Before we start, I think we might need a refill," Gaby said.

Chapter 7

"Now that the time is here, it's not as easy as I thought it would be," Gaby said. "What I'm about to say happened a long time ago. It's something I never thought would happen to me, but one lapse in judgement changed my life forever. I was so scared at the time, but now I know it's one of the best things that ever happened to me. So, make sure your glasses are refilled because we're about to go back in time. To the 1990s, to be exact."

Gaby looked at herself in the mirror, and even though she'd only just turned twenty, she looked a lot older. The fifteen minutes she'd had to get ready hadn't been enough time to hide how tired she looked from the constant juggling of her university studies and a part-time job as a waitress at Sizzler. She'd been asked to work back, and although she would have preferred to come home earlier, she didn't want to knock back an extra hour's pay. The books she needed for next semester weren't cheap, and she needed to start saving now. She sighed as she reached for her perfume and then turned up the radio to block out her thoughts, just as the DJ was announcing the next song.

"We've had a lot of requests for this song, so I'm going to play it one more time. Here's one of the biggest selling songs of 1998 – I don't want to miss a thing by Aerosmith."

Gaby leaned over and turned the radio off again. She hated that song. Oliver had always turned the radio up whenever it came on because they'd danced to it once. She'd been so happy that night.

"Are you ready, Gaby?" Evie yelled down the hallway.

"Just looking for my lipstick," Gaby yelled back.

"Did you know Anna is bringing that English guy tonight?"

"What English guy?"

"The one she told us about last week. I think his name's Chris. He's the one whose mum moved out here and somehow became friends with Anna's mum."

"Oh yeah. So why is he coming?"

"Anna's mum asked if she could take him out one night, and I think he's leaving soon, so it has to be tonight."

That was so like Anna's mum, Gaby thought. She was always looking out for everyone, including Gaby, whenever she'd gone to Anna's house. Even when Anna's dad died of cancer six years ago, and she was upset a lot of the time, she'd still stop and talk to Gaby whenever she saw her. And since he died, she hadn't shown any interest in being with anyone else. She was so different to Gaby's own mum, who she could hear talking to Evie in the kitchen, along with the sound of another empty bottle going in the bin.

"Are you girls going out tonight?"

"Yeah, we're going to City Rowers," Evie said.

"That sounds like fun. Brad and I are going out to dinner in an hour. We might join you afterwards."

"Don't even think about it," Gaby said as she walked into the kitchen.

"Why not?" she said as she lit a cigarette.

"Because I'm not going clubbing with my mother. It's too embarrassing. Do you have to smoke in the house?"

"Yes, I do. It's my house remember. Can you make me a drink? I'm going to have a bath before I get ready. There's another bottle of bourbon in the pantry."

It's probably the only thing in the pantry, Gaby thought. It was her mum's turn to buy the groceries, but she had a habit of getting out of it, and Gaby hadn't had a chance to go this week. The house needed a clean too. Tomorrow, she thought. I'll worry about it tomorrow. At least she'd had a chance to get one load of washing done, so she had something to wear that night. Gaby only had two reasonably good outfits. She'd love to buy more, but her mum didn't contribute much to the running of the house, and sometimes Gaby had to take money from her mum's purse so she could buy the necessities like food. Her mum's idea of necessities was bourbon and cigarettes. Gaby wondered if she would come home tonight or if she'd go back to her latest boyfriend's place. She was hoping it would be the latter because Gaby didn't like him, and she hated it when he was around

"Come on, it's time to go," Evie said. "We haven't been out dancing in ages. You're usually working or studying on a Saturday night."

"I wish I didn't have to, but if I don't study, I won't pass, and if I don't work, I don't eat."

Evie put her arm around Gaby. "You're not allowed to think about any of that tonight. You're only allowed to think about having fun."

As they stood in the bathroom, they did a final check. Gaby thought she looked ok in her black pants and red top. It might not have been as trendy as what other people were wearing, but it would have to do. Her shoulder-length brown hair was up, and she was wearing flat black shoes because she couldn't walk in heels.

"Is my make-up ok?" Gaby asked.

"Yep, you look gorgeous."

Gaby took one more look in the mirror to make sure her makeup was alright and wished again that Anna had been there to do it for her. She was so much better at it, and she would have hidden the dark circles under her eyes and added some healthy-looking colour to her cheeks. As she stared at her face, she debated whether or not to take off the red lipstick but knew she'd never hear the end of it if she did. Laura had bought it for her because she thought the brown one Gaby always wore didn't brighten her face enough. As she left the room, she picked up the beautiful gold bracelet that Evie, Laura and Anna had given her for her eighteenth birthday two years ago. It didn't really go with her watch and its battered black leather band or her two-dollar earrings, but it was one of the few nice things that Gaby owned, and she hardly ever went anywhere she could wear it.

"Come on," Evie said when they arrived at the club. "Let's go have some fun."

Gaby walked through the door and straight away felt that she was different to everyone there. The club was packed with beautiful people in beautiful, expensive clothes, and her outfit had come from Target, and she'd bought it at the Boxing Day sales. She doubted anyone here had ever been to the Target Boxing Day sale.

"I don't think this is our sort of club," Gaby yelled over the noise and thumping beat of the music.

"Of course it is. Oh, I love this song. Come on, let's dance."

That only made Gaby feel worse. She didn't like dancing. No matter how much she tried, her body just wouldn't move the way she wanted it to. If it hadn't been for Evie talking her into coming, she'd be at home right now studying. She had an exam the following week that she needed to prepare for. But she stayed on the dance floor because Evie loved to dance, and she'd lost track of the number of times Evie had done things for her. Only last week, Evie had driven her to work because her car needed to be fixed, and she hadn't saved enough money yet to pay for the repairs.

"There you are," Anna yelled over the music. "Laura and I have been looking everywhere for you. Gaby and Evie, this is Chris."

As soon as he spoke, Gaby noticed his thick, English accent, which she thought sounded sexy. She also noticed that he was very good looking. While they were dancing, Gaby found it hard to take her eyes off him, and she wondered if anything was going on between him and Anna. She hadn't said anything but that didn't mean there wasn't. Gaby wasn't interested in dating—she'd broken up with her boyfriend Oliver three months ago, and she was still upset by it. He had been the first guy she'd let see her home life, and he'd made her laugh and reminded her that life could also be fun and not just constant hard work.

"How long have you been travelling, Chris?" Gaby asked as they all walked away from the dance floor and went to the balcony outside.

"Almost two years now."

"Wow, that's great. Do you think you'll keep travelling for a while longer?"

"Yeah, there is still so much to see. I guess I'll eventually feel like I've seen enough and be sick of living out of a backpack. That's when I'll go home."

Gaby thought about what it would be like to travel the world, go wherever you wanted, and only have one backpack to be responsible for. No matter how hard she tried, she couldn't imagine how it would feel. She didn't get to think about it for very long before Evie stood up.

"This music is awesome. Come on, let's go back and dance."

Gaby shook her head. "I think I've embarrassed myself enough for a while. I'll stay here."

"I'll stay too," Chris said. "I'm not the best dancer, and I don't think I need to show anyone that again."

Gaby watched Evie, Laura, and Anna return to the dance floor. Maybe she'd been wrong about Chris being interested in Anna. It didn't happen often. Whenever Anna was around, every guy in the room would look at her, although she never seemed to notice. Usually, if a guy came up and spoke to her, she'd be polite for a minute or two and then introduce him to Laura, Gaby or Evie, whichever one of them was there and let them take over the conversation.

"So, where's your favourite place so far?" Gaby asked.

"Thailand. It's such a beautiful country, and the people are really friendly, and it's so cheap, which is great when you're on a budget. And it was the first country I went to that was completely different to home."

"Was there somewhere in Thailand you liked the most?"

"Yeah, but it's not what most people would say. I went out to the River Kwai because my grandfather was a prisoner of war and was forced to work on the railway. He died there and is buried in the cemetery at Kanchanaburi. I promised my dad I'd go and see his grave. He was only twenty-four when he died. Never got to see my dad because he was born seven months after his dad shipped out. Might have even been dead by that time. No one is sure when he died. Sometime between June and August in 1943."

"Did you find his grave?"

"Yeah, I did."

"Did you feel sad?"

"Yeah. I never got to meet him, and my dad grew up without a father."

"What about your grandmother?"

"She died during the war too. A bomb landed in her street in south London, not far from the house, and destroyed the front room where she was sitting. The back rooms were left standing, and that's where dad was sleeping. Only two more metres, and I wouldn't be here now."

"That's really sad."

"Yeah, but it was fairly common at the time. Dad was raised by his mum's older sister and her husband."

Gaby didn't know anything about her grandparents or any other relatives. Her mum hadn't spoken to her parents or brother in years, so Gaby had never met them. And she would never know the relatives on her dad's side because she didn't even know who he was. Maybe she had a grandfather who'd fought in the war, perhaps even been forced to work on the railway like Chris' grandfather. She'd always wanted to know about her family, but her mum never talked about anyone, and no one had ever tried to contact her.

"Have you told your dad you went there?"

"Yeah, I did. He was pleased about it. So were the rest of my family. They all want to see the photos I took."

"How many are there in the rest of your family?"

"Five—two brothers and three sisters. I'm the youngest by six years and a surprise to my parents."

"Wow, that's a lot."

"What about you?"

"I'm an only child."

The conversation was going somewhere Gaby didn't want it to go, so she changed the subject back to Chris' travels for a while.

"Would you like another drink, Gaby?"

Gaby nodded, and Chris walked towards the bar. He was really lovely, and she enjoyed talking to him, although it was more like shouting because of the music.

"That was so much fun," Laura said after she'd bounded over and stood next to Gaby. "I love dancing."

"Me too," Evie said.

"Great, then next time, it can just be the two of you," Anna said. "I don't like being out there where everyone is looking at me. And speaking of everyone looking at you, Gaby, isn't that your mum over there?"

Gaby turned to look where Anna was pointing. "Shit."

"What's wrong?" Chris said as he handed her the drink.

"Nothing. It's just really hot in here, and I'm tired. I might go."

Gaby skolled her drink and grabbed Chris' hand before pushing her way through the crush of people. The others followed, and they managed to sneak out before they were spotted. On the way outside, Gaby whispered in Anna's ear and asked if anything was going on between her and Chris. Anna shook her head, and out of the corner of her eye, she could see Evie smiling at her.

Back in the lounge room in Mt Tamborine, Gaby paused for a moment to refill her glass. She'd thought that once she'd started telling her story, it would get easier, but it hadn't, even though each word she said got her one step closer to the end. She was aware of exactly how many times she'd crossed, then uncrossed her legs, put her wine glass down and then picked it up again. She'd even stood up at one point and walked over to the window, though with the way she felt, she wouldn't have been able to say it looked peaceful the way Anna had. Nothing looked or felt peaceful. As she looked around the lounge room in the house on the top of the mountain, she could tell by the looks on their faces that they were all remembering that night. Before her mum had turned up, Gaby had been having a great time. If she had known what would happen that night, she wondered if she would have gone out. She was hopeful that by sharing her secret, she'd be more at ease with it. Telling her friends would be the easy part though. A shiver went down her spine as she thought about the impact it would have on her family when they found out.

"After seeing mum, all I wanted to do was get out of there and go home because I knew it was the one place she wouldn't be. And Chris offered to come with me."

Gaby paused again as every detail of what happened when they got there ran through her head. She wasn't one to blush, but she could feel her face getting warm. She shifted in her seat, trying to get comfortable again and then took another sip of her wine. That would have to be the last sip for a while. She didn't want to be drunk while she was sharing her secret. It was too important not to focus entirely on what she needed to say. If only it wasn't so tempting to drink the whole glass and then fill it up again.

"Are you ok, Gaby?" Anna asked. "We don't have to go on if you don't want to."

"I'll continue. I'm the one who suggested this in the first place, and I knew what I was doing when I did. As long as everyone else is happy to continue."

All three nodded, although Gaby could tell they were all feeling nervous. She knew that they were waiting to hear what she said to gauge whether the secrets they had were more shocking than her own. It was ironic that Evie had mentioned Chris in the car on the way to Mt Tamborine. It had been a long time since she'd said his name to anyone and a long time since she'd thought of him as a person in his own right with a life of his own and not as someone forever linked to her life. She supposed he went back to London eventually. He was probably married now, with a family of his own, and she doubted he'd thought of her at all since that night.

"Ok then. Grab a top-up if you need one, and then I'll continue."

Three glasses were topped up, and then everyone settled back into their seats.

Chapter 8

Gaby sat in the back seat of the taxi, cursing her mum for turning up at the club. Sometimes Gaby wished she would go away and not cause her any more trouble. As she sat back in the seat, she heard the same song she'd heard while getting ready – *I don't want to miss a thing.* It was the last song she wanted to hear, so she concentrated on giving directions.

"Left here," Gaby said to the taxi driver. "Then first right. It's the second house on the left."

"Is this your house?" Chris asked

"Mine and Mum's."

"Do you think she'll come home soon?"

"No. When she goes out, she stays out."

"I can't imagine my mum going to a nightclub. She's more likely to head down to the local pub for a pint and then be home by 8pm."

"My mum's a bit different to most."

"Must be nice having a mum who still likes to go out and have fun and not be bothered about acting her age."

Gaby didn't answer. She liked the idea of a mum who just went out for one drink at the local pub and then came home. One drink for her mum was what she did before leaving the house in the morning. As Gaby turned the key in the front door, she began to feel nervous. She hadn't had a lot of experience with men. Oliver was the only guy she'd slept with, and she wasn't sure if she was supposed to do something or wait for Chris to do something. Gaby wasn't sure what to say either, so she said the first thing that popped into her mind.

"Do you want a drink?" she asked.

"No. Unless you do."

"No, I'm fine."

Gaby took a deep breath and decided to kiss him before she lost her nerve. She was surprised at how good it felt, so she kept kissing him and then led him down the hall to her room. She stumbled over the hallway runner and fell into the wall, but they kept kissing. At the end of the hall, she kicked the door open and fumbled for the light switch, but the light was too harsh, so she turned it off. She pulled Chris' shirt up over his head, not bothering to take the time to undo the buttons, and his hands went around her back and reached for the clasp on her bra. Gaby was glad she'd turned the light back off. The bra she had on was old and faded, with the stitching starting to come undone. She pulled Chris down onto the bed and took what she wanted, forgetting that she was doing something her mum had done time and time again.

The next morning, the light shining through the open curtains woke her. She slowly peeled her eyes open and quickly shut them again. Her mouth was dry, and her head was pounding. She reached over to pick up the glass of water on her bedside table and touched a shoulder instead. Why had she let him stay? She should have sent him back to Anna's in a taxi last night. Slowly Gaby crawled out of bed, careful not to disturb him and went into the bathroom. There were no noises in the house, and Gaby hoped the shower wouldn't wake Chris. She needed to get him out of the house before her mum came home. The warm water felt soothing against her skin, and she stood there for five minutes, letting it run over her to wake her up. It also gave her time to think about how to ask Chris to leave. She'd enjoyed last night but wasn't sure what she was supposed to do now because she'd never had a one night stand before. But she didn't have a chance to think about it for very long because she heard her mum's voice as soon as she turned the water off.

"Do you want a coffee?"

Shit, Gaby thought. Her mum had told her last night as they were leaving the house that she was spending the night at Brad's and wouldn't be home until late morning. Brad was the latest boyfriend and the one Gaby hated the most out of all of them. Hoping that it was Brad who answered, she almost started to cry when she heard Chris' voice.

"Coffee would be great."

"I'm Joyce, by the way."

"Hi, I'm Chris."

"How do you have your coffee?"

"White with two."

"I detect an English accent there, Chris. Where are you from?"

"London."

"Always wanted to go there. Never had the chance to travel. Is it a nice place?"

"Yes, it's a great city."

"Is Gaby awake?"

"The bathroom door is shut, so I think she's taking a shower."

"Grab a seat; jug won't take long to boil."

The bathroom door swung open, and Gaby's mum stuck her head in.

"Cute," she said before shutting the door again.

Good morning to you too, she thought as she hung up the towel. Gaby could hear them all talking in the kitchen. She wished she could stay in the bathroom until all three had left, but she knew that wasn't an option and that they were waiting for her. She could feel the grin on her mum's face from here. She'd be checking Chris out from every angle. Gaby supposed she had better go and rescue him and try to get him out of the house as quickly and painlessly as possible.

"Morning," Gaby said as she walked into the kitchen. "Any hot water left?"

"No, but boil the jug again," her mum said. "I'll have another one in a minute."

"Have a good time last night, Gaby?" Brad said.

Her mum slapped him on the arm. "Behave Brad."

Gaby scowled at him, and Chris looked down at the floor.

"So, Chris, where did you two meet?" Brad asked.

"At a club."

"Really," Brad said. "When?"

"Last night."

"Shut up, Brad," Gaby said. "Leave him alone."

"Don't talk to Brad like that," her mum said.

"Tell him not to talk to Chris like that. It wouldn't hurt him to learn a few manners."

Her mum glared at her. "You apologise to Brad."

Gaby shook her head. "Wouldn't hurt you to learn a few manners either."

"Leave her alone, Joyce," Brad said. "She's just grumpy. She mustn't have had enough sleep last night."

"Grow up, Brad," Gaby said. "Come on, Chris, we can have our coffee in the lounge room."

Gaby set her cup down on the coffee table and sat on the recliner. Her hand started playing with the tear in the material on the arm, the foam showing through the brown and beige fabric.

"How long have they been together?"

"About four months."

"Oh, I thought they'd been together longer than that. They seem to get on really well."

"Four months is a long time for my mother. I give it another few weeks."

"I heard that, Gaby," her mum called from the kitchen.

Gaby ignored her. Instead, she looked over at Chris. Thankfully he wasn't too bad in the morning light. And he still seemed like a nice guy. Maybe it would have been good if he was staying in Brisbane.

"Anything planned for today?"

"Anna's going to take me to the Sunshine Coast. Somewhere called Mooloolaba."

"That'll be nice. I should probably get you back there then. I'll go and grab my car keys and drive you."

"Thanks. That'd be good."

Gaby said a silent prayer of thanks to Anna for having planned a day trip. Now Gaby didn't need to think of an excuse to ask him to leave before they both started feeling awkward around each other. She didn't want to give her mother or Brad the chance to say anything else either.

"He seemed nice," her mum said when she got back.

Gaby nodded.

"Are you going to see him again?"

"No, I don't think so."

"That's a shame. Maybe you'll meet someone else soon. Come on, Brad. It's 10.30am. We're wasting valuable racing time. I don't want to be late today. Got down to the track yesterday, and someone else was standing in my spot."

"You got any money?" Brad asked. "I'm a bit broke this week."

You're a bit broke every week, Gaby thought. If he didn't spend his money on alcohol and gambling, then maybe he wouldn't need to scab so much off her mum and then she might be able to give Gaby more money for the household expenses. She was tired of having to make what little money there was go far enough, and she hated having to think about it every day.

"So, was he any good?" Brad asked.

"Fuck off."

"What's wrong, Gaby? Don't pretend to be something you're not. Just like your mother, you are."

"I'm nothing like my mother."

"What's that?" her mum asked as she came back into the kitchen.

"Nothing," Gaby replied. "You have a good time."

"I will. See you later sweetie."

Gaby looked around at the mess the house was in and sighed. As she pushed the vacuum across the lounge room floor, she couldn't get Brad's words out of her head. It's not true, she told herself over and over again. The more she thought about what he said, the harder she pushed the vacuum, not even noticing that she was going over an area she'd already done. When the carpet was done, she shoved the vacuum back in the cupboard, not caring that she'd knocked the broom over, and then slammed the door shut.

Gaby yawned as she sat in her cultural studies lecture. When it was over, she looked down at her notebook and saw she'd scribbled a note across the top of the page to remind her to ring Evie that night after she got home from work. Gaby hadn't answered the phone yesterday when it rang because she knew one of the calls would have been from Evie wanting to know all the details, and she wasn't sure what she wanted to say yet.

"Didn't want to answer your phone yesterday?" Evie asked when Gaby called her that night.

"I was busy."

"Sure you were. At least you called today."

Gaby still wasn't sure what to say, but she decided to get the conversation over and done with.

"So, details," Evie said.

Gaby could almost feel her grinning down the phone line. "What sort of details?"

"You know exactly what sort of details."

She knew Evie wouldn't say anything to anyone else, so she told her about Chris and about what happened after they got to her place and what had happened the next morning.

"Saturday night sounds good. Sunday morning sounds terrible. You must have wished that a hole would appear in the floor and swallow you up."

"It was awful. Why yesterday, of all days, did mum come back early and bring Brad with her?"

Gaby could still see the smirk on Brad's face and hear what could almost be described as pride in her mum's voice when she'd said Chris was cute.

"I'm never doing anything like that again."

"You're young and single and without a potential boyfriend in sight. Are you sure you won't ever do something like that again?"

"Yes, I'm sure. Now can we change the subject, please?"

"What are you up to tonight?" Evie asked.

"Study and housework. What about you?"

"My parents are out, and James is at a friend's house, so I'm going to take over the main bathroom, turn the bubbles on in the spa bath and steal a glass of mum's champagne. I don't feel like studying tonight."

Gaby didn't feel like studying either, but she had no other time to do it.

"Are you going to see him again?"

"I don't think so. He's leaving soon, and we didn't talk about seeing each other again."

"So what about Oliver?"

"Nothing to tell. I've seen him a few times since we broke up, but we're not back together."

She'd been thinking lately about the day they'd first met while waiting in line for coffee at university. Three days in a row, they'd been there at the same time. He was studying civil engineering, and his lectures were around the same time as her English and Cultural Studies lectures. On the third day, they'd sat together to drink their coffees, and after that, they started spending their breaks together. And when he asked her out, she didn't have to think too long before saying yes.

"Does it still hurt?"

"Yes, but not as much as it did three months ago when he said he wanted to break up. I guess he's not the one for me."

After Gaby hung up the phone, she felt bad about lying. It did hurt as much as it had three months ago.

Over the next few weeks, Gaby did nothing but study and work, and she felt tired all the time. For the first time ever, she'd thought about not going to her lecture, but she got up and went anyway. On the way from her lecture to her tutorial, Gaby stopped to go to the toilet.

"Hey Steph," the voice in the next cubicle called out.

"Yeah," the voice from the cubicle on the other side of Gaby replied.

"You got any tampons?"

"I think so. Yep. I'll pass it along. Excuse me, can you pass this to the cubicle next to you."

"Sure," Gaby replied, reaching to get the tampon and then passing it along.

"Thanks."

Gaby had forgotten about that. Hers must be due soon. She made a mental note to check the calendar when she got home.

"Gaby, can I see you before you go," Professor Morton said at the end of the tutorial. "Have you thought about what you want to do when you finish your degree? You don't have long to go."

"Not really. I've thought about a few options but haven't really settled on anything."

125

"Is continuing your studies one of your options?"

"I'd like to if I could."

"Good, because I think you should continue on until you get a PhD. You're one of the smartest students I've ever had the pleasure of teaching, and I think you would make a great lecturer. You should consider it as an option."

"You think so?"

"Yes, I do. Have a serious think about it. I'll see you next week Gaby."

Gaby had thought about doing more study, but she hadn't considered working towards a PhD, and she wondered if she could do it. Professor Morton seemed to think so. She would have to give it a lot of thought, but maybe this could be her future. It would also be something else to think about besides Oliver. He'd called and said he wanted to see her, and she'd agreed. He'd told her he'd made a mistake and he missed her, and he thought they belonged together. After listening to him and realising that he meant what he was saying, she agreed to get back together because she hadn't stopped loving him, even though she'd told her friends she had.

"Mum?" Gaby called out as she opened the door.

No answer. Monday night, two for one drinks until 9pm down at the club. She threw her bag on the bench and opened the fridge. Lunch was a long time ago, and she pulled out the ingredients for a salad. Next to the fridge was the calendar, and Gaby remembered that she'd wanted to check the dates. It was the 12th today, and Gaby thought she must have counted wrong last month. 1,2,3,4…..26,27,28. No, that had to be wrong. That would have made it last week. So she counted again 1,2,3,4…26,27,28. No, she had counted right. She just must be stressed or something. There was no other reason for it. The only time she'd had sex in the last month was with Chris, and they had used a condom. Not the second time you didn't, the voice in the back of her head said. Shit, she thought. It wasn't possible. There had to be another reason her period was late. She repeated that to herself as she lay in bed, wide awake, all night, tossing and turning. It didn't stop the sick feeling in her stomach though.

Gaby stood in the toilet with just a t-shirt on, opened the box and read the instructions carefully because she had to do it right. Once she was sure she knew what she was doing, she put the empty container beneath her, but she was so nervous about the result that for a long time, she couldn't fill it. When she finally did, she placed it on the bench in the bathroom, took out the indicator stick, inserted it through the foam ring then put the stick in the container. Now all she had to do was wait for one minute. She walked out of the bathroom because she couldn't stand looking at the test kit. Her whole future was linked to that one small, thin strip of cardboard, and deep down, she already knew what the result would be. Gaby went and stood outside in the fresh air, leaned against the railing on the back verandah, and took a few deep breaths. If only time could stop right now, she would be happy.

One blue line meant negative, and two blue lines meant positive. There it was, clear as anything, two blue lines. Gaby sank down to the floor, curled up into a ball and rocked back and forth. It was a few minutes before the tears started, but it took more than a few minutes for them to stop.

"Have you given any more thought to your future?" Professor Morton asked a week later.

The tutorial had just finished, although Gaby wasn't sure what had been discussed because she hadn't been paying attention. Ever since the two blue lines had appeared, she hadn't been able to think of anything else.

"I have. But I haven't made any decisions yet."

"It's good that you're giving it a lot of thought. It's a big commitment. Let me know when you've made a decision, and I'll see what I can do to help you."

Finishing her degree was the only option she had. She'd come so far, and she couldn't stop now. If what her doctor had calculated that morning was right, she should have her final exams completed before the baby was due. But she would have to push any thoughts for further study out of her mind. Gaby had two hours before her next lecture, so she went to the library where it would be quiet so she could think. No matter what she did, her life had changed forever. This was probably the most important decision she would ever make, and for the first time in a long time, she felt like a child herself. As far as Gaby could see, she had three choices. She could have the baby and raise the child on her own, give the child up for adoption or not have the child at all. She wished there was someone she could talk to. Oliver was out of the question, and her friends didn't have the life experience she needed right now.

Those three options were still going through her head the next day as she pushed the shopping trolley down the aisles, crossing items off the grocery list as she went. She'd just put the last thing in the trolley when she heard her name and turned around to see Evie. They hugged each other, and Evie looked at Gaby's trolley.

"I hate grocery shopping."

Gaby nodded. "Me too. It takes so long."

"I can think of lots of other things I'd rather be doing on a Saturday morning."

"Where's Scott? I thought he usually helped with the groceries."

"He's playing football. This is the third week in a row he's done that."

"I guess he's got out of doing the housework today too."

Evie sighed and nodded.

Gaby knew Scott hadn't done his fair share since the day they moved in together, but it was hard to sympathise as it was no different to what Gaby had been doing for years.

"Earth to Gaby," Evie said, smiling. "Are you ok?"

Gaby felt bad straight away for thinking what she just had. Evie was her best friend and had always been there whenever she'd needed her. "Sorry. Too many things to think about."

Evie gave her a hug. "Is there anything I can do to help?"

Gaby shook her head.

"Is it just the usual stuff? You seem sad."

Gaby shook her head again and gripped the handle on the trolley even tighter because she felt if she let go, she'd fall over. She wanted to tell Evie, but she'd burst into tears in the middle of the canned goods aisle if she said something right now.

"Are you sure? You really don't seem like yourself."

"I'm ok. Just tired."

Gaby could tell by the look on Evie's face that she didn't believe her. But they knew each other well enough for Evie not to push the point.

"I need to go. I've got a lot of study to do when I get home."

Evie hugged her again. "Ok. Call me though if you need anything."

Gaby pushed her trolley away and knew, without turning around, that Evie was watching her. But she didn't look back. Instead, she took several deep breaths and forced herself to walk at a steady pace. When she got to the checkout, she placed each item on the conveyor belt, one at a time. What she wanted to do was throw them on, as many as she could manage at once and tell the checkout operator to go as fast as she could. As soon as she'd paid, she pushed the trolley towards the car, slowly at first, and then faster once she realised Evie was nowhere in sight. Opening the boot, she shoved all the grocery bags in, piled them in a heap instead of placing them in neat rows like she usually did and then drove off. She hated lying, but she didn't know what else to do. Except go home and shut herself away.

Over the next week, she found it hard to concentrate on anything. She'd hardly slept or eaten, and she hadn't spent any time working on her assignments. She couldn't focus at work either and had made a few mistakes for the first time since she'd started her job. It had been hard to act normally around Oliver too. All she could think about were the three choices that were open to her. On Friday morning, Professor Morton stopped her after the tutorial and asked to speak with her.

"I don't want to pry, Gaby, but I couldn't help but notice how distracted you've been. You're usually involved in every discussion, but you haven't said a word in any lectures or tutorials, and you've never asked for an extension on an assignment before. You're the only one of my students from whom I never expected to hear that request. Is everything ok?"

Gaby hadn't realised it had been so obvious. Here was the perfect opportunity to speak to someone who could give her good advice. Although she was scared to say something, she needed help and didn't know where to turn, so she told her what had happened and how she was feeling about it all.

Professor Morton handed her a box of tissues and said matter-of-factly that it wasn't the perfect situation, but things in life rarely were.

"Come and see me next Wednesday during my lunch break. I'll think about your situation and see what options I can come up with. In the meantime, try not to be so hard on yourself."

Gaby nodded and left her office. It felt good to have someone in her corner. However, she still had to tell Oliver, which terrified her more than talking to Professor Morton.

It took her a week to work up the courage, and after she'd told him, he said he needed time to think. Gaby wasn't sure what he was thinking about. She couldn't imagine him hanging around now, even though he'd told her several times he thought they belonged together. One mistake was going to ruin the two most important things in her life.

She didn't hear from Oliver for two weeks, but then he rang and asked if he could come over. It was the longest two weeks Gaby had ever experienced. On the day he said he would come, Gaby paced up and down the hallway while she waited for him. She made herself a cup of tea but couldn't drink it. She turned on the TV, but nothing could stop her from counting the minutes, each one bringing Oliver closer to her house. She sat on the lounge chair with her knees tucked up under her chin until she heard a knock on the door. As she got up, she'd put the tissue she'd been drying her eyes with into her pocket.

"Hi," she said as she opened the door.

"Hey," Oliver said. "How are you?"

"Ok."

"You've been crying."

"There's a lot to cry about. Would you like a coffee?"

Oliver shook his head, so they walked into the lounge room and sat down. Neither of them said anything. They just looked at each other for a while, then Oliver looked down at the floor. Gaby knew what he would say, and she couldn't stand one more minute of false hope. That would make the tears start again.

"Just say what you need to. I know it was stupid of me to think you might want to still be with me."

He didn't say anything, and Gaby suddenly felt sick in her stomach. She only just made it to the bathroom before she threw up. After she'd rinsed her mouth with water, she looked at herself in the mirror. Her life was ruined, and it was all her fault. She took her time walking back down the hallway, and when she got back to the lounge room, Oliver handed her another tissue and then sat down beside her.

"I know what you think I'm going to say, but first, I have to tell you something."

And for the first time, Oliver told her about his parents. His mum had fallen pregnant just before she'd met her future husband, and six months later, they'd got married, and he'd raised Oliver as his own. No one other than their families and very close friends knew Oliver wasn't his.

"I haven't been able to think about anything else since you told me. I asked Dad why he made the decision he did, and he said he couldn't imagine his life without Mum in it, so it wasn't a hard choice for him to make."

Gaby looked at him and thought about what she'd just heard. She wanted to feel disappointed that he hadn't felt he could share that with her, but she just didn't have the energy right then. It was something they could talk about later. If he was still around.

"The thought of having a baby in my life when I'm just about to turn twenty-one is terrifying."

Gaby stared straight ahead, too scared to look at him. "You're not the only one who thinks it's terrifying."

Oliver reached over and held her hand. She could hear him trying to slow his breathing, and she could feel him shaking, even though he was trying to hide it.

"This is the hardest decision I've ever made, and even though I've made it, I can't get the words out. I need a minute. I'm going to get a glass of water. Do you want one?"

Gaby shook her head and watched as he left the room. She pulled her knees up under her chin again and hugged her legs. She felt like she was standing on the edge of a deep, dark hole and was only just stopping herself from falling in. When Oliver came back into the room, he still didn't speak for a minute or two, but then he turned to Gaby.

"I'm not going to walk away. I don't know how this will work or even if it will work. But I need to at least try. I think we're meant to be together, and what if I never feel that way again?"

Gaby looked at him, too scared to speak. Did she just hear what she thought she had?

"Are you sure?"

"No, but I'm going to do it anyway. It was talking to Dad that helped me make my decision. My parents were the same age as we are now, and they're still together. And I want what they have, so I have to try."

"I'm scared."

"Me too. It's going to be really hard."

Gaby just nodded. There was no other way to describe the future. She just hoped they could actually make it. She reached over and took hold of his hand. For the first time in weeks, Gaby could see a way forward. She just needed to address the issue of what they were going to say to people.

"Why didn't you tell me about your parents?"

"Mum asked me not to. It still upsets her, and she thought if I told you, then you would think differently about her, and she doesn't want that."

"I'm hardly in a position to think differently about her. I'm in exactly the same situation she was."

"I've seen how hard it's been on my mum any time the topic has come up, so I'm going to do the same thing Dad did and let people assume. I might not always feel like that, but for now, I won't say anything unless someone asks me directly. I won't lie though."

Gaby would have leapt in the air if she wasn't still feeling so sick. Would it be possible to just let people assume? Would anyone actually ask outright?

"Really? You would do that for me?"

Oliver nodded. "I thought about that a lot too after talking to Dad. He let people assume, and he said it was the right thing for him to do. He also said it was my decision to make, and it took me a few days to make it, but if I'm going to do this, I want to do it from the beginning."

Gaby couldn't believe what she was hearing. She knew it was possible he would change his mind, although she couldn't think about that now. One thing at a time. The only thing she wanted to think about was that Oliver would be in her life.

Back in the lounge room in Mt Tamborine, Gaby paused and looked at each of her friends before she continued. She was almost at the end, and she was grateful for that. She didn't think she could keep talking much longer.

"You all know Professor Morton helped me apply for the scholarship that allowed me to get my PhD. She also helped me get a place at the university-run child care centre. What you didn't know was that Daisy wasn't Oliver's daughter. We never said she wasn't. We just let people assume that she was; that on one of those occasions we saw each other between breaking up and getting back together, we had sex."

Gaby had lost count of the times she'd been worried that someone would figure it out. Not because she was worried about being judged for falling pregnant from a one night stand, but because someone might say the one thing that scared her the most—that she was no different to her mother, even after everything she'd done to get as far away from that life as possible. The one person she thought she would give her the most grief was her mum, but she assumed Daisy was Oliver's like everyone else and the only thing she'd said to Gaby was that she was too young to be a grandmother.

"As Daisy got older, we were scared about how she would react if she found out. We knew we had to tell her, but we couldn't figure out how. We were worried that she would think she wasn't as much a part of the family as Grace and Lucas. But we have to tell her. She has a right to know. That's why I agreed to take part in this. I was hoping that saying it aloud to you would help me find the words I'm going to need when I tell Daisy."

It hadn't worked out as Gaby hoped though. Talking about what happened wasn't going to make any difference when telling Daisy. At least she would have Oliver. She wouldn't have been able to go through it all back then without him, and she wouldn't be able to face what was to come without him now.

"I still pinch myself to this day that Oliver made the decision to stay. I won't say it's always been easy. We had a lot of arguments, and there were a lot of times when Oliver was unsure about the decision he'd made and thought about walking away."

The other worry in the back of her mind all those years ago, and for at least the next ten years, was that Oliver would change his mind and leave. What he'd offered to do was more than most people would ever do for another person. He'd said to her once that back then, he'd been naïve about what it actually meant and how their lives would change. If he'd been older and had more life experience, he might not have made the same decision. Gaby had to sit down when he'd said that. She only got back up again when he said that he couldn't imagine his life being different and that he was glad he'd been naïve, no matter what they'd had to deal with over the years. It was eight years since they'd had that conversation, and she could still remember every single detail—what room they'd been in, what time of the day it was, what she'd been wearing. She also remembered that for the first time since Daisy was born, she felt secure in the knowledge that Oliver wasn't going anywhere.

"That's why I was a little bit upset when Laura made that remark earlier about not commenting on having moments with your husband. We've had plenty of moments over the years because of the consequences of the decision Oliver made. There was even a time about fifteen years ago, before Grace and Lucas, that I thought he was going to leave. But he didn't, and we worked through it, just as I know we'll work through this."

Gaby looked at each of them and tried to guess what they were thinking. They were all doing a good job of not reacting, but she could imagine the thoughts racing through their minds.

Especially Evie. Gaby could still clearly picture the day of Daisy's christening. It wasn't something she would have done, but every child in Oliver's family had been christened, and neither of them wanted the inevitable questions that would be asked if Daisy wasn't. Evie had held Daisy as the water had been poured on her head and she hadn't made a sound. She just kept staring up at Evie. It was as if a bond had formed at that moment and had never been broken. Laura and Anna would look differently at Daisy now, and there was nothing she could do about that. She knew them well enough to know they wouldn't do anything to give away her secret so she wouldn't have to ask them to be careful around Daisy. But Evie, she would have to talk to her and soon. Not about being careful—Evie would never do anything to upset Daisy—but about how upset she must be feeling right now. Gaby could see it in her face even though she tried her best to hide it. There would be an opportunity to talk before they left, so she pushed the thought to the side while she finished speaking.

"The passing years have taught me something else as well. I've realised that I'm not my mother. The same thing may have happened to both of us, but I made choices that were good for me and good for my family, and I'm happy with the life I have. And I know now that she's happy with the life she has. She is who she is, and she'll never change. I've accepted that, just as I've accepted who I am, and I don't have to repeat her patterns. I've created the life I wanted for myself."

Chapter 9

After Gaby finished speaking, there was silence. Evie got up and went into the kitchen to get another bottle of wine. Laura followed her to the fridge to get more snacks. Neither of them said anything. When they came back into the room, Evie filled up everyone's glass except Anna, who put her hand over the top of hers. Laura filled up the bowls of snacks on the coffee table, sat down, and stared at the fire. Evie stared intently at her glass but didn't take a sip. It was Gaby who broke the silence.

"I can tell that I've shocked you all. It wasn't easy to say what I just did. Apart from Oliver, you are the only people who know. I realise that Daisy should have been the first to know, but I've just been putting it off. She hasn't seemed herself lately, and I didn't want to add to whatever is going on. I don't know how Daisy will take the news or how we'll move forward as a family once she does know."

Anna and Laura looked at each other, unsure of what to do or whether they should say anything. Evie didn't look at Gaby at all.

After a minute or two, Anna got up, went over to Gaby and put her arm around her.

"I know we're not supposed to say anything, but I want to say we'll all be there for you if you need us."

Laura nodded. "Absolutely. Any time you need anything."

Gaby looked at Evie and waited for her to say something, but she didn't. Instead, she just nodded in agreement and then changed the subject.

"I know that took a lot of courage to say what you did, but I think we need to stick to the rules and continue before Anna, Laura or I work ourselves into such a state that we won't be as brave as you were when it comes to our turns. So who wants to go next? I'd rather not if that's ok. I just need a while to think about what I've just heard."

Anna was still holding on to her wine glass, and she started twirling it around, staring intently at the wine that she'd only had a few sips of. Laura reached for a cracker and cheese, but instead of eating it, she put it down on the armrest of her chair. She looked at it for a moment, picked it up, took a small bite and then put it down again.

"I'll go next," Anna said. "If I don't do it now, I'll chicken out and never have my turn, and that wouldn't be fair on everyone else."

"You don't have to go as far as I did," Gaby said. "That was just something I needed to share to help me figure out how to handle the situation. And before you start, I just wanted to say something about the rules. I know we agreed that we wouldn't speak again about anything we say in this room if we didn't want to. But part of the reason I told you all my secret is that I'm hoping you can give me some advice on how to tell Daisy. Not now. Tonight I want to stick with what we agreed to. And it doesn't apply to anyone else. Just me. I'm happy to not talk about what any of you say after this if you don't want to."

"Of course we'll talk about it with you and help come up with the best way to tell Daisy," Anna said.

Laura nodded. "I'm happy to help too. That also applies to Anna and Evie. If there is something either of you needs help with, we can talk about it any time. Or we can stick to the rules and not say anything."

Gaby looked at Evie, but again she just nodded and didn't say anything. "Thank you. I really appreciate it. And Laura, the same goes for you. It's up to each one of us whether we never again mention what's said tonight or if you want to talk about it in the future. I've taken up enough of Anna's time, so I think we should let her speak now."

Anna wasn't sure where to start. From the minute she heard Gaby open up, she knew what she needed to say, but she didn't know how to say it. She looked over at Gaby and thought she got through her story all right, and she seemed ok. Her hands weren't shaking like Anna's were, and she was sure that Gaby's mouth wasn't dry, nor was there any sweat dripping down the back of her neck. Anna looked around the room and realised everyone was waiting for her to start. The only way she was going to be able to do this was to plunge straight in before fear paralysed her, and she couldn't speak at all. So she did.

"I had an eating disorder."

Anna felt sick the minute she said it. There was no turning back now. She could feel her stomach churning and the sweat starting to pool in her palms. She looked at her half-full wine glass and wondered if it would help calm her nerves if she took another sip but decided against it. With her stomach feeling the way it was, the wine would probably come straight back up.

"You were right, Laura. You knew, but I denied it. When I think about the number of times you said you were concerned whether I was eating or not and the number of times I lied, I feel terrible. But I felt like I couldn't say anything because I would seem weak. I thought I was fat and ugly. And that everyone else thought that too. I kept thinking that if I lost a little more weight, everything would be all right, and I wouldn't have to hide what I was doing anymore. I kept focusing on the day I would unveil my new thin figure, but even though I lost weight, I never thought it was enough, and I always had a few more kilos to go. It took me almost a year to go and see a doctor and ask for help, and even now, whenever I get stressed I start to control what I'm eating. Not like I used to and not

150

all the time. But even though it's been twenty-one years since the problem got out of hand, I still struggle with it sometimes. So now that I've started, I guess the best thing to do is take you back to when we were all in grade twelve."

Anna looked at the outfits on her bed. She was supposed to go to Laura's first show tonight, and everything she owned made her look fat. She'd gone through her entire wardrobe five times and hated everything. Tonight was a big deal for Laura, so she had to find something. At seventeen, Laura was the youngest person to display some of her drawings and paintings at the local art show. Anna wished she was good at something in the way Laura was with her art, but so far, she hadn't discovered what it was. She did know what she wasn't good at though—losing weight. She'd been on a diet for the past four weeks, and she didn't look any different. It was like she only had to look at food, and she put on weight. She tried on all the dresses again and picked the one she thought hid the most. It was a deep navy blue, and every time she wore it, she thought about her dad. Navy blue had been his favourite colour. As soon as she thought about him, her heart ached, and the tears threatened to roll down her cheeks, just like every other time. It had been four years since he'd died, and she hoped that eventually, she'd be able to think about him without being upset. Everyone told her that she'd be able to do that one day, but so far, the pain hadn't gone away.

Laura spotted Anna as soon as she walked into the gallery and ran over to her. "What do you think?"

"Your paintings look amazing," Anna said as she gave Laura a hug. 'I'm so proud of you."

"Thanks. I'm so glad you came."

Anna hugged her again. "There's no way I would have missed this. Is Gaby here yet?"

Laura shook her head and then scanned the room. "I haven't seen her. Oh, hang on, she's just coming in now."

Anna watched as Laura ran over and hugged Gaby before turning to say hello to the person who walked in behind her. On her way over to Anna, Gaby looked around the room at all the artwork.

"I've never been to an art show before," Gaby said. "Maybe I should have put a dress on."

"You don't like dresses."

"I know, but maybe I should have got one for this."

"You look great how you are."

"How long have you been here?"

"Not very long. I wanted to come a bit earlier, but I had to do some washing."

Gaby sighed. "Me too. When do things get easier?"

"I don't know. I hope it's soon."

Anna and Gaby walked around the room, looking at everything on display. There wasn't a lot they actually liked, except for Laura's artwork, of course.

"What's that meant to be?" Gaby asked, pointing at a sculpture.

Anna shrugged her shoulders. "No idea."

They stared at it for a while, trying to figure it out until they were interrupted by a waiter with food, and Gaby grabbed one of everything he had on the tray.

"I'm starving. I haven't had dinner. Do you want anything?"

Anna stared at the tray. Everything looked so good, and the smell made her mouth water. She shook her head though. "No, I had some dinner before I left, so I'm not hungry."

Anna hoped that Gaby couldn't hear her stomach rumbling. She hadn't eaten anything since the apple at lunch, and she was starving. It was so hard to stick to her diet, but she didn't have a choice. She had to stay on it until she got down to the size she wanted to be.

"Look at Laura over there, smiling and talking to people about her art. It's so wonderful," Gaby said. "I'm so happy for her."

Anna nodded. "Me too. She's worked so hard, and she's so talented."

"And she knows what she wants to do with her life. I wish I knew that."

"I thought you wanted to go to university and become a teacher."

"I don't know. I can't make my mind up. How am I supposed to know what I want to do for the rest of my life? I'm only seventeen."

Anna didn't know what she wanted to do either, and she was eighteen. She'd always thought she would automatically feel more like an adult when she turned eighteen, but she didn't. There were still so many things she was unsure about. If her dad was still alive, she would have asked him. He'd always made her feel better when she wasn't sure about something or when she didn't know what the right thing to do was. There had never been anything she couldn't talk to him about, although if he was still with her, she wouldn't have told him about her diet. She knew he wouldn't have liked it, and she wouldn't have been able to get him to understand that she had no choice.

"I don't know what I want to do either," Anna said. "I'm hoping I have it figured out in the next five months before we finish school."

Anna had gone through so many options, but nothing seemed right to her. It scared her that she was almost finished grade twelve and next year would have to either get a job or go to university. She wished the right career for her would just pop into her mind one day, and she'd be happy with it. All of the options she'd previously thought of were still going through her head when the waiter came back. She smelt the food before she saw it, and if she stayed too much longer she'd give in, and she didn't want to do that. She told Laura and Gaby that she was tired, even though she wasn't, and she left ten minutes later. When she got home, she rode on the exercise bike for half an hour. She would rather have done aerobics, but she didn't feel up to standing and jumping around.

The next day she really did feel tired. As she sat on the grass overlooking the sports oval with her friends at lunchtime, she struggled to keep her eyes open. She should have gone to bed instead of exercising, but if she hadn't, she would have been awake for hours feeling guilty. For some reason, she felt really lethargic too, and she didn't know why. In the background, she heard the bell sound and she slowly got up off the grass and started walking towards the buildings. She didn't want to go back into a classroom because the sun was warm, and it was making her feel better. As she headed to class, she thought she should have gone for a walk instead of sitting down. Now she had to spend the next two hours sitting still in a cold, dark classroom, which wouldn't burn any calories at all.

"What have you got now?" Laura asked

"Accounting. What about you?"

"Economics. I'll see you after school. Are you going to aerobics tonight?"

"Yeah."

"I should come with you sometime."

"I don't think you'd like it. Remember how much you hate exercise."

"I know, but I don't do anything."

"You don't need to. Look how skinny you are."

"I still should do some exercise. It's supposed to be good for you. See you after school."

Anna was glad Laura wasn't coming with her. If she started exercising, she'd become even skinnier, and the difference between their sizes would be even more noticeable. For a brief moment, she wondered why she didn't have a best friend who was overweight like she was, but she quickly dismissed the thought. She loved Laura, and she felt lucky to have her as a best friend. She just wished Laura wasn't so skinny.

"Hey Evie," Anna said down the phone that afternoon after school. "How are you feeling?"

Evie sighed. "Still sick. I hate being sick. And I hate that I missed Laura's show last night. I wanted to be there with her too."

"She knows you would have been there if you hadn't been unwell."

"Yeah, I know. I rang her just before and asked all about it. It's not the same though. Did you have fun?"

"Yep. I didn't like some of the artwork but looking at Laura's paintings hanging on the walls at the gallery was amazing."

"I wish I could have been there. Laura's so lucky to be able to paint and draw like she does. I'm not the least bit artistic."

"Neither is Gaby and I. We said that to each other last night."

"You might not be artistic, but there are plenty of things you're good at. Look how well you're managing on your own, taking care of the house and yourself and still going to school. That's a talent."

"How is that a talent?"

"You obviously have great organisational skills, and you're a lot more grown-up than the rest of us. I'm sure I'd do a terrible job of looking after a house. I can't even be bothered making my bed in the morning."

If Anna didn't do that every morning, it would just be one more thing to add to the list of chores to do at the end of the day, and with her mum away, there was no one else to do it. Just like there was no one else to clean the house, buy the groceries, do the washing, pay the bills or do the hundred other things she had to fit in around her schoolwork. Anna didn't think she was handling her situation as well as her friends thought she was. At least she could talk to Gaby about everything she had to do because Gaby understood what it was like.

"You always look amazing too when we go out," Evie said. "Laura said you looked beautiful last night. She said you looked like one of those Botticelli angels."

Anna almost dropped the phone when Evie said that. She remembered them from art class, and they were fat in all those paintings. So when she got off the phone, she started exercising. First running, then bike riding, then aerobics. By the time she went to bed she felt exhausted, and when the alarm went off at 6.00am the next day, she struggled to get out of bed. The first thing she did was look in the mirror, and what she saw disgusted her. All she could see were rolls of fat—on her stomach, thighs, backside, even on her arms. She turned away from the mirror because she couldn't stand looking at herself anymore, then she got dressed in a baggy tracksuit and went downstairs. As she pulled out the cleaning products from under the kitchen sink, she wondered how many calories housework burned. She was vacuuming when the phone rang.

"Good morning," Laura's voice came down the phone. "What are you doing?"

"Cleaning the house."

"Yuck."

"I know, but I have to clean before Mum arrives. I don't want her thinking I'm not looking after our house."

"Guess that's a good reason to clean. How's your pop going?"

"He's ok, but he finds it hard to do a lot of things now."

"At least he's got your mum."

Anna's mum had moved back to Mackay earlier that year to look after her ailing father, and Anna had been living in the house on her own. She didn't want to move during her last year of high school, and after a lot of persuading and a few arguments, she'd managed to convince her mum she'd be ok on her own. It was only after she'd reminded her that she was eighteen and didn't need to ask her permission anymore that she'd finally given in.

"Yeah. It's not easy looking after Pop, but she's been catching up with friends she hasn't seen in a long time, so she's really liking that."

"Is she still as skinny as ever?"

"Probably. She was the last time she came down to visit, and I doubt that would have changed."

"Your mum is always so glamorous, and she has the most amazing figure. I'd love to look like that when I'm her age."

"You and me both."

"You've got nothing to worry about. You're gorgeous, exactly like your mum. Anyway, I'm driving to school today. Do you want me to pick you up?"

If she got a lift with Laura, she could still fit in a run. "That would be good."

"All right. I'll be there about 8.15am."

Anna hung up the phone, put away the vacuum and went up to her room to get her Walkman and look at herself in the mirror again. It used to be in her mum's room, but Anna moved it to her room because it was bigger than hers. She looked at herself for a few minutes and then headed down the stairs, running her hand along the railing, remembering the day her dad had painted it. It was six years ago and she remembered pestering him to let her help. He eventually gave in and let her paint a section. Then, when he thought she wasn't looking, he painted over the same area again to fix it, so it looked like the rest. He never said anything to her. Instead, he always told anyone who commented on the new railing colour that Anna had helped paint it. Thinking about it made her smile. She was so glad her mum hadn't wanted to sell the house. That was something her mum thought about but decided not to because she didn't know how long she'd be gone. Her pop had good days and bad days and the doctors couldn't say how long he had left. Her nanna had been dead for three years, and her uncle had died in a car accident when she was five years old. Her mum was the only one left to care for him. Sometimes Anna hated that she was so far away. She'd already lost one parent, and it would have made her feel better to have the other one around all the time, but there was nothing she could do to change that. And there was nothing she could do to bring her dad back, so she pulled on her joggers and went for a run, partly to exercise and partly to stop thinking about her dad.

When she got back, she felt light-headed and had to lean against the basin in the bathroom for a few minutes before she could get in the shower. While she waited for the dizziness to pass, she looked at herself in the mirror. Laura was wrong; Anna was nothing like her mum.

After her shower, she still felt a little bit dizzy but walked into the bedroom anyway and opened the wardrobe doors to get her uniform. Hanging up beside it was her mum's jeans, the ones she'd worn when she was Anna's age. Her mum had decided to have a clean-up before she went to Mackay and found them in one of the boxes stacked in the garage. She had wanted to throw them out, but Anna wouldn't let her. Every morning she held them up against her in front of the mirror. She was determined to fit into them one day. As she reached in to get the jeans, she suddenly felt the room start to spin and her vision clouded over, and all she could see were spots. She grabbed onto the wardrobe door to steady herself, but the room wouldn't stop spinning. Everything went dark, and she could feel sweat building up all over her body and a shooting pain running down her back. She cried out, but there was no one there to help her. Her heart started beating faster in her chest, and her breath became shallow. No matter how much she tried, she couldn't get enough air into her lungs. The last thing she remembered was the pain as the back of her skull hit the wardrobe door as she fell.

Chapter 10

Anna opened her eyes and, for a moment, didn't know where she was or what had happened. She tried to sit up but instantly felt nauseous, so she lowered herself back down and concentrated on breathing as deeply as she could. After a few minutes, she was able to crawl over to the bed, pull herself up and collapse on the mattress. She lifted her arm slowly and reached up to the back of her head where she could feel a lump. That explains the headache, she thought. She lay still until she started feeling better, then turned her head as gently as she could to look at the clock. Laura would be there in about twenty minutes, so she crossed her fingers and prayed she would be ok soon. A voice in the back of her head told her if she'd eaten something, this wouldn't have happened. The same voice told her to get up and go and eat something. A different voice told her not to. The voices went back and forth until, eventually, the voice that told her not to eat won. She slowly sat up, had a few sips of water, then got dressed and went downstairs to wait for Laura, taking time to sit with her head between her knees until she felt almost back to normal. The dizziness had gone by the time Laura knocked on the door, but the headache was still there. And she felt stiff and sore all over from landing heavily on the timber floor. As she walked to the door, she put a fake smile on her face and told herself not to let Laura know what had happened.

The morning dragged on, and Anna had trouble focusing on her classes. Nothing made sense. Biology was her favourite class, especially when the topic was anatomy, but when she looked down at what she'd written, there wasn't much there. The more she learnt about the human body, the more she hoped she would discover ways to take control of hers. At the end of the lesson, she got up and felt her head spin again, so she stood at the desk for a few moments pretending she was still packing up while waiting for the lightheadedness to pass. As the next class walked in, one of the boys asked the teacher if they would still be dissecting frogs. Just the thought of that made Anna feel sick. She walked slowly out of the classroom and just made it to the toilets across the hall before she vomited. The only thing that came up was water, but it still hurt the back of her throat. She held onto the sides of the toilet bowl until the vomiting stopped then tried to stand. She got about halfway up before everything went black. The next thing she knew, she was lying in the sick room with a cool face washer draped across her forehead.

"You gave us a fright," the school nurse said. "Lucky I found you when I did. I don't think you'd been lying there long. If I hadn't seen your foot sticking out under the toilet door, you might still be there."

Anna remembered going to the toilet to vomit but nothing after that. Twice in one day, she thought. For a moment, she started shaking, scared by what had happened, but then she took a deep breath and told herself not to be silly. It was just a coincidence. Maybe she was coming down with something. It had nothing to do with her diet. Nothing would make her change that.

"Do you know what happened?" the nurse asked.

"I was in biology and I heard a boy talking about dissecting frogs, and it made me feel sick. I needed to throw up. I think I bumped my head when I was getting up."

"Some people don't react well to the thought of dissection. I'll check your head while you're here to make sure everything is ok."

Anna lay still while the nurse felt her head, touching it all over until she found the lump from that morning.

"It's only a small lump, so that's good. You'll get a headache from it, but that should be about all. I'm going to keep you here until the end of the day, just to make sure."

Anna didn't tell the nurse she'd had a headache all day or that she'd taken several tablets, but they hadn't done anything to make the headache go away. At least she'd had a nurse check out her head. If something else had been wrong, she would have been told. For the rest of the afternoon, she lay in the sickroom and sipped on water. The nurse offered jellybeans to replace the sugar she thought Anna would have lost from throwing up. When she wasn't looking, Anna spat the jellybeans out of her mouth, wrapped them in a tissue and put them in her bag. After the school bell rang at 3pm, the nurse checked her again and let her go. She walked to Laura's car and waited for her to arrive, the whole time willing her to hurry up because she just wanted to go home and lie down.

"Hey," Laura said as she pulled her car keys out of her bag. "How were your classes this afternoon?"

Anna didn't want Laura, or her other friends, to know she hadn't been in class and was grateful that this was the one afternoon of the week they didn't have any classes together. "Boring. What about yours?'

Laura laughed. "The same. I hate science. Why can't I just have art class all day?"

Anna got in the car slowly and tried to get comfortable. She was still sore from the first fall, and the second one had only made it worse. She just wanted to get home and hop into the bath because she knew the warm water would make her feel better. She stared out the window as Laura drove, cursing under her breath every time they had to stop at a red light.

"You're quiet," Laura said. "What's wrong?"

"Nothing, I didn't sleep well last night."

She'd actually fallen asleep straight away, but Laura didn't know that, and it was a good excuse for not talking much.

"You didn't sleep well the other night either. And you look a bit pale. Are you feeling all right?"

Anna nodded.

"Maybe you're trying to do too much with looking after the house and going to school."

"That's probably it."

"You need to take care of yourself. I worry about you and everything you're trying to do."

"There's nothing to worry about. I'm fine."

"Are you sure?"

"Yes, just tired like I said."

Anna was happy for Laura to think she was tired. It had only been the day before that Laura had commented about Anna not eating very much at lunch. She would never understand because she'd always been skinny.

The night before her mum arrived, she checked that every room in the house was neat and tidy. When she'd finished, she headed upstairs to begin her nightly ritual of standing in front of the mirror and looking at all the things that were wrong with her body. About halfway up, the dizziness hit her, not as bad as earlier in the week but enough that she had to sit down, put her head between her knees and wait for it to pass. The voice in her head came back and told her she should eat something, but she ignored it. Instead, she stayed on the stairs until she felt ok and then went back to the kitchen to make herself a black coffee. As she waited for the jug to boil, she couldn't stop thinking about a piece of bread. Her stomach grumbled and ached, and it was like she could feel the bread calling her. Just one slice won't hurt, she thought. Then the other voice that was often in her head said that it would, and she shouldn't eat anything. She'd never reach her goal if she did.

She walked out of the room, but the bread was all she could think about. She tried watching TV, but that didn't take her mind off the bread. By the time she heard the jug boil and went to make the coffee, she felt dizzy again and had to hold on to the kitchen bench. The voice returned and kept saying, eat the bread, eat the bread. Finally, when she couldn't take it anymore, she threw open the fridge door, grabbed the piece of bread and shoved in it her mouth, not even tasting it, just chewing fast and then swallowing. After the bread was gone, she sank down onto the kitchen floor and started crying. Why had she given in? She would never fit into her mum's jeans if she kept eating like she did. The bread suddenly felt like lead in her stomach. She rushed to the bathroom, knelt down in front of the toilet and stuck her fingers down her throat.

Straight away, she started gagging and felt like she couldn't breathe, so she pulled her fingers out. But there was no way she was letting herself fail at this as well. So she pulled herself back over to the toilet and tried again and again until she threw up. When she'd finished, she got up, washed her mouth, cleaned her teeth and looked at her face in the mirror. She heard the phone ring in the background but let it go to the answering machine. From the bathroom, she could hear Evie's cheerful voice.

"Hey Anna, just seeing if you were home. I've got the place to myself. Mum and dad decided to go away for the weekend, and James isn't here either, so I thought I'd ring for a chat. Call me back."

Anna had often wondered what it would be like to have a brother like Evie or two sisters and a brother like Laura. Her dad got sick for the first time not long after she was born. By the time he'd finished the treatment that was supposed to take away the cancer, her parents hadn't been sure whether to try for another child in case it came back, which it eventually did. The thought of her dad made her eyes overflow with tears. Her life would be so different if he was still there, and they lived together like a typical family. For as long as she could remember, she hadn't been happy with her weight, but her dad told her every day how beautiful she was. After he was gone, there was no one to tell her. No one she believed anyway. Anna wiped the tears from her eyes, turned away from the mirror, cleaned the toilet and then went to bed. When she saw Evie, she'd pretend that she'd forgotten to ring her back.

The next day, her mum arrived at 3.30pm. Anna had been dressed and waiting by the front door for the last thirty minutes.

"Hi mum," she said, giving her a hug as she came in the door. "Did you have a good trip?"

"I did. I stopped in Rockhampton for morning tea and then Miriam Vale for lunch. There wasn't a lot of traffic on the road, so I had a good run. The house looks great."

"Thanks."

"You're doing such a good job, but I still hate leaving you here by yourself."

"I'm eighteen, and the neighbours check on me, and my friends all live nearby. You have to stop feeling guilty. Pop needs you more than I do and I don't want to change schools in my last year. I'm fine on my own."

"I know. You always were very grown up and capable of looking after yourself even when you were young, but I still don't like it."

"Everything is fine. Put your bag upstairs, and I'll make you a cuppa."

Anna looked at her as she walked up the stairs, and even after ten hours in a car, she looked like she'd just got ready to go out instead of just arriving after a long road trip. Anna looked down at her own outfit and wondered why she'd bothered. She would just have to keep going until she looked the way she wanted to. As she boiled the jug, she remembered she still needed to do some economics homework, but she couldn't remember what chapter she was supposed to read, so she rang the person who would know.

"Twelve and thirteen," Gaby said. "Has your mum arrived yet?

"Yep, just now."

"You must be happy to see her. What are you going to do while she's here?"

"Don't know. Didn't make any plans. She's only here for a few days, and apparently, I'm not allowed to skip school to spend time with her."

Gaby sighed. "At least she's taking your education seriously. My mum wouldn't even know if I went to school."

In the background, Anna could hear the sound of breaking glass.

"Can you hang on a sec?"

Down the phone line, Anna could hear Gaby talking.

"I'll get it. Sit down again. Mum, sit down. Don't go over there. You haven't got any shoes on. I'll clean it up in a second when I've finished talking to Anna."

Anna heard mumbling but couldn't make out the words.

"Sorry," Gaby said. "I'll have to go."

"Your mum all right?"

"Yeah. She just got back from the pub. She'll pass out in a minute and I'll be able to go back to my homework."

Anna hung up and thought about what Gaby had to do. Apart from wishing she looked like her mum, Anna had nothing else to complain about. Her mum had always been supportive of her. She wasn't the one who commented on Anna's size. It was something Anna did to herself.

"How's school?" her mum asked.

"It's all right," Anna replied, pouring the boiling water into the coffee cups. "I'm doing well in all my classes, and I'm on the tennis team now."

"I used to play tennis when I was younger. Are you enjoying it?"

"Yeah, it's a lot of fun."

"Are you still playing netball?"

Anna nodded.

"You're becoming very sporty. Don't overdo it though. You look like you've lost some weight."

"It's just this jumper. It's too big for me. Do you want to go outside to the verandah?"

Her mum nodded, and Anna followed her out the door, pulling her jumper down as far as it would go so she could hide as much of herself as possible. They sat on the swing chair that had been there for years. It was faded now, but Anna's dad had made it, so neither wanted to throw it out. Anna often came outside and sat in the chair, sometimes for hours.

"What do you want to do later for dinner? I'm not really in the mood to go out after ten hours of driving, so I might order a pizza."

Anna couldn't remember the last time she'd had pizza. Just the thought of it made her mouth water. It was so unfair that her mum could eat whatever she wanted. She shook her head though and told a white lie. "I had pizza for lunch and ate way too many slices. I'm still full. So I might just have toast."

"What sort of pizza did you get?"

Anna thought quickly. "Ham and pineapple."

"That was your dad's favourite. I haven't had one of those in ages. I might order one anyway because I'll be hungry at dinner time."

Anna looked away as soon as her dad was mentioned. She didn't want her mum to see how upset she still was. She'd dealt with so much after Anna's dad had died, and she'd finally begun to look happy again, so Anna didn't want to say anything that would cause her to worry.

Anna and her mum stayed outside and chatted while they drank their coffee and then went inside when the sun had set. When the pizza arrived, Anna said she had homework to do and went up to her room and shut the door so she couldn't see it. She could still smell it though. And it was torture.

The next day Anna had planned to go to the markets with Laura and Evie. She'd wanted to cancel, but her mum told her not to.

"You'll only be gone for a couple of hours, and it will give me a chance to go next door and see Martha while you're gone. We can spend more time together when you get back."

Wanting to spend time with her mum wasn't the reason Anna didn't feel like going. Even though she'd had an early night she was feeling tired, and not even the two cups of black coffee she'd had made her feel more awake. It took her so long to get ready that she was still in the bathroom when Laura and Evie arrived. She heard them talking to her mum and then she heard them laughing together. Anna thought how nice it would be if they kept laughing and forgot she was there so she could go back to bed and sleep. The thought didn't last long because she heard Laura bounding up the stairs. She quickly pulled her baggy shirt down and stepped away from the mirror where she'd been standing looking at her stomach.

"Morning. I was just saying hello to your mum. Evie's still down there chatting. Are you ready?"

Anna nodded. "Almost. Just need to put my shoes on."

"Is that a new shirt?"

"Yes, I bought it last weekend."

"It's nice. Looks a bit big for you though. Have you lost weight?"

"Just a little bit from being sick. That's all."

"You sure that's all it is?" Laura asked. "You're not trying one of those silly diets like the one you tried earlier in the year are you?"

Anna shook her head. She thought to herself, yes, she was on a diet, but it wasn't a silly one, and she didn't want to talk about it with the one person she knew who'd never been on a diet in her life. One of two people, she corrected herself. Her mum had never been on a diet either.

"It's just that tummy bug I had. Let's go to the markets."

Anna hated every minute at the markets, especially lunch. Laura and Evie ate hamburgers while she got the smallest salad she could find.

Laura screwed her nose up. "Don't understand how you can eat that. I can't stand salad."

Evie shook her head. "Me either."

Anna didn't want to talk about food, so she changed the subject. "Where have your parents gone this weekend, Evie?"

"Just up the coast. How come you didn't ring me back the other night?"

"Sorry, I forgot," she said quickly, hoping Evie wouldn't say anything else. "Do you want to look at some more stalls when we've finished eating?"

They both nodded. Anna knew that would change the subject from food and the unreturned phone call. Laura and Evie loved shopping, and they thought Anna was strange because she told them recently that she didn't really like shopping anymore. Not since the day she'd gone shopping trying to find a new dress to wear to Laura's art exhibition.

"What about this one," the shop assistant had said.

Anna had tried it on and looked at it from every angle. "I'm not sure."

"It's a lovely colour on you, and the cut is very slimming."

Anna had turned to look at her, and the assistant had smiled knowingly.

"We all look for that in a dress don't we? Something that makes us look skinnier than we are."

Anna had taken the dress off, mumbled something about thinking about it and quickly left the store.

"I want to go and try that dress on we saw at that stall near the entrance," Evie said.

"Ok," Laura said. "There was one there that I really liked and I saw one that would look great on Anna."

Anna shook her head. "I don't want to buy anything. I can't afford it this week. Before we go anywhere, I need to go to the toilet."

Inside the cubicle, she stuck her fingers down her throat.

"Are you all right, Anna?" Evie asked.

Anna stood up quickly. She hadn't realised that Evie had followed her in.

"Yes, I'm fine. Just got a funny taste in my mouth, so I'm trying to spit it out. I'll be out in a minute."

Anna leant against the cubicle wall and hoped that Evie believed her. She waited another minute and then opened the door. Evie wasn't there. Anna could see her through the window, waiting outside with Laura. When she walked outside, Laura asked her if she was ok, and Anna told her the same thing she told Evie. As they walked off towards the stall with the dresses, Anna saw them look at each other, but they were soon distracted by clothes.

"This is the one I thought would look great on you, Anna," Laura said. "You should try it on."

The woman who owned the stall held the dress up and told her she could try it on behind the curtain at the back.

"I can help you if you like," she said. "It can be tricky sometimes to get the straps in the right position."

Anna shook her head. "No, I don't think so. I don't really need another dress."

"No one will see you behind the curtain if that's what you're worried about," she said.

Anna shook her head again. "No, that's not it. I just don't think it's the right sort of dress for me."

Laura looked at the dress and then at Anna. "What are you talking about? It would look great on you."

"I don't want to," she said for the last time and then she stormed off.

Laura and Evie both chased after her.

"Sorry," Evie said. "I didn't mean to make you feel bad."

"Me either," Laura said.

Anna felt bad about yelling at her friends, but she just wanted to be alone and away from the pretty clothes that would never look good on her.

They only stayed another fifteen minutes after that. As she got out of the car, when they arrived back at her house, Laura asked her if she was ok, and she nodded.

"You just haven't been your usual happy self lately. Are you sure everything's ok?"

Evie chimed in from the back seat. "I noticed that too."

"There's nothing wrong. I just feel tired from being sick, and I just want to lie down."

"You've been tired a lot lately," Laura said.

Evie leaned forward in between the front seats. "Maybe you should go to the doctor."

Anna shook her head. "I don't need to go to the doctor. I'm not really sick anymore. A few more days, and I'll feel better. Now I have to go because I told mum I'd spend the rest of the day with her."

She waved as they drove off. She could see them talking, and she knew they were talking about her. It didn't matter though, because it wouldn't be much longer now.

In the kitchen, there was a note saying that Martha had been out in the morning, so they were spending the afternoon together and then having an early dinner. Anna breathed a sigh of relief. The change in her mum's plans meant she could tell her when she got home that she'd already had dinner. As she stood in the kitchen, she suddenly felt very dizzy and had to hang onto the bench. Once the dizziness passed, she went upstairs, ran a bath and lowered herself gently into the warm water. When the water went cold, she emptied the tub and refilled it. She was still there, the water cocooning her when her mum came home.

"Anna," her mum said, as she knocked lightly on the bathroom door, "how much longer are you going to be?"

"I'll get out now."

"Great. I haven't had a chance to spend a lot of time with you today. See you downstairs in a minute."

Anna climbed out of the bath. As she was drying herself, she looked down at the bruises on her arms, the ones that had been there since she fell in the toilet cubicle at school. She quickly pulled her jumper over her head so she couldn't see them anymore and then went downstairs. It was close to midnight before she got into bed. Her mum had wanted to keep talking, and Anna had to remind her it was a school day tomorrow. Before she headed up to bed, her mum gave her a hug goodnight, and the sleeve of her jumper was pushed up.

"What happened to your arm?"

Anna quickly pulled the sleeve back down. "Last week's netball game was a bit rougher than it usual, and I got knocked over by one of the players on the other team."

"Does it hurt? Did you go to the doctor?"

Anna shook her head. "It looks worse than what it is. I hardly felt anything. Good night."

"Good night. Are you sure you don't need to get your arm checked?"

Anna shook her head, "No, it will heal soon." She hugged her mum and walked out of the kitchen. She'd have to be more careful about making sure her clothes covered what they needed to.

"Are you ready, Anna?" her mum called up the stairs. "Laura's here, and you don't want to be late for school."

"Down in a minute," Anna called out.

She reached for the cleaning products under the sink and quickly cleaned up the vomit on the sides of the toilet bowl. She'd had no choice but to eat some of the cereal her mum prepared for her, but as soon as she finished it, she ran up to the bathroom. As much as she loved seeing her mum, she was glad she was going home tomorrow so she wouldn't have to hide what she was doing anymore.

"You can blame me for Anna running late this morning. We were up late last night, talking. Do you want some more breakfast before you go, Anna? You didn't finish all of your cereal."

"I'll just take something with me. I haven't got time to sit down and eat. Come on, Laura, we'll be late for school. I'll see you tonight."

When Anna got home that afternoon, a note on the kitchen bench said her mum had gone to buy some groceries. Anna sighed. She didn't want any more food in the house. She walked up the stairs, stopping at the door to her mum's room. She listened for a moment but couldn't hear any noises, like a car pulling up outside or the garage door opening. She walked in and opened the wardrobe door. All the clothes her mum had brought with her were hanging up. One by one, she pulled them out of the wardrobe and tried them on. Not one of them fit, no matter how much she breathed in, tugged at them, twisted them and tried to pull shirts over her head or pants up her legs. When she'd finished, she put each one back, careful to make sure they were in precisely the same order. Then she closed the door and went into her room, shutting the door, throwing herself on the bed and pummeling her fists into the mattress. All her hard work still wasn't enough. She was never going to fit into those jeans. The same ones her mum had been wearing the day she met her dad.

The following morning, Anna got up early to say goodbye. "It's been great seeing you. Have a good trip back to Mackay and drive safely."

"I will. Make sure you look after yourself. And make sure you eat lots when you feel better. You look like you've lost too much weight and it doesn't suit you. I'm worried."

"I'm fine. Now go so you can get back to Mackay before dark."

"Plenty of time to get back. It's only 4.00am. You should go back to bed. It's dark and cold outside, and you don't have to be at school for a few hours."

"I'll wait until you go, and then I'll go back to bed."

Instead, Anna waved until her mum was out of sight, walked back into the empty house, put her sneakers on and went for a jog. How could she say that Anna had lost too much weight and it didn't suit her? When she'd stood beside her mum in the bathroom that morning and looked in the mirror, it had shocked her how much fatter she still was. The mirror didn't lie. She would have to eat less and exercise more if she was going to fit into those jeans. That thought stayed in her mind as she continued running and stayed there even after she got home and had a shower. As she towelled herself off, she caught sight of her naked body in the mirror and hated what she saw. In frustration, she banged her fist on the wall and put a hole in the plaster. A sharp pain ran down her arm and, for a minute, she thought she had broken a bone. Blood from her hand started running down her arm, the room started spinning then she fell to the floor. Tears from the pain streamed down her face, and she sobbed. She lay on the cold, hard tiles, a towel wrapped around her hand to stop the bleeding. The tears and the pain wouldn't stop, and she didn't know whether she needed to call an ambulance. Eventually, the pain subsided enough that she could move, but she stayed on the floor with her arms clamped around her knees that were pressed tightly against her chest, rocking from side to side. Through the bathroom door, she could see the photo of her dad that she had beside her bed and thought about what he would say if he saw her now. He'd be so disappointed in her, and he'd be upset with her too. Anna couldn't stand that thought and, for the first time, she really started questioning what she was doing, not half questioning it and then ignoring it like she'd done up to now. She was sick all the time, had no energy and was lying on the bathroom floor, frightened and alone and hating herself for what she was doing. And hating the thought that if there really was a heaven, her dad would be looking down at her now, and that was the worst thought of all. As the tears started streaming down her face again, she got angry. All she ever did was think about food and exercise and how she was having too much of one and not enough of the other. There was no room in her life for anything else, and she couldn't handle it anymore.

"I don't want to do this," she screamed over and over again.

She pulled herself up off the bathroom floor and got the scissors out of the bottom drawer of the cabinet. In the bedroom, she threw open the wardrobe door and pulled out her mum's old jeans. With her uninjured hand, she started cutting into the denim and then pulled at the fabric as much as she could, holding it in place with her elbow instead of the hand she'd just hurt.

"No more," she kept screaming. "No more."

She kept cutting and tearing until there was nothing left but ragged pieces of material, which she threw on the floor and jumped on. When her anger subsided, she looked at the photo of her dad again then did what she knew he would want her to do. So she quickly rang her doctor and made an appointment before she changed her mind. Then she rang Laura and told her she was going to the doctor, but not why, and said she wouldn't be at school that day.

Anna looked at the others sitting so still in the lounge room in the house at Mt Tamborine, listening to every word she said.

"It took me a long time to stop obsessing about food and about my size. I still do it sometimes. I'm not sure I'll ever be free of it. My therapist said I would always have those thoughts in the back of my mind; the trick is to learn to control them and to realise and accept I would never be a size eight. I kept telling myself that if I was thinner, everything would be ok. But being thinner wouldn't bring my dad back, and it wouldn't make it any easier to deal with the pressure I felt living on my own and trying to look after a house and still go to school."

She paused for a moment and shifted in her chair. She'd hardly moved the whole time she was talking, almost like she'd been frozen in place. But now that she'd finished, she felt like her muscles were starting to thaw out.

"It was really hard at the time. I remember feeling like I couldn't keep up with everything and that I wasn't doing anything properly, just making halfhearted attempts. I wanted there to be something that I was doing right, something I was succeeding at. It gave me a sense of power and control, deciding what I could and couldn't eat, how much exercise I was doing."

Even though it was so many years later, Anna could still clearly remember how alone she felt.

"When it started getting out of control, I wanted to tell someone, but I was so angry with myself for not being able to get to the weight I wanted. I thought you would all think I was weak, so I never said a word. I just kept telling myself that I'd get there in the end, then I could tell you all because you'd be able to see I'd succeeded. It was only after a few sessions with the doctor that I realised how wrong I'd been to think like that. It took a while for me to change the way I thought, and by the time I did, I'd begun to feel ashamed, and I didn't want anyone to know, so I kept it to myself all these years. You might think that's a silly reason and that I should have told you all long before this, but I was too scared and too worried about what you would all think. I'm even more worried now, but my secret is out in the open, and I can't hide it again."

Chapter 11

Anna looked around the room at her friends. No one spoke, and she was glad of that. Even though she'd been the first one to offer support to Gaby, she couldn't bear it if anyone said anything to her. While she was speaking, she didn't have time to worry about what her friends were thinking. Now she had plenty of time to think about it.

"I'd like to stick to the rules, so please don't say anything."

Sticking to the rules tonight didn't mean that at some point, they would want to talk about what she'd said. But she would worry about that when the time came. What she'd just done was hard enough. She didn't want to make it worse and end up crying, which would happen if anyone said anything.

"And I just need to leave the room for a moment."

Evie watched as Anna got up and left the room. There was no point getting up and following her because she knew Anna would walk away from her if she did. Instead, the three of them sat there, not speaking until Anna returned. While she was gone, Evie stood up and put another log on the fire. It didn't need it, but she had to do something. Sitting still made her nervous, especially now that it was only Laura and herself to go. Behind her, she heard movement, but she didn't turn around. Instead, she just kept staring at the fire. She only turned around when she heard Anna come back and watched as Anna walked by the chair she had been sitting in and went to the one in the darkest part of the room. When she was settled, she turned to the others.

"Who wants to go next?"

Laura looked at Evie. "I don't think I'm ready."

Evie shook her head. "Me either."

"You'll both be fine," Gaby said. "Anna and I have spoken, and we're ok."

Anna didn't say anything, but from the look on her face, it was easy to tell that she wasn't as ok as Gaby said she was.

Evie and Laura looked at each other again. Neither of them said anything and the silence became uncomfortable. Finally, Laura spoke.

"I'll do it. Just give me another minute to collect my thoughts."

Laura had started feeling sick halfway through Gaby's story, wishing now she'd never agreed to take part. She'd been hoping that the secrets wouldn't be as big as they were, that they would be something like the start of Gaby's story— a one night stand. Not finding out that the daughter of one of her best friends had a different father from what everyone thought. And listening to Anna without saying anything had been so hard. Laura had been right all those years ago. She'd known it deep down but hadn't pushed hard enough. Before Gaby or Anna had spoken, she'd toyed briefly with the idea of making something up but knew that wouldn't be fair to either of them. As much as she hadn't planned on telling them her biggest secret, she now felt like she had to.

"After Sebastian and I split up, I lost my way for a while. I suppose a lot of people do when a relationship ends. At the time, I felt more upset than I ever had before, and I was sure that no one else had ever been hurt like I had. Of course, that's not true, but when you're at that place, you wonder if you'll ever be happy again."

Laura stared at the fire as the details came back to her. She'd been expecting it. Not on a conscious level, but somewhere in the back of her mind she'd known something wasn't right. It happened just before Max's second birthday. Small things she noticed at first—when he went to the pub to catch up with his mates he stayed out longer. His fortnightly golf game became weekly. He went back to spending a lot of time on the weekend watching sport rather than spending time with them. Laura hadn't known for sure if it was a temporary relapse or a permanent one until the day he moved out, and she became a single parent.

"I'm sure you all remember that it was a hard time for me. My husband decided he no longer wanted to be part of our family, and Max was too young to understand where his dad had gone. But you didn't know exactly how hard it was. I didn't talk about some of the things that were going on, including what I'm about to tell you. The first time I felt like I wasn't coping was about three weeks after Sebastian had gone. I think I was still in shock before that. Anyway, I won't put off sharing my secret any longer, so I'll start where it began, two years ago, after Sebastian left."

Laura had come home from work feeling tired, more tired than she'd felt in a long time and all she wanted to do was sit down, but Max was hungry. If Sebastian had still been there, she would be able to sit down. He finished earlier than she did, so he always started dinner before she got home. But now it was up to her, every day. She opened the fridge to see what there was, but after perusing the shelves, it looked like it would be takeaway tonight. There was a bottle of wine though, so she poured herself a glass and sipped it while she went through the takeaway menus. While she was on the phone ordering, Max started crying. "Hungry mummy. Hungry"

"We'll have dinner soon."

"Now. Now."

"Not now, but soon."

Max threw himself on the floor and thumped his fists into the carpet. Not tonight, she thought. She opened the fridge again and gave him a piece of cheese. And she topped up her glass while she was there. Halfway through the second glass, she began to feel better.

After they'd eaten she put Max to bed, ran a bath and poured herself another glass of wine. There wasn't much left, so she took the bottle into the bathroom with her. There was no point putting only a small amount back in the fridge. That night she fell asleep straight away and didn't cry. The next morning's headache was nothing compared to not crying herself to sleep. So that night, she did the same thing and then the night after that. And each morning, she continued to get out of bed with a headache, but she didn't care.

"I'll just wrap that up for you," Laura said on Friday afternoon to the only person who'd bought something from the gallery all day.

Even on slow days, she usually sold a couple of the craft pieces that the gallery also stocked, but no one else had come in to take her mind off Sebastian being gone. Instead, she'd walked around the gallery several times to try and wake herself up. After a few nights of drinking wine to put her to sleep, she knew she couldn't keep doing it, so she stopped. Instead, she just lay in bed and cried. She still couldn't believe he'd decided that their life wasn't for him and left.

"Thank you, and I hope you come again," Laura said as the customer walked out the door.

Laura locked the door and turned the sign around. As soon as she did, the tears started. The customer had bought a painting for her husband as a birthday present. Twenty-two years they'd been married, she'd said. And they were still as happy as the day they got married, she'd continued. Laura stayed in the gallery until the tears stopped, and then she headed for the train. Near the train station was a bottle shop. Laura stood outside for a few minutes before walking in.

With the wine hidden in the bottom of her bag, she picked up Max from childcare, taking a moment outside to pull herself together to make sure she wasn't going to cry again. She wouldn't let Max see her cry. He did enough of that himself, and it broke her heart every time, so she put on a cheery demeanour until she put him to bed. Only then did she let the tears escape. And open the bottle of wine.

Later that night her phone rang, and she saw Sebastian's number. She didn't have the strength to talk to him, so she let it go to voicemail. When she listened to the message later, he'd said he wouldn't be coming over on the weekend to see Max as planned. Something had come up and he wouldn't be able to make it. It took all the restraint she had not to call him back and yell at him. Instead, she went to the fridge and poured herself a glass of wine. When she woke up on the couch at 2am, the TV was still on, and the bottle was almost empty.

It was five weeks later before Sebastian actually turned up to spend time with Max. The only time she'd had anything to drink during that time was one night when her friends came over to see her. While they were there, she'd only had two glasses. After they'd gone, she'd drunk the rest of the bottle, trying to forget how happy they all were and what easy lives they had.

Sebastian only stayed for an hour and spent most of the time in the yard, pushing Max on the swing and watching him on the trampoline. Laura didn't know if it was because he didn't want to talk to her, but she didn't want to go outside and find out. But the longer she watched, the angrier she became. When he came inside she knew she couldn't let him go without saying something.

"Is that all the time you have to spend with Max? Do you have any idea how much he misses you?

"What's wrong with the time I've just spent with him?'

"It was only an hour, and you haven't seen him in over a month."

"I can't stay any longer. I have somewhere I need to be."

"Somewhere? It's the middle of the day."

"Yes, somewhere."

Laura looked at the way he was dressed and smelt the cologne he was wearing and realised that's why he wouldn't tell her where he was going. He was heading out on a date.

"So you've got time to go on a date but not to spend with your son?"

Sebastian looked sheepish. "I didn't say I was going on a date."

"I can tell by the way you're dressed. How could you? You only just walked out on us."

"I don't want to talk about this now. It's none of your business anyway."

"None of my business? It's only been twelve weeks since you decided you didn't want us anymore. I'm still your wife, in case you'd forgotten already."

"We're not together anymore."

"I realise that. I'm the one who is here with Max every day while you're out having fun."

Laura thought of the few times she'd been out since Sebastian had left. She either had to rely on her mum to look after Max or take him with her, but because of his age, it was too hard to take him anywhere at night. She'd learned that when she'd had dinner with Anna, and Max had thrown a tantrum in the middle of the restaurant at 7pm because he was tired. They left shortly after, and she hadn't tried to do it again. From then on, if her friends rang and said they wanted to see her, she invited them to her place.

However, more often than not, she'd cancel at the last minute because she didn't feel up to socialising.

"I don't understand why you want to tear our family apart."

"I'm doing what's best for me."

"Exactly. What's best for you? What about what's best for your family?"

"I don't want to talk about this anymore. I've made my decision. I'll call when I can come and see Max again."

Laura watched him walk out the door and slammed it shut behind him. Checking first to see if Max was still outside, she went into the kitchen and looked for a bottle of wine before realising she didn't have any. She leaned against the fridge and clenched her hands. Even though he'd gone, she couldn't stop thinking about him and the life they used to have. It had been one adventure after another—travel, parties and weekends away. Jobs were only for making enough money for their next trip, and chores were something they did when they had time. By the time he'd reached his early thirties though, his focus had changed, and suddenly, he wanted a wife and a child and a backyard. The thought of Sebastian dating someone made her feel sick. She walked next door, asked her neighbour Maureen if she wouldn't mind watching Max for ten minutes, then got in the car and drove to the bottle shop. While she was in the shop, her phone rang.

"Afternoon," Anna said. "What are you up to?'

"I'm at the shops. What about you?"

Laura didn't see any point in saying exactly what shop.

"At work. I had someone call in sick."

"You always fill in when someone's sick."

"I know, but I like my job, and it is my nursery. But I'm not working tomorrow, so I thought I'd see if you wanted to catch up for breakfast."

Laura didn't feel up to pretending that everything was ok, so she told a white lie.

"I can't. I told mum I'd bring Max over to see her tomorrow morning."

"She'll love that. Have you seen her since you went over last week on the anniversary of the day your dad died?"

"No, she's been doing a few extra shifts volunteering at the Salvos store so we haven't had a chance to catch up again."

"It's great that you still spend that day together. I'm glad I get to do that with my mum too. Sometimes I think it was fate that you and I became friends when we did because we had each other when our dads died."

"Whatever it was, I'm glad we did. It was a lot to deal with at fourteen, and I wouldn't have got through it without you."

"Me either. I'm so glad you were there for me."

In the background, Laura could hear voices.

"Oh no. Sorry Laura, but some customers have just walked in, and there's no one else here to serve. Can we catch up soon? I'll call back and organise something."

Laura listened to the dial tone. She wanted to ring her back and say, *yes I'm fine, Anna. Doing really well. Not feeling overwhelmed or lonely at all.* But even if Anna had asked, Laura probably would have lied about that too. It just would have been nice to be asked. And the conversation had her thinking about her dad and what it had been like when he died. It wasn't only their ages that

Laura and Anna had in common. Both their dads had died of cancer—Anna's dad of lung cancer and Laura's of bowel cancer. While the types of cancer were different, they both knew what it was like to watch their fathers go through the treatment, and it had been good to have someone who understood and to talk to.

The afternoon went slowly, and by 5pm, she'd drunk most of the bottle of white wine. Sebastian seeing someone else was something she just couldn't deal with. By that night, the pain had dulled, but it hadn't gone completely. With nothing to do but cook dinner for Max and then put him to bed later, she opened the fridge to see what there was. She didn't like cooking, and if Max hadn't been there, she probably would have toast every night. Her cooking repertoire consisted of spaghetti bolognese, tacos and whatever sauce came out of a packet that only required meat and vegetables to be added. If she had the money, she'd take Max out for dinner more often. While Sebastian had been providing some money, it was for Max, and it was exactly half of his expenses and not a dollar more. Nothing in the fridge grabbed her attention except the wine bottle.

An hour later, she'd bathed Max, put a packet of pre-made pasta and sauce in the microwave and then fed him. After putting him to bed, she took the leftover pasta out of the fridge, heated it up and then spent the next ten minutes pushing it around her plate instead of eating it. The red wine she opened to go with it went down much easier, even easier than the rest of the white she'd had earlier when she couldn't decide what to cook. She only went to bed after the second bottle was empty.

When the alarm went off the following day, she dragged herself out of bed, dragged Max out of bed, and then dragged them both out of the house. At the gallery, she looked at herself in the mirror. There were bags under her eyes, her hair needed a wash, and her clothes could have used a quick iron before she'd left the house. But there was nothing she could do about it except count down the hours until she could go home. Laura had always loved her job. It allowed her to paint when it was quiet, she could talk to the customers about art, and she got to spend her days surrounded by paintings and drawings and sculptures. Lately though, none of that held any interest for her and she couldn't wait for closing time to come around.

After what seemed like much more than eight hours, she was finally able to shut the door and head to the train station. On the way, she stopped at a bar to delay going home to a house with no husband.

As she stood at the station waiting, she heard an announcement saying the train had been delayed and would be another ten minutes. Laura's shoulders sagged, and she looked around for a seat. A young couple sat down next to her. They were holding hands, smiling and laughing. She lasted only a few minutes before she got up and moved. There were no more seats, so she leaned against a post and prayed for the train to come. When it finally arrived, she grabbed a window seat, rested her head against the wall of the train carriage and stared out the window. The train had only just pulled out of the station when she heard her name and turned around.

"Hey, Gaby. What are you doing on the train?"

"My car's in for a service, so it's public transport for me today. How are you?"

"I'm ok. What about you?"

Gaby flopped down in the empty seat beside her. "Busy."

"So no different to every other day?"

Gaby laughed. "Exactly. Are you sure you're ok? You look exhausted."

"Max hasn't been sleeping well lately."

"I remember those nights. Has he been spending any more time with Sebastian? You look like you could use a rest."

Laura shook her head.

Gaby reached over and squeezed her hand. "How are you going with it all?"

"Some days are harder than others, but really, I'm doing ok."

"I'm glad. It will get better you know."

Laura wanted to believe Gaby, but she couldn't. Gaby had never been through anything like what Laura was dealing with now, so she just nodded in agreement.

"Can you smell anything?" Gaby said. "I swear I can smell alcohol."

Laura shook her head quickly. "I can't smell anything."

"Must be imagining it then. You'll have to come over so Max can play with my kids, and you and I can sit still for a while and have a coffee or a wine. Grace and Lucas like having Max around. They feel like they're playing older sister and brother."

As tempting as the thought was of sitting and drinking wine while Max played for a few hours, Laura wasn't up to spending time in Gaby's happy home.

"That sounds lovely, but I've got a lot on over the next few weeks."

"So have I. We'll find a time though that suits us both."

They spent the rest of the trip talking about work and their kids. Gaby tried once more to check how she was and asked about Sebastian seeing Max, but Laura changed the subject. She was grateful when the train pulled into her stop and that Gaby hadn't made any more mentions of smelling alcohol.

As the train pulled away, she saw Gaby wave through the window. As lovely as it was to see her, the thought of Gaby going home to her husband and children was almost too much to bear. She walked home from the station much faster than she usually would, and as soon as she shut the door behind her, she sank down on the floor and rested her head against the wall. The tiles underneath her felt cold, but she didn't have the energy to pull herself up. She sat there for a few minutes and then got up, walked into the kitchen and opened the fridge. For a moment, she panicked when she saw the bottle holder was empty, and then she remembered she had a few bottles of red in the cupboard. She knew she was drinking too much, but she didn't care anymore and didn't try to talk herself out of doing it. Her evening glasses of wine were the only thing making her feel better at the moment. She told herself she'd cut down soon. In the meantime, she still had an hour before her mum dropped Max off, so she went out to the back yard, sat on the grass and stared at the trees, the glass of red in her hand the whole time.

The next week Gaby called. "I know I said I'd get you over, but Evie called this morning and is keen for the four of us to catch up. We thought breakfast would be good. Anna is free next Sunday, so are Evie and I, so that just leaves you."

Laura paused before answering. She couldn't keep saying no to every invitation because eventually, one of her friends would push her on it, so she agreed. But come Sunday morning she wished she hadn't. Ten seconds after the alarm went off the pounding in her head started. The two nearly empty wine bottles in the kitchen reminded her of the cause. Max had stayed with her mum last night, so she'd been on her own with no one else to be responsible for or to take her mind off Sebastian being gone. Before leaving, she poured the last of one of the bottles into a hip flask and put it in her handbag, then poured the last of the other into a glass and drank it while she was getting ready. Her headache and the time of the day mattered less than psyching herself up to pretend everything was ok.

"Earth to Laura," Anna said not long after they'd arrived at the cafe. "You look tired."

"That's what I said to her on the train last week," Gaby said.

"I'm fine. Just busy with work and Max."

"How is Max?" Evie asked.

"He's really good. He had a sleepover at grandma's last night, so he's being thoroughly spoilt."

Evie laughed. "Yes, I can picture your mum spoiling him the whole time he's there. It's nice that he gets to have sleepovers at her house."

Laura nodded. "He loves going and she loves having him. And it gives me a break for a night which is nice."

"Guess that means there hasn't been any change with Sebastian?" Evie said.

"No, he still doesn't see Max very often."

Evie shook her head. "I can't understand how he can be like that."

"I can't either. Every time I think about it I remember my dad and how great he was."

Anna reached over and rubbed Laura's arm. "He would have loved Max."

"I know. I wish he was here. I still miss him all the time."

There wasn't a day that went by when she didn't think about her dad. He was only forty-two when he died, but cancer didn't care about age, just as it hadn't with Anna's dad, although Anna's dad had fought it for years before he died. With Laura's dad, it had been quick and merciless. Diagnosed in May and dead in October. It hadn't been enough time.

As she sat and listened to the conversation going on around her and heard about the movies they'd seen, the restaurants they'd been to and the concerts they'd attended, she didn't join in the conversation. There was nothing she could add. She couldn't afford any of those things at the moment, and her days were mostly filled with taking care of Max, going to work and looking after the house. A feeling of exhaustion started washing over her as she thought about all the things she needed to do each day, and she just wanted to be on her own.

"I'm going to head off."

"We've only just got here," Gaby said.

"I've just realised the time, and I said I'd pick Max up early."

Evie stood up and gave her a hug. "It was lovely seeing you. Let's not leave it so long next time."

Anna and Gaby both nodded and then hugged her goodbye as well.

"Drive safe," Anna said. "I'll call you later."

As she drove away, she was sure her friends were talking about her, but that was one more thing she didn't care about at the moment. All she cared about was getting through each day and the one thing that helped her do that. Halfway home, she pulled over and took a sip from the hip flask she'd taken out of her handbag and hidden in the car before she'd gone into the café.

True to her word Anna called that afternoon. Laura had come straight home after the café. Max was still with his grandma, who'd said she'd drop him home around 5.30pm. She hadn't felt the need to share that with her friends, and she didn't feel bad about lying so that she could leave the café. The first thing Anna said was that she was worried about her.

"There's nothing to be worried about. I'm fine, and so is Max.'

"You say that, but I don't believe you."

The last thing Laura wanted to talk about was Sebastian, so she told Anna again that she was doing ok and then changed the subject. She was in the middle of asking Anna about the new garden she was creating in her backyard when she realised that she had slurred a couple of words.

"Sorry," she said quickly. "I'm speaking faster than I'm thinking. That didn't come out right. I meant to say I'll have to come over and have a look when you're finished."

"Is that all it is?' Anna said, laughing. "You sure you didn't stop at the pub on the way home."

"You know I wouldn't do that with Max around."

"I know. I was just teasing. Don't get your knickers in a knot."

For the second time during the conversation, Laura wanted to change the subject. "I haven't heard that expression in a long time."

"I hadn't either, but I had a customer in the other day, and I overheard her say it on the phone. I liked the sound of it, and you just gave me the perfect opportunity to use it."

Anna laughed again when she'd finished speaking, and Laura wondered when she would laugh like that again. She didn't say that to Anna. Instead, she told her she had some chores to do and needed to hang up.

"Ok," Anna said. "I'll call you again during the week."

Laura leaned against the kitchen bench, her hands clenched. *Couldn't you tell that I'm not all right*, she thought. *You're supposed to be my best friend; you should be able to see through my lies.* She picked up her wine glass and took a big gulp, then rinsed the glass and put it away. Her mum would be dropping Max off soon, and she didn't want any wine glasses lying around.

Over the past few weeks she'd begun to understand some of what her mum went through when her dad had died. Trying to protect her children, keep the house running, put food on the table, go to work and all the while trying to keep up a façade so her children wouldn't see how sad she really was or how hard it was for her. As much as she was hurting, she had to admit that it couldn't be as bad as what her mum had dealt with. Sebastian had chosen to leave them, to stop being a husband and father. Until his last days, her dad had fought to be those two things.

By the time Max was dropped off, it was almost an hour later than it should have been because they'd stopped at Max's favourite ice cream shop. Laura was glad her mum was doing something nice with Max. She wanted him to spend as much time as he could with people who loved him in the hope that it would make up for the time that Sebastian wasn't spending with him.

"Here we are," Laura's mum said. "A bit later than what I said, but Max was enjoying his ice cream."

"Ice cream yummy," Max said before running off to his room to find some toys.

"Thanks. I appreciate you taking him."

"I thought you could use a break. Have you heard from Sebastian? When is he coming to spend time with his son?"

"I don't know. He cancelled the last visit."

"How can he do that to his own child? I can't believe he's turned out to be the person he has."

Laura didn't say anything. Everyone wanted to talk about Sebastian today, except her.

"I should start preparing Max's dinner. Ice cream won't tame his hunger for long."

"Ok, I'll head off and leave you to it."

Laura walked her mum to the door, but she stopped before walking through.

"What's that smell?"

Laura shrugged her shoulders. "I can't smell anything."

"Smells like alcohol."

"I did some cleaning when I got home. It must be the cleaning products you can smell."

Laura waved to her mum as she drove off then quickly closed the door. How could she have possibly smelt the wine Laura had been drinking? She'd cleaned her teeth to mask the smell on her breath. Next time, she'd have to be more careful.

Max was tired after the day with his grandmother and didn't stay awake long after he'd had dinner. Laura turned on the TV to stop her thinking too much about how her life had changed so suddenly. Nothing interested her, but she kept flicking anyway, finally settling on a nature program that had some beautiful scenery. The wine bottle was sitting on the coffee table in front of her, and she filled up her glass every time it was empty. Before long, it was the bottle that was empty as well as her glass. She didn't feel tired so she went and opened another bottle and settled back in front of the TV. The amount she was drinking didn't even register anymore. She just kept filling her glass. Later she heard the phone ringing. Who would be calling at this time of night, she wondered? She struggled to open her eyes and looked at the clock, but it wasn't on the bedside table where it usually was. She tried to sit up but felt stiff and sore. It took her a moment to realise she was on the floor, wedged between the lounge chair and the coffee table, and not in her bed.

Beside her, two empty wine bottles lay on the floor, and another half-empty bottle was sitting on the coffee table. Using the table to steady herself, she tried to get up, but her head was spinning like a carnival ride. Before she could stop it, the retching started, the contents of her stomach spreading out across the carpet. In desperation, she pulled herself up and dragged herself towards the toilet, trying to catch the vomit in her hands until she got there.

When there was nothing left to bring up, she lifted her head from the toilet bowl and gasped for air. Her head was pounding, her mouth was dry, and her throat felt like she had swallowed razor blades. Letting go of the toilet bowl, she pulled herself to her feet, walked slowly into the kitchen and poured herself a glass of water. The glass shook as she tried to raise it to her lips, and the water hurt as it went down. When the glass was empty, she stared at the carpet. She had to clean it up. In case Max woke during the night.

As she scrubbed, tears began rolling down her cheeks. She brushed them away and cleaned faster. Max must never know. When all traces were gone, she hauled herself into bed, this time, not brushing away the tears. Or the disgust.

Chapter 12

The sun shining through the window woke Laura. As she slowly sat up, she could still taste the vomit in her mouth. The clock on the wall said 6.15am. Luckily Max was still asleep. What if he'd found her last night? She had to stop drinking so much. Struggling to her feet, she went into the bathroom and cleaned her teeth twice before showering and then getting her first cup of coffee for the day. Even after toothpaste and mouthwash, there was still a faint trace of vomit. Her head was pounding, and when she held her hand out in front of her, she could see it was shaking. When she got the shaking to stop, she walked into the kitchen, got the last remaining bottle out of the cupboard and threw it out.

Not even the strongest coffee was going to help her that morning. She almost stopped to buy a bacon and egg muffin after dropping Max off, but the thought of food started her stomach churning. As she walked into the gallery, she wondered if she should have called in sick but this was self-inflicted, not the flu. So she opened the gallery and got ready for customers, all the while feeling worse than she had in a long time. Ten customers came in during the morning but time still seemed to pass slowly. After lunch Laura's phone rang and it was her boss, calling from her other gallery.

"Can you go to the 2.30pm meeting with the artist instead of me? I'm double booked but really interested in seeing what works he has produced lately."

"Yes, I can go. I'll need to close up though."

"That's fine. It should only take an hour, maybe an hour and a half."

"All right. Do I need to take anything with me for the meeting?"

"No, just let me know what you think of the works he shows you and if you think they'd be suitable for us."

Laura walked into the bathroom and splashed water on her face. It didn't do much to change the way she felt. She looked at her reflection in the mirror and realised she couldn't go to a meeting the way she looked, with bloodshot eyes and pallid skin. She could only imagine what that morning's customers must have thought when they saw her. Luckily she had some makeup in her drawer. After applying concealer, foundation and blush, she looked much better. A liberal dab of perfume helped as well. As she locked up the gallery, she tried to remember what her boss had said previously about this artist. Hopefully, enough details would come back to her on the way to the meeting.

"Road works again," the taxi driver muttered under his breath. "We might be here a while."

"I can walk the rest of the way; it's just around the corner. I've got a meeting to get to."

"No worries, that'll be $12.10."

Laura jumped out of the taxi, took a few deep breaths and started walking along the footpath. She was coming up to 'their' restaurant. If it hadn't been for the road works, she could have driven by quickly. She cursed under her breath for not thinking about that before she got out of the taxi because even though she tried not to, she looked over. The same striped awning, the same tables and chairs outside, the same row of plants dividing the restaurant and the street. A waiter came out through the doorway, and she realised it was Andrew, 'their' waiter. He was always friendly, ready to have a chat, and he remembered things you told him on previous visits. He walked to the corner carrying a tray with two plates and placed it down on 'their' table, where a couple sat holding hands. She felt the tears start and she desperately tried to stop them. She had to get to this meeting, so she wiped away the few tears that had escaped and started walking again. She'd only taken a few steps before she realised the man sitting at the table was Sebastian and opposite him, holding his hand, was a woman.

Laura felt like she'd been hit in the chest. Every part of her wanted to run over and start screaming. *This is our restaurant. What are you doing here with her? How could you? It's only been five months.* Instead, she turned and ran back the way she'd come. Tears were streaming down her face and she could hardly see where she was going. She didn't see the tree root breaking through the concrete footpath, and she tripped and fell. Blood was trickling out of her knee, but she didn't feel any pain. She just sat there and cried until a voice beside her asked if she was all right. Laura looked up and saw an elderly lady looking down at her.

"I'm fine. I just tripped," she said as she got up, brushed her clothes and picked up her handbag.

She put her sunglasses on her face to hide her red eyes before walking into the bottle shop just a few doors away from where she had been standing. Even after last night and how she still felt, the only thing she wanted was wine. She picked up the first bottle she came to and then hailed a cab. The cabbie looked at her in the rear-view mirror.

"Off to a party?"

"Something at work this afternoon."

"That'll be nice," he said.

Laura didn't respond and spent the rest of the trip staring out the window. Sebastian had clearly been on a date. They had both looked too friendly with each other to be colleagues, and they had been holding hands. She wondered if it was the same woman he'd gone on a date with that day he'd come to see Max. When she got back to the gallery, she left the front door shut and the closed sign facing out, poured a large glass of wine and let the tears flow. She wanted to go home but knew she had to stay in case her boss rang before closing time. If she did ring, she hoped it would be much later so she could come up with a reason why she missed the meeting. At the moment, she couldn't think of anything else but what she'd seen at the restaurant. She wasn't sure how long she sat there before she heard continued knocking on the door, and most of the wine was gone.

"The opening hours on the door said you should be open, so I thought I'd check."

Laura let the customer in and watched as the woman walked around the gallery. She stopped in front of every painting and stared at it for a while before moving on. Laura recognised the type. She wasn't really interested in art but was trying to act like she was because there was a blank wall at home that needed something. A painting would say to her friends that she was cultured. Laura wished she would pick something and leave.

"Can I help you at all? Is there something, in particular, you're looking for?"

"Nothing particular, but I'll know it when I see it."

I hope you see it soon, Laura thought. All she wanted was another glass of wine to wipe out the memory of Sebastian sitting at that table with that woman. She couldn't remember how much was left in the bottle, but she was sure there was something.

"I like this one," the woman said. "What can you tell me about it?"

Laura got up from her desk, steadying herself for a moment, and walked over, hoping she looked in control and not like she was wobbling.

"It's by a local artist. We've been exhibiting her work for a number of years. She gets her inspiration by walking around the city streets and looking at the people and the buildings. She has an excellent eye for detail and uses lots of colour."

"I like the idea of a local artist. I'll take it. Has there been a party in here? I'm sure I can smell alcohol."

Laura panicked for a moment. She'd been so upset at seeing Sebastian the only thing she'd thought of was having a drink, not what would happen if a customer walked in. She turned away from the customer and took the painting off the wall.

"No, you must be smelling the cleaning alcohol I use for my own brushes."

"Do you paint?"

"Yes, I do."

"Is there any of your work hanging in the gallery?"

"Those four on the far wall are mine."

"They look nice. Not really my taste though."

I don't think you have any taste, Laura thought. You've just picked the painting with the brightest colours. Laura wrapped the painting, took the money, shut the door behind the woman and leant against it. What had she been thinking? If her boss found out she'd been drinking at work, she'd lose her job. It was one slip, she told herself, and she'd never do it again. With everything else going on in her life, she couldn't afford to lose her job. She needed the money and she couldn't think of another job where her boss would be happy to let her paint when it was quiet. Not that she'd done a lot of painting since Sebastian left. She usually found so much joy in creating her art, but it had been a while since she'd picked up a paintbrush. No other customers came in that day, and she hid the empty bottle in her bag and took it with her when she left. It was only after she got outside that she realised she'd been so caught up in the pain of seeing Sebastian that she'd forgotten she'd driven that day instead of taking the train. You shouldn't be driving, she told herself. It's not far though, she thought, and if I keep focused on the road and the car, I'll be fine. Just before she opened the door her phone rang and she looked at it and saw Evie's name. She almost let the call go to voice mail but answered at the last minute.

"Just calling to see if it's knock off time for you. I've just finished with a client who's around the corner from you, so I thought I'd see if you wanted to catch up quickly before going home."

Laura was in the middle of thinking up an excuse when Evie said the magic words.

"There's a new wine bar that's opened up two streets away from your gallery. We could catch up there."

Ten minutes later, she was sitting opposite Evie.

"How did you find out about this place?"

Evie looked up from the drinks list. "From the client I just saw. He sees it on his morning walk, and he mentioned it. I can't decide what to order. What are you having?"

Laura knew she should say a soft drink, but she didn't. "A glass of the Pinot Grigio."

"That sounds good. I'll do the same."

After the waitress took their order, they talked about their day. Laura left out some of hers.

"It's nice to catch up," Evie said. "I haven't seen you since our annual weekend away."

Laura didn't want to talk about that weekend. There were things she couldn't remember. They'd all had hangovers, but none as bad as hers. Evie, Anna and Gaby only had a few drinks, but because none of them were big drinkers, it didn't take much for them to get a hangover. Laura hadn't drunk much either—in front of them. Later in her room was a different story.

"It was such a fun weekend," Evie said

"It always is. What are you doing this weekend?"

"Haven't decided yet. What about you?"

"Same."

Probably the same as the previous weekends, Laura thought. Staying in pyjamas all day, drinking and sitting around the house whenever she could get away with it and whenever Max was occupied and wouldn't see her.

"How's Max? Is he still liking daycare?"

Laura nodded. "He's very social, so he likes to be around other kids."

Evie laughed. "I wonder where he gets that from."

"He is a lot like me."

"Has Sebastian seen him lately?"

Not since the time he left early to go on a date, Laura said to herself. With the same woman he was having lunch with today. She was sure of it. To Evie though, she just shook her head.

Evie reached across the table and grabbed her hand. "Maybe he'll get better at visiting soon."

Laura doubted it, but she nodded anyway. "I hope so. Max really misses him."

"I'm sure you could use a break once in a while too. If you ever need me to take care of Max for a day or two, let me know. He's so adorable. I'd be happy to do that."

Laura took a sip of her wine then put the glass down on the table, too quickly though, because some of the contents spilled.

Evie laughed again. "Taxi! You've hardly had any. Are you feeling ok?"

"Yes, just not paying attention," Laura said quickly.

"Is that all? Are you sure you didn't have a long lunch today and forgot to mention it?" Evie teased.

Laura didn't say anything. It couldn't be noticeable. She'd become very good at hiding it.

"Hey, I was just joking."

"I know. Sorry, it's been a long week. I might head off if that's ok."

Evie nodded. "Of course. I can't stay any longer either. We're having dinner with Nick's parents tonight."

"No wonder you need a glass of wine."

"I could use another one, but I'm the designated driver, as always."

After they'd hugged goodbye and Laura started walking away, she thought about taking a taxi but decided, as she had earlier, that she'd be fine.

Driving slowly and cautiously, she was only a few minutes from home when she saw the RBT on the side of the road. Her heart started pounding, and she started shaking. If she got pulled over, she would lose her licence. She kept driving and looked straight ahead, still going as cautiously as she could. The closer she came, the sicker she felt. When the policeman waved at her to pull over, she thought she might actually be sick. Laura's hands were shaking so much she was surprised she was able to pull over like she would any other day. Several cars were in front of her, and two police officers were moving down the line, testing two drivers at a time as they got to the front of the line. She watched as the first two blew into the bag and waited while the officers checked the reading. Both drivers were waved on, putting Laura closer to the front of the line. She watched the process repeat, but this time something was different. The driver at the front blew into the bag and the police officer took longer to check the reading. Then the driver had to blow in the bag again. After reviewing the reading for a second time, the police officer waved the driver to a spot just off to the side of the line. Laura watched as the driver, who looked to be in his early twenties, moved his car to where he was directed and then got out and stood beside it. Another police officer walked over and started writing things down. The details Laura assumed, like how much over the limit he was. Oh my God, Laura thought. That's going to be me. I'm going to be waved over to that spot and have to get out and stand beside my car. And all the other drivers still in the line would see her and know what she'd done

"Afternoon," the policeman said. "We're doing random breath testing. Have you been pulled over for a test before?"

Laura nodded.

"And have you been drinking today?"

"I had some wine after work."

It was the first thing that came to mind. She couldn't bring herself to admit the truth. Especially not to a policeman. She didn't even want to admit it to herself. Laura watched as he pulled the plastic off the breathalyser then slid it through the car window. Laura blew in the bag, gripping the door handle tightly as she did and praying for the first time since high school when they had to go to weekly chapel services. That wasn't going to save her though. She should have taken a taxi, but it was too late to think like that now. She was going to be way over the limit.

"You'll have to try harder," the policeman said. "It's not registering."

Laura inwardly groaned, feeling it must be so obvious to the policeman, before trying again.

"Still not registering. Try it once more."

Laura couldn't believe this was happening. She was still gripping the door handle as she tried for the third time. If she let go, she wouldn't be able to stop her hands from shaking. The sweat on the back of her legs made them stick to the seat and her hair was plastered to her neck. She was sure the policeman could see the panic in her eyes and hear the deep breaths she was taking to try and calm down. Her eyelids were blinking as she watched him look at the breathalyser, and she tried to come to terms with the fact that she was going to lose her licence. He must be able to tell she'd been drinking, even without the breathalyser.

The policeman looked through the window at her. "I'll be back in a minute."

Why was he walking away? It must be bad if he has to go and talk to one of his colleagues, Laura thought. Then she had a distressing thought. What if she went to jail? Oh, God. She wouldn't cope in prison. And she'd lose her job and wouldn't be able to provide for Max. Max, she thought. That would be the worst of it. He'd grow up with a mother who'd spent time in jail. When he got older, he'd be teased or even bullied because of it. And who would look after him? Her mum loved spending time with Max, but she was sixty-eight and having Max full time would be too much to ask of her. And then she had a worse thought. If she went to jail, Max would go to Sebastian. He was Max's father, so she assumed that's what would automatically happen. Sebastian could then decide she was an unfit mother and go through the family court and get custody of him full time. She would be reduced to supervised visits.

What had she done? Instead of having another glass of wine, she should have told Evie what had happened. She would have offered her support, probably even cancelled her dinner plans to stay with Laura even though it wouldn't have been popular with Nick. She would have driven Laura home and stayed until she was ok. And then she wouldn't be in the situation she now found herself. Through the window, she could see the policeman turn away from his colleague and walk towards her. For a brief moment, she had the crazy thought of driving off. She'd definitely be arrested then.

"This breathalyser is faulty, and we've used all the plastic tubes that you breathe into, so we can't perform the test. You can drive on."

Laura wound up the window, and the policeman waved her back onto the road. She drove carefully and slowly until they were out of sight, then she let herself shake. She gripped the steering wheel tighter so she didn't lose control and just kept staring straight ahead. Pulling over would have been the sensible thing to do. The shaking, as well as the alcohol, was affecting her driving but all she could think of was getting home. At that moment, nothing was more important. *You can do it,* she kept repeating to herself over and over. Soon her street came into view.

"Almost there," she said aloud as if it was more believable saying it out loud than in her head.

As soon as she pulled into the garage and shut the door, she started sobbing. She wasn't sure how long she sat in the car, but it was a while before she pulled herself together enough to get out of the car and walk inside to the lounge room. And then she had another thought, worse than any of the ones she'd had while she'd been pulled over. It wasn't just her licence she could have lost or the time that would be taken from her if she had been arrested. If she'd had an accident, she could have hurt someone else. How could she have lived with herself if she'd hurt someone, or even more horrifying, killed someone? And then she realised if she'd had an accident, it could have been her that was killed, and Max would grow up without a mother.

"I hate you," she whispered, then again, louder.

She repeated it again and again, each time louder.

"I hate you, I hate you."

She picked up the cushions on the lounge chair and threw them across the room.

"How could you leave us?"

Anger coursed through her veins and if she saw Sebastian now, she would probably throw something at him. But he wasn't there. So, she opened up the cupboard where all the mementos of their time together were stored and proceeded to destroy everything. Photos, letters, and cards were torn into tiny little squares and then thrown into the bin. As she tore up all the memories, she realised that all this time she'd been angry about the wrong thing. She should have been angry with herself for reacting the way she had and drinking excessively to dull the pain. It was only a relationship break-up. They happened every day, and people survived. She could have ended up in jail today. Or dead. And all because Sebastian decided he didn't want a family anymore. He was the one who had made the choice, and yet Laura had been punishing herself. He wasn't worth any of this. From the box under the phone, she pulled out several sheets of notepaper and a pen and began writing down everything that was causing her pain. Laura poured all of her feelings onto that page, and when she finished, took the paper, held it over the kitchen sink and lit it with a match. As she watched it burn she pictured all the hurt inside her floating away with the smoke, and she let it go. She cleaned up the mess, grabbed every bottle of wine she had and took them outside to the bin.

Back in the lounge room at Mt Tamborine, Laura was conscious of the wine glass beside her chair. She hadn't picked it up the whole time she was telling her story, and it would have been a bad idea to pick it up now.

"What I'd done scared me so much, but at the same time, it was a wake-up call and I made an appointment with my doctor. It was the hardest thing I've ever had to do. Sitting in the waiting room, I was so nervous. I didn't want to admit to anyone how weak I'd been, how stupid. I thought she'd yell at me and tell me all sorts of terrible things and say I was a bad person, but she didn't."

Laura remembered how calmly her doctor had talked to her and went through the available options to help her. Just before she left the appointment, her doctor had taken the opportunity to remind her of the damage heavy drinking would do to her body. That was something she'd blocked out at the time. And still did.

"She recommended that I see a counsellor and prescribed some anti-depressants, which I took for three months. I didn't tell anyone I was taking them. I hid them in the bathroom cupboard behind my deodorant. I'm a lot better now, and I haven't taken any medication for a while."

She hadn't thrown them rest out, though, just in case.

"I was lucky that what I was doing only lasted a few months. It would have been much harder to stop if it had been longer. After seeing the counsellor a few times, I started painting again. I was sitting in the reception area, waiting for my counselling appointment, and I heard a piece of classical music that inspired me. Something about it made me see colours and images in my head. I went home from that session and painted for three hours. It made me feel so happy."

Laura looked around at her friends and knew she had to address what they were all thinking. Especially Evie. The way she was looking at her made Laura uncomfortable like Evie knew what she'd done the night before. And on lots of other nights.

"I can tell by the looks on your faces that you're thinking about the wine I had earlier, but I've hardly had any in the past twelve months. I stopped just after Max turned three. Now, if I drink anything, I limit myself and I'm very careful about that. I don't want to end up back where I was."

Laura thought back to the previous night and what she'd done and felt guilty for a moment. What she'd said was mostly the truth. She didn't think leaving last night out of the story was a big deal. She hadn't exactly lied, just stretched the truth a little. Now that she'd had her turn, she could sit back and relax a little and maybe have another sip of wine. If she only had a few sips, she didn't think anyone would say anything. She'd hardly had any at all since they'd arrived.

Chapter 13

"Before I finish, I just want to say that I know what I was doing wasn't a good thing, but a lot has changed over the past eighteen months," Laura said. "Things have improved with Sebastian and he's taking more responsibility with Max. I've done some of my best paintings and sold several through the gallery. And you all know I've been teaching an art class once a week. I'm in a much better place, and I'm grateful for that."

She didn't add that she still had some issues to deal with. And that even after everything she did the day she was pulled over, she still missed Sebastian. Saying what she had was hard enough. She only got through it by saying what she did so that her friends would think everything was ok now. She turned towards Evie, who looked terrified because it was now her turn.

"It will be fine," Laura said.

"I know. I can't back out. I'll share my secret. I just need to go to the toilet first."

Once she shut the door, she no longer tried to stop herself from shaking. She put the toilet lid down, sat on it and crossed her arms and legs, trying to keep them still. Then she quickly stood up and lifted the toilet seat because she suddenly felt sick, but after a minute or two with her head over the bowl, nothing happened. She would have run away if she wasn't stuck on top of a mountain. It didn't matter what she'd agreed to or that everyone else had taken their turn. When she was certain she wasn't going to be sick, she leaned against the wall and tried to slow her breathing. There was no way out of it. She knew she could tell a different story—make something up—but she wanted to stop, just like Laura had.

By the time she got back to the lounge room, she still wasn't ready to speak. What scared her the most was what their reactions would be and if what she had to say would change the friendship they had.

"Are you ready, Evie?" Gaby asked.

"Just one more minute, and then I'll start. This has turned out to be more serious than I first thought."

"That was because of me," Gaby said. "But I needed to say what I did."

Anna nodded in agreement. "So did I."

Evie tried to get comfortable but the chair seemed harder than it had an hour ago. No matter which way she sat, it just didn't feel right. She took a sip of her wine and then a large gulp. Evie glanced around the room at her friends, all waiting for her to begin, so she took another mouthful of wine then started.

"About fifteen years ago, when I was still with Matthew, you might remember a woman named Chelsea that I met through work. She was the one who was into the rave scene."

She paused for a moment, looked around the room, and saw three heads nod.

"I didn't know much about it, but the more Chelsea talked about it, the more interested I became. She said to me at the time that it was a release, a chance to leave the world behind for a night and just feel nothing else but complete happiness. Her job as an ambo was stressful like mine, and she said going to raves was what kept her sane. I liked the sound of that. Work was hectic, I had no free time, I hadn't seen any of you for months because I'd been working weekends and things were tense with Matthew."

Things were often tense with Matthew, she thought to herself. She didn't need to tell her friends that at the time, their relationship wasn't as good it had been at the start. She'd had a lot of conversations about it back then. But, like with her grandmother, she hadn't taken any of her friends' advice either.

"So when Chelsea invited me along to a rave one night, I went. And while I was there, I tried speed."

Evie stopped for a moment and waited for her friends to forget the rules and chastise her for what she'd just said. Especially Gaby. There was no way she would stick to the rules after they left the room. It wouldn't be tonight, but it would definitely be tomorrow. No one spoke though. They didn't even let the shock they must be feeling show on their faces, so she kept going.

"I was so nervous about taking it. I'd never tried drugs before except for the occasional joint. What if something happened? In the end, I broke the tablet and just took half because I thought that would be safer. And with Chelsea there, I figured I'd be ok because she was an ambo and used to dealing with all sorts of medical dramas. And she said it was common with a lot of people she knew, using something to block the stress and pain caused by what they saw on a daily basis."

Thinking about it now, she realised how easily she'd been talked into it. If she'd been stronger, maybe she still wouldn't be having problems now.

"Once it kicked in I had the most amazing feeling of euphoria, and I immediately forgot all the things in my life that were causing me pain or stress. I had so much energy that I could barely keep still. Most nights I came home from work after dealing with all of my client's problems and just collapsed on the lounge, so it was wonderful to have so much energy."

She could still clearly remember the first tablet's effect on her and how much she hated it when it began to wear off. She'd started with just half a tablet, but she'd wanted to stay in the place where she was, so she'd taken the other half.

"I'd never liked dance music before but suddenly I loved it. I danced for hours because I couldn't stop. When the sun came up, I was so disappointed because I wasn't ready to go home. Chelsea said we didn't have to go home because she knew where a recovery

251

party was. So, I followed her to a small club in the Valley where a DJ played techno music until 10am. Afterwards, Chelsea and I walked around the streets for another hour. I could still feel the speed in my system and I couldn't sit still. The Valley was crowded on that Sunday morning and I remember that I felt so happy, like I was floating on a cloud. I didn't want to let go of the night before or the way I felt."

That morning, all those years ago, Evie had stood in the bright morning sunlight after Chelsea dropped her off and looked up at her house. Matthew had gone away for the weekend so she didn't have to worry about explaining why she'd been out all night. Sometimes she wondered if the seven-year age gap was too much, although sometimes he seemed a lot older than thirty. She didn't want to think about that now, not while she was still feeling the last of the effects from the tablet. Once inside, she turned on the stereo and danced in the lounge room, lost in her own happy world. Eventually, she turned the music off and went to have a shower because she was meeting her friends at Gaby's house for lunch. Before walking out the door, she took one last look in the mirror and checked that her pupils were back to their normal size. Chelsea had warned her about that, but she hadn't understood until she looked in the mirror after taking the first half of the tablet and saw that her pupils were massive.

"Grab a seat," Gaby said to her when she arrived for lunch. "We're having champagne. Do you want one?"

"Yes, please. Are we celebrating something?

Anna shook her head. "No, I just felt like champagne, so I bought a bottle. Did you know there's no fat in champagne?"

Evie laughed. "I didn't know that. Considering we're all skinny, I'm not sure I need to know that."

Before she had a chance to say anything else, Laura rushed through the door and collapsed in a chair.

"Sorry I'm late."

Anna laughed. "You're always late."

"No I'm not."

"Yes, you are," Evie and Gaby said in unison.

"Leave me alone. I didn't get much sleep last night."

"Were you out with Sebastian again?" Anna asked.

Laura nodded. "He's so much fun to be with. I'm having a ball."

"Glad to hear you're having fun," Gaby said. "We stayed home and watched a movie. You can't go out on a Saturday night when you have a three-year-old."

"But she's an adorable three-year-old," Evie said.

"Not when she's throwing a tantrum like she did last night at bedtime. What did you get up to last night, Evie?"

"Matthew was away last night, so I went dancing."

Evie thought it best not to go into details in case anyone asked questions, so she didn't say anything else. Instead, she started sipping her champagne.

"That sounds like fun," Laura said. "When are we eating?"

Gaby stood up. "I'll bring it out now."

Evie turned her head and watched Gaby walk inside. "Do you need a hand?"

"No, stay there. Everything's done, and there are only two dishes to carry."

Evie was in no hurry to go home. Sitting in the sun sipping champagne with her friends was a lovely way to spend a Sunday afternoon. It made her feel happy. Not as happy as she'd felt last night, but it was the closest she could get without taking another one of those magical tablets. And the longer she stayed, the less time she'd spend having to listen to Matthew say she hadn't ironed his shirts correctly or that she hadn't put enough water in the pot plants.

At work the following morning, Evie had a client struggling with an addiction to a drug prescribed by his doctor. She'd only been a qualified social worker for a couple of years and had just started taking on some more complicated cases independently. This was the first time she'd seen someone who had an addiction without one of the senior social workers with her. At last week's meeting, her boss had told her she was impressed by Evie's work ethic and natural ability for the job and was confident she could start treating her own clients. She'd been nervous before the client walked in, but once they started talking, she relaxed and began developing a rapport. At the end of the session, he'd organised a time to see her later in the week. She told Matthew when she got home that night, excited.

"It's good that it went well," he said. "But don't get too carried away. Not everyone will be like that, and it could just be that you had a good client."

She watched him as he walked out of the bedroom. Or it could have something to do with being good at my job, she thought.

The next day, Chelsea called and told Evie they were going out that weekend and that it would be like nothing Evie had experienced before. The more Chelsea talked about the plans for the weekend, the more excited she became. Evie, on the other hand, became more nervous. She'd been thinking a lot lately about what they'd been doing, or more specifically, what they'd been taking. Evie knew what she'd been doing was dangerous and stupid. She kept telling herself that she needed to stop but saying it to herself and actually doing it were two very different things.

"Sounds great," Evie said after Chelsea had finished describing their upcoming night out.

"You don't sound too enthusiastic about it," Chelsea said.

"I am. It will be fun."

"Still not convinced. What are you worried about? That Matthew will find out."

"No, he'll be away. It's what we've been taking. It's scaring me a little bit."

"Is that all? No need to be scared about that. You'll be with me, and you know what I do for a job. We wouldn't be doing it if I didn't think it was ok. And we've never had any issues before."

Evie thought about what Chelsea had said after they'd hung up. She wanted to believe Chelsea was right, but a little voice kept saying just because Chelsea said it was ok didn't mean that it was.

The closer it got to the weekend, the more Evie thought that she probably shouldn't be taking anything. The fact that they'd done it several times before and nothing had happened didn't comfort Evie as much as she would have liked. By Friday morning, she'd decided she would ring Chelsea and say she wouldn't be taking speed. She'd still go because she'd already paid for the ticket, and it was too short notice for Chelsea to find someone else to go with. Evie was happy with her decision as she headed off to work. She'd make the call during the first break she got. But the day was busier than expected. By the time her last client left, she felt very pleased with herself. That client, plus two others she'd seen that day, had told her how grateful they were for what she was doing for them and how much she was helping them. Her boss overhead the comments and added to them, saying Evie was doing a great job. Evie practically skipped out the door and down to the car park where Matthew was waiting for her.

"You look happy," he said. "What's put that smile on your face?"

So Evie told him about her day and the positive comments she'd received.

"Good to hear you're getting feedback like that and that you're helping people in your own way."

"What do you mean, in my own way?"

"It's not like you're saving people's lives like I am. Most of the people you help are there because they've got to a place where they can't help themselves. They've made a lot of bad choices."

"Just because someone has made bad choices doesn't mean they don't deserve help."

"I didn't say that. But the help I give people can be the difference between life and death."

Evie spent the rest of the trip home not saying anything and wishing she'd never mentioned her day in the first place. When they got home, she watched Matthew pack. She then shut the door behind him as he headed off to the airport on his way to the outback clinic he volunteered at when he had a few days off from the hospital. She didn't offer to drive him. And she didn't ring Chelsea.

Evie checked that the laces on her shoes were still tied and that her hair was still in the tight plait she'd put it in an hour ago. It was the May Day long weekend, 2001, and they'd arrived at Adventjah, the night Chelsea had been telling Evie about. The hesitation she'd felt earlier about taking a little something to get her in the party mood had disappeared. As they stood in line to get in, Evie had trouble standing still. She just wanted to get inside and start dancing. She could hear the music from where she was standing as the techno beats escaped from the pavilions in the Exhibition grounds at Bowen Hills. Her feet started to move but she forced them to stop because she needed to stay in control until they got past the security on the gate. She was already wired. Usually, it takes a while for the tablet's effects to kick in, but tonight it had kicked in straight away. "What's the holdup?"

"They're checking ID," Chelsea said. "Just be thankful we got here when we did. Look at the queue behind us."

Evie turned and looked at the line that stretched up along O'Connell Terrace and around the corner into Brookes Street. There was supposed to be around six thousand people coming tonight. She turned back around and looked through the gate at the Exhibition grounds. She'd been there so many times when the Ekka was on. Ever since she was a kid, she loved coming during those ten days in August when the grounds were filled with rides, show bags, food, and displays in all the pavilions. There weren't any show bags tonight, but there were rides and displays in the pavilions, just not the sort they usually contained. Instead of giant pumpkins and new cars and camping equipment, there would be people letting go, releasing themselves to the music and letting it wash over them. In the words of Faithless, *this is my church, this is where I heal my hurts, for tonight God is a DJ.* This is where Evie healed her hurts, where it all slipped away, and she was free. She had no thoughts of her clients and the stress she often felt when trying to help them. And no thoughts of Matthew, who never seemed to have any time for her lately.

Through the gate, Evie could see the stalls selling clothes and accessories. She thought how much she'd like a new pair of pants with lots of pockets to stick all her stuff in so she wouldn't have to carry anything. As it was, she had her money, cigarettes and lip balm all crammed into one pocket. Next to the clothes stalls were the food stalls, and Evie often wondered how well they did on a night like this. She never felt like eating, and she didn't think many other people did either unless you counted sucking on Chupa Chups as eating. Further along, she could see a stand selling glow sticks. She loved dancing with them, the way the colours swirled through the air in the dark pavilions. That stand would be her first stop.

"Almost in," Chelsea said. "Got your ticket ready?"

"Yes. Your pupils have dilated already."

"So have yours. Not surprising considering we took a whole tablet instead of taking half like we usually do."

They handed their tickets over, showed their ID and then they were in. They'd only moved a few metres, but already the atmosphere changed. Everywhere they looked, people were milling around, laughing, talking and dancing in the street. Evie immediately felt relaxed and instantly forgot what Matthew had said to her in the car that afternoon. She was so used to him telling her she never did anything right that she didn't even argue about it anymore.

"I really like those glow in the dark orange pants at that stall," Evie said, pointing just ahead of them. "Do you think they'd suit me?"

Chelsea nodded. "Absolutely, although the ones you've got on are great too."

Evie was wearing her blue cargo pants with the yellow trim, a yellow stretchy singlet top and a pair of dark blue sneakers. Even though it was autumn, there was no reason to rug up because she would soon be sweating. And it was a nice change to go out dressed comfortably instead of dressing up to go to a regular club.

"Are you ready to start dancing now?" Chelsea asked.

"Absolutely. Let's go."

From the minute they stepped into the dark pavilion, Evie felt her mood change, and she let the music and its driving beat wash over her. Her feet moved of their own accord, knowing what to do from so many nights before. Evie and Chelsea didn't talk. They just danced; harder and faster as time went on. All around them, people were doing the same. Evie was spellbound by the flashes of light as the hundreds of glow sticks in the pavilion weaved through the air. After an hour of continuous dancing, they forced themselves to stop and go outside to get some water.

They found a spot on the grass and sat among the other revellers taking a break. Even though they'd only just sat down, Evie was having trouble sitting still. Her feet were tapping and her fingers started to twirl the glow sticks. She wanted to move, but Chelsea said she needed another minute before they got up, so she started observing the people swarming around them. There were so many different types of people, and that was one of the things she loved the most about the dance scene. Everyone looked as if they belonged, and everyone was accepted. It didn't matter who you were, what your job was or what your personal life was like. Evie watched a guy walk by dressed as a traffic controller, complete with the reflective orange vest and a few metres behind him, a girl with glitter in her hair and on her face, wearing a tutu and butterfly wings, and carrying a wand. Evie thought wearing butterfly wings in this crowd must take special skills because there had to be four thousand people there already and it was only 11.30pm. Evie was sure those wings would be in the bin by sunrise the next day.

"Okay, let's go," Chelsea said.

And up they got in search of the next dance floor.

The first pavilion they went into wasn't very crowded. The DJ was playing trance music, but it was too early for that. Evie wanted something fast and heavy. The next pavilion was more crowded, but it still wasn't what she wanted. The jungle rhythms weren't hard enough, so they headed back to the main pavilion just inside the gate. As they got closer, Evie heard the music, and it was exactly what she was looking for. They walked inside and the crowds of people swallowed them. Evie felt like she had arrived in another world. On the stage, the DJ was lost in a trance, like he had to keep the music coming and couldn't stop. Whistles scattered through the crowd sounded in time to the music. She'd never tried using a whistle. She preferred glow sticks because something about them amused her. The pretty colours and the way you could move them through the dark and create mesmerising patterns in the air. They also gave her something to do with her hands, which she usually had trouble keeping still.

They pushed through the crowd and got as close to the stage as possible. A light display threw different shaped patterns against the back wall. The music got louder, and four fire eaters came out from the back of the stage, spewing fire from their mouths. Evie watched them, amazed at their skill and then behind them, four more people ran out onto the stage. They were contortionists, and they began to twist their bodies into poses most people could never hope to achieve. The fire eaters moved between them, adding flames behind the contorted bodies. Evie was entranced by what she saw, even slowing down her movements to take in everything. The DJ became more frantic, manipulating the turntable to produce the sounds that accompanied the show. The audience was still dancing, arms and legs moving wildly, but their eyes were on the stage. Claps and cheers and whistle blows rang out as each new trick was performed, but no one stopped dancing. The beams of light swirled faster and faster, turning into a myriad of shapes and patterns.

Evie was watching with everyone else when suddenly the light made the shape of a pentagram, and a shiver ran down her spine. She turned to Chelsea to see her reaction, but there was none. She was lost in the same trance as all the others. Everywhere Evie looked, people were staring at the lights, transfixed. It suddenly dawned on her that they were worshipping just like the Faithless song said. The pavilion was the church, the DJ the priest and the music was the choir bringing the sounds their souls were craving, reverent looks on their faces. She wasn't sure why, but Evie suddenly needed to get out of there. She tapped Chelsea on the shoulder and pointed outside before turning and pushing through the bodies and running out.

"What's wrong?" Chelsea asked, catching up to her.

"I just needed to get out. It was scaring me in there."

"Why?"

"I'm not sure. I was fine until I saw the pentagram on the back wall. It scared me. This will sound very strange, but I felt like there was something evil in there."

"Did you take another tablet?"

Evie nodded. "Just half though. I'll be fine in a minute. I just need some fresh air."

But Evie needed more than that. What was going on in the pavilion was still freaking her out. She wasn't a religious person but what she saw in the pavilion made her think of everything she'd learned in Christian education classes in high school about heaven and hell. She hadn't thought much about it since leaving school, but at that moment, it felt like the devil was real and was being worshipped at this very moment by a large number of drug-fuelled worshippers. She took a few deep breaths. It was just a side effect of the tablet, she told herself. She'd just imagined it. It must have been a hallucination. Even if it was, she was still scared.

"Ready to go back inside?" Chelsea asked.

Evie shook her head. "I want to go home."

"But it's only early."

"You stay. I don't like what just happened, and I want to leave. And I don't feel very well."

"Just sit down for a minute and have some water and you'll be fine."

But Evie wasn't fine. Everything around her had slowed down, and everything she looked at was blurry. She could feel the bile rising in her throat and realised she was going to throw up. She went to run to the toilets, but her legs wouldn't work. Evie covered her mouth as she began to retch. Chelsea grabbed her under the arm and steered hertoward the loos.

"How much further?" Evie asked.

"Not far. Come on, you can make it."

Kneeling on the floor, her arms locked around the toilet bowl, Evie threw up for what seemed like an eternity. Just when she thought she couldn't possibly throw up anymore, it started again. Evie had never been so sick in all her life. She kept telling herself that everything would be fine when she finished throwing up, but it was getting harder to breathe. Gulping in huge gasps of air in between retching, Evie tried to calm herself. Chelsea stood behind her and held her hair back for her until she had nothing left to bring up. They sat next to each other on the floor and leaned against the cubicle wall. Evie focused on her breathing because she felt like she needed to take in as much air as possible.

"You all right?" Chelsea asked.

"Not really."

They walked back outside and found a spot where they could lie down on the grass.

"Maybe you shouldn't have taken the extra half a tablet," Chelsea said.

Evie just nodded and looked around her. Chelsea was right, but she didn't feel up to speaking. No one was lined up at the gates anymore, and the grounds were filled to capacity. People were squeezed in everywhere, and they'd been lucky to get a spot on the grass. A couple of people stopped to ask if she was all right, and some stayed to chat. It was heart-warming to feel so comfortable with people she had just met. The only people she usually felt that comfortable with were her school friends. Evie would have loved some of her friends to come with her, but she could never invite them because they would see the tablets she took each time, and none of them would be happy. Gaby would be horrified and would be on her case for as long as it took to get her to stop. Anna would never take anything that would make her lose control, and even though she knew Laura occasionally smoked pot, she would never touch anything else. So that just left Evie. On her own again. She turned to Chelsea, still sitting beside her.

"I want to go home."

Chelsea shook her head. "I've been waiting for this for weeks. Just one more pavilion, and then we'll go."

Evie didn't want to, but Chelsea had already walked off. She watched her for a minute and then followed. They stopped in front of the trance pavilion, the same one they'd walked past earlier, where the music was slower and more hypnotic, and Chelsea said this was what she wanted now. From the doorway, she watched Chelsea walk to the middle of the room and start dancing. She was beckoned over a few times but Evie didn't want to dance. She just wanted to go home. Next to her was a girl in a slip dress wearing butterfly wings like she'd seen earlier on another girl. She had two glow sticks tied to pieces of elastic, and she twirled them around her as she moved. She looked so peaceful. Evie wondered briefly if she could do that. It looked so pretty, but she doubted she had the grace to pull it off. She'd probably keep hitting herself in the head with the glow sticks. The room was less crowded than the other ones they'd been in, and after a while, Evie forgot about wanting to go and let the music pull her back in. She didn't know how much of the tablets were still in her system, but it was enough to lead her to where Chelsea was dancing. She moved more slowly than she had before and let herself become lost in her own world, not thinking but instead entranced by the girl beside her making patterns in the dark with glow sticks.

They stayed in the same pavilion until 4am when the music stopped, and it was time to go back to the real world.

When Evie got home, the house was in darkness, and she cursed under her breath that she hadn't left a light on. All she wanted to do was get inside, but she couldn't find her keys in the dark. The street was quiet and none of the houses had lights on. A bird flew by and she jumped at the sound of its wings just above her head. As soon as the door was open, she turned on all the lights and took her phone out of her bag, keeping it close by in case she needed it. Not that she would ring anybody. The events of the night were not something she would share with anyone.

Even though she no longer felt sick, Evie didn't want to go to bed just yet. So she wandered through the house, looking for things to do.

Nothing appealed to her until she walked back into the kitchen and saw how dirty the windows were, and she had a sudden urge to clean. She pulled out the glass cleaner and a cloth from under the sink and started slowly, but as the cloth moved through the dirt, she started cleaning faster until the first window was clear. She felt a sense of satisfaction when she looked through the clean glass, so she started on the next and then the next until all of them were done.

When she'd finished, she washed her hands but couldn't get rid of the smell of the cleaner. She scrubbed and scrubbed, but it wouldn't come off. She kept scrubbing until her hands were raw, but she still couldn't get rid of the smell and started crying in frustration.

As the tears streamed down her face, she suddenly felt so alone, like she was the only person in the world. The quiet tears turned into sobbing, and she dropped to the floor, huddled against the kitchen cupboards and buried her face in her hands to muffle the noise. She cried until she thought there couldn't be any more tears, but they still came. The floor was cold and hard. She pulled herself up onto her hands and knees and crawled across the hallway from the kitchen into the spare bedroom, onto the old mattress in the corner, then curled up into a ball. The only thing she could think of was wanting to go home, and she kept whispering that to herself over and over again. But this was her home, and there was nowhere else for her to go. She certainly couldn't go back to her parent's house because they would only make her feel worse. She couldn't go to one of her friends' houses because while she knew they'd help her, how could she explain what was wrong when she wasn't even sure herself. She could only assume it was the speed. Evie had never felt so alone in her whole life.

Suddenly she felt sick and ran to the bathroom, but after throwing up earlier, there was nothing left. She sat on the bathroom floor, hugging the toilet bowl, sobbing. In her head, a voice started to speak. *You're on your own. You have no one. Matthew doesn't love you. Your family doesn't love you. Your friends just tolerate you. No, they don't. They care about me. And so does Matthew, and so does my family. No, they don't. You don't love Matthew. You don't even like him. Why am I still with him? I need to break it off. Your friends will support you. Maybe they won't. Of course, they will. How would my family react? They like Matthew. Go away. Go away.* Evie huddled up even more and prayed for the sun to come up. *No more. You're worthless. You know you are. No. No.*

Evie felt like she was suffocating. She couldn't breathe. She had to get out of the room. Do something else, anything. She ran to

274

the lounge room and turned on the TV. She wanted to scream and started rocking herself back and forth on the lounge chair. *Snap out of it. Stop it now, stop it.* Over and over she yelled in her head until it finally stopped, but she stayed on the lounge chair until the sun started to rise.

As the sunlight filtered through the window, she began to feel stronger and told herself to have a shower and make a coffee, then she'd feel better. In the kitchen, the cleaning products and rags were still on the bench, so she put them away because she couldn't look at them. The noise of the jug boiling held her attention, and she stared at it, watching the steam rise from the top. When it was ready, she filled the cup and held it in her hands, warming them because she felt so cold. She shuffled into the bathroom and ran a bath, filling the tub with inviting warm water.

Evie never had a bath in the morning, but she felt like she needed a bath now, not a shower, as the water shooting from the nozzle would be too violent. She undressed slowly as if she was in pain and gingerly stepped into the bath, sinking under the water and letting it warm her. The bath made her feel calm. And safe. Things looked clearer now in the morning light, and she tried to understand

what had happened during the past few hours.

Chapter 14

Back in the lounge room at Mt Tamborine, Evie looked around the room at her friends. She could only imagine the thoughts that must be going through their heads. Out of all the secrets, she knew hers was the worst. And she hadn't finished telling it yet.

"Chelsea went overseas to work after that night, and I didn't do anything like that again. What happened scared me too much. I put the whole thing down as a youthful act of rebellion and thought that was that. I won't go into all the details of the next few years. You know Matthew and I got divorced. His work was more important than I ever was."

At the time Evie had thought that was that. Chelsea had gone, and she stopped going out. But then Matthew left and she met Nick, and her life changed again. She owed it to the others to keep going. Her story had three parts. She'd said part one and she would say part two, but no matter how much she felt she owed it to them, to be honest because they had been with her, she wouldn't be saying part three.

"After Chelsea had gone, I put it all behind me. I thought that's where it would stay. But a year ago, Chelsea came back from working overseas. We caught up for a coffee not long after she arrived. I told her about the divorce from Matthew and getting married to Nick. I never told her what happened when I got home that night after Adventjah. I just wanted to forget all about it."

Until now, she hadn't thought about that night for years. Even though she'd just spoken about what happened, the way she'd felt at the time didn't come back to her.

"Chelsea talked about all the places she'd been to and the things she'd seen. She was the one who brought up the subject of raves and how we used to go. She said, wouldn't it be funny if we did something like that for old times' sake. While the thought of going out dancing again appealed to me, I didn't want to do what we used to, and I made that clear to her. And she said that was fine with her. She hadn't taken speed in years. She'd replaced it with prescription amphetamines."

The day she caught up with Chelsea had been lovely. It had been nice talking about everything that had happened in the past fifteen years. When she'd first got the message that Chelsea was coming back to Brisbane, she thought maybe they'd catch up at some point. But Chelsea had contacted her as soon she got back, saying she wanted to slip back into her old life because she'd moved around so much that now she just wanted to settle into a routine and not have to make new friends. Evie had been surprised at how comfortable it was being around her after so long. It was like they'd seen each other only last week. Evie had been thrown by the mention of prescription amphetamines though. When she asked Chelsea what she was taking and why, she'd said she was taking Dexedrine, which Evie knew was used to treat ADHD, and that she didn't take it very often, just when she went out partying. On the way home in the car, Evie realised the situation wasn't all that different to fifteen years ago when she and Chelsea were out partying. Evie was in a relationship with a man who didn't seem happy to be with her. She remembered what a release it had been when she went out on those nights with Chelsea and forgot her problems for a while.

That was how she found herself agreeing to go out with Chelsea the following weekend, and on that Saturday night, it was like no time had passed. Everything she remembered from all those years ago was there. The only difference was that Dexedrine didn't have the same kick as speed. But it didn't matter. Evie would never take speed now. On the other hand, a prescription drug couldn't really do any harm. That's what she told herself over and over the whole time they were out.

By the time she got home the following day, her watch said 7.00am. As soon as she slipped her key into the front door and opened it, she knew Nick was home. He'd told her his plane didn't land until 7.30am, so she thought she'd be home in plenty of time. But the bathroom door was shut, and she could hear the water running. She tiptoed by the bathroom, walked into their bedroom and quickly got changed into shorts and a t-shirt, then went to the laundry and hid the clothes she'd been wearing in the bottom of the laundry hamper. Nick never did the washing, so he wouldn't find them there. Then she walked quickly back to their bedroom and checked her face in the mirror. She couldn't see anything that would give away what she'd done last night, but with Nick, she could never be too careful. Evie heard the bathroom door open and took a deep breath.

"Where have you been? I thought you'd be here when I got home."

"I went for a walk. You said your plane didn't land until 7.30am."

"The flight time was changed. We landed at 6.20am and there weren't many people queuing for taxis."

"How was your trip?"

"Busy. It always is. What have you been doing while I've been away?"

"Not much."

"That doesn't surprise me. I'm going to try and sleep for a couple of hours."

Evie watched as he lay down on the bed and closed his eyes. She should have come up with something better to say, but she didn't want him asking questions about anything she'd done while he was away. There was no way she was going to mention what she'd done last night. Evie leant against the bed and felt the happiness from last night drain away. She walked out of the room, shut the door and went and made herself a coffee. While she was on the verandah drinking it, she heard her phone ring. And it was in the kitchen. She got to it as quickly as she could, but Nick was already standing there, the phone in his hand.

"I told you I want to try and get some sleep. Why didn't you have this with you?" he said as he looked down at the screen. "And tell your friends they shouldn't ring at this time of the morning. I'm going back to bed. Try and be more considerate next time."

Evie waited until he'd gone back down the hall and shut the bedroom door before going back outside, sitting down and taking a few deep breaths. Then she rang Laura back.

"Good morning," Laura said down the line. "You were quick to call me back."

Evie yawned. "Morning. I was just out on the verandah having a coffee and almost made it to the phone on time."

It wasn't exactly the truth, but it was close enough, Evie thought.

"Sounds like you had a big night."

"Just caught up with an old friend. Stayed out much later than I planned."

"I know how that goes. You plan on catching up over a glass of wine, and the next thing you know, you've ordered a bottle. And then you think, this is fun, why don't we stay a bit longer and have a cocktail."

"That's it."

"Good thing I'm just leaving now to pick you up then. You've still got time to have another coffee if you need it."

"What are you picking me up for?

"We're meeting Gaby and Anna in the Valley for yum cha, remember."

Evie had forgotten about that. They'd made plans three weeks ago, and even though she'd written it down in her diary, it had completely slipped her mind.

"I don't really feel up to it."

"You should have thought of that before you went out last night, so no sympathy from me. See you in half an hour. I have to drop Max off at mum's first."

Evie hung up and tried to talk herself into going. At least it would get her out of the house so she wouldn't be there when Nick woke up again. She tiptoed into their room to get an outfit from the wardrobe then headed for the shower. The warm water ran over her as she lathered the shampoo in her hair and then turned around, leaned back and let the water wash the shampoo, sweat and anger away. The water felt soothing, but it didn't make her feel any better. And she couldn't stop thinking how easily she'd fallen back into old habits.

"Good morning," Laura said when she arrived. "You look tired. Shouldn't have stayed out so late."

"I know. Can you keep your voice down? Nick is still asleep."

"No time to hang around anyway. You ready?"

"I'll just grab my handbag."

As they drove through the streets, Evie tried her best not to think about Nick and how she'd had to ask Laura to be quiet. She hated that she had to do that. And she hated that Laura knew why she had to do that.

"It all looks so good," Laura said as she eyed off the trolleys of food whizzing around the restaurant.

Evie looked at the trolleys but she wasn't the slightest bit hungry. So, she told her friends she'd had too much to drink last night and just the thought of food made her feel like being sick.

"We've all been there," Laura said. "Loneliest time ever when you've got your head over the toilet bowl. Some food might make you feel better though. It always does for me, especially a big greasy breakfast."

Evie shook her head. "I'll leave it. Shame though. I love yum cha too. I should have behaved myself a bit more last night."

Gaby nodded. "Drinking too much isn't good for you."

Laura laughed. "As if you haven't done it before."

"It doesn't happen very often."

Evie thought about what Gaby would say to her if she knew that it wasn't alcohol she'd had last night, considering she wouldn't even take a headache tablet unless she really needed to. Gaby wouldn't have yelled, but she wouldn't leave Evie alone until she'd promised never to do it again.

"Who did you go out with last night, Evie?" Gaby asked.

"I don't know if you remember my friend Chelsea? I used to see her a lot before she moved overseas. She's just recently come back."

Gaby nodded. "I never met her, but I remember you saying years ago that you used to go out dancing with her."

"Did you go dancing last night?" Anna asked.

Evie nodded. "It was fun. I haven't been dancing in a long time."

Laura laughed again. "That's what happens when you have a few too many drinks. Were you the oldest people there?"

Evie smiled. "Yes, but we didn't care."

And they hadn't cared. They just wanted to have fun and be happy for a while.

"Where did you go?" Laura asked.

"Just to a club here in the Valley. I can't remember what it's called. I've never been there before."

"Any good?"

"Yeah, it was pretty good."

"Isn't it dangerous in there at night?" Anna asked.

Evie shook her head. "I didn't see anything that was dangerous."

"I'm still not sure I'd want to go out in the Valley at night," Gaby said. "I keep hearing stories about lots of fights and bad behaviour, mainly because there's a lot of drugs around."

"I didn't see anything like that."

Evie hated lying but there was nothing else she could say. It was only a little white lie anyway. She wasn't hurting anyone by saying it.

By the time Laura dropped her back home, Nick had gone out. The note on the kitchen bench said he'd gone to Stewart's place to help him fix his car and watch football, so he wouldn't be home until that

287

night. Evie said a silent thank you prayer and went and lay down. She didn't sleep, but she turned the bedroom TV on and watched a couple of Sunday movies until it got dark. Then she got out of bed so Nick wouldn't think she'd spent all day doing nothing.

Evie fell back into an old pattern and went out with Chelsea whenever Nick was away. It had been happening for about three months when Evie had to cancel one Saturday night because Nick's work trip had been pushed back. Evie was actually glad that she couldn't go out. The conversation she'd had with Chelsea the day before was still playing on her mind. Whenever she thought about the conversation, she broke out in a sweat. The person Chelsea usually got the tablets from had gone interstate for a few weeks, and none of her other sources could help out. So she'd asked the one person she knew who had easy access to them through her work. Evie.

"It will be easy," Chelsea said. "You're at the hospital all the time to see your clients. And you know the nurses really well.

They're so used to seeing you there that no one would think twice if they saw you."

"You're at the hospital all the time too."

"But I only go to emergency, which is always swarming with people. I never go near the dispensary."

"I never go near the dispensary either."

"You wouldn't have to. Surely you know of a patient that takes Dexedrine and you could grab a packet when they're not looking."

"I've never done anything like that before. I really don't think I can."

"How many times when we were younger did I supply you with party drugs when we went out? And not asked you to pay. You'll be fine. Just do it this once."

Evie wasn't happy that Chelsea had tried to guilt her into getting the tablets but what she'd said was true. Maybe there was another way Evie could get the tablets.

A few days later, she hadn't thought of another option, and she really needed a night out. Nick was always harder to live with when he travelled a lot. He was a homebody at heart, but he didn't want to change jobs. Sometimes it was only once a month. Other times, like now, it was twice a week. So later that day, she found herself at the hospital.

"Hey there, Evie. How are you?"

Evie turned around and saw one of the nurses she knew and often chatted with. "Yeah, good. I'm good. What about you?"

"Same. Are you here to see one of your clients?"

"Yes, but I don't have a lot of time today so I can't stop and chat. Sorry."

"That's all right. I'll see you next time."

Evie's breathing slowed down a little as she watched the nurse walk away. She wanted to turn around and walk out of the hospital, but Chelsea's voice was in her head, so she kept walking down the hallway until she found the person she'd come to visit. A visit she'd timed to coincide with when the nurses went around to the patients and gave them their afternoon medication. He hadn't been expecting Evie to visit but was pleased that she had, and she was surprised how calmly she was able to talk to him. They'd been speaking for about ten minutes when a nurse, who Evie didn't recognise, walked in. She asked Evie to leave the room for a few minutes.

"Just need to check a few things and give him his medication," she said. "You can come back after I'm done."

Evie waited outside while the nurse was in the room. The longer she waited, the more she could feel herself shaking, so much so that she was sure someone would notice. The shaking had become worse ever since she'd seen the box of medication in the nurse's hand, and Evie knew from her client's file that one of the packets in the box was Dexedrine. After a few minutes, the nurse walked out and Evie took a deep breath and walked back into the room. The package of medication was still there.

"I don't think the nurse has finished yet."

"Oh, ok. I'll go out again."

As she turned, she knocked the box off the table over the end of the bed, and all the medication fell on the floor.

"Oh my god. I'm so sorry. I better pick these up before the nurse comes back."

Evie picked up all the boxes as quickly as she could, and when she found the Dexedrine, she slipped two tablets out of the box and into her pocket. She couldn't risk anymore. She hurriedly put the box back on the table and walked out of the room. She'd only just reached the hallway when the nurse returned.

"Only a few more minutes," she said.

Evie just nodded. She couldn't think properly to form a sentence. She was feeling too sick about what she'd done. She waited until the nurse had finished, went in, said goodbye, then walked out of the hospital as quickly as she could, not making eye contact with anyone. When she reached her car, she jumped in, locked the doors, rested her head against the steering wheel and waited for the shaking to stop.

That Saturday night, Evie went out with Chelsea to try a new club in the Valley with the two tablets burning a hole in her pocket. The first opportunity she got, she told Chelsea she would never do anything like that again. As much fun as going out was, and as much as she needed it to deal with her home life, she'd rather stay home than steal tablets again.

"It's not that big a deal," Chelsea said.

"To me, it is. I haven't thought about anything else since I did it, and I won't do it again."

"But I don't think I'll be able to find any for next weekend."

"Then we'll have to go without. Besides, Nick isn't away next weekend, so I can't go out."

"The next time he's away then."

"Chelsea, I'm not stealing again. I could lose my job if anyone found out."

"You'd lose your job anyway if your boss found out what you're doing tonight. Or what you did two weeks ago. Pretty sure it wouldn't do your relationship any good either."

Evie shuddered at the thought of anyone finding out. She loved her job. Not only would she lose it if her boss found out, but she'd also find it hard to get another job. No one would hire a social worker who took recreational drugs, even if they were prescription. And it would be worse if anyone at work found out what she used to do when she and Chelsea were younger. And Nick. If he found out it would take things from bad to intolerable. Evie knew she had to find a way to stop, no matter how much of an escape it was.

"If you're worried I'll tell someone, I won't. I'm in the same boat remember. We'll just have to think of another way you can get the tablets."

"Chelsea, I don't want to get the tablets."

"It's always up to me."

"That's because you know people who can supply those things. I don't."

"Not anymore. The last person I know who could get them went interstate, and I've just found out he's not coming back. So from now on, it's up to you."

"But I don't want to."

"Stop thinking like that. You'll be fine. How many more have you got on you?"

"None."

"What do you mean none? Why not?"

"I was too scared to get anymore."

"What are we going to do for the rest of the night? The one we've taken will wear off soon. You'll have to do better next time."

Evie watched as Chelsea turned and walked away. No matter what she said, Chelsea didn't seem to understand there wouldn't be a next time. Evie began to wonder if Chelsea was really her friend or if she'd met up with her after all these years because she thought Evie could be useful to her. After ten minutes, when Chelsea still hadn't come back, Evie went looking for her and found her in the toilet.

"It's all good now. I found some. Just one and a half, but that will have to do. You can have the half."

Evie looked down at the half tablet in her hand. It was hard to see because the toilets were dimly lit. This will be the last time, she thought to herself as she swallowed it. I'll stop after this.

Chelsea walked out of the bathroom without saying anything else.

The longer they danced, the happier Evie started to feel. She had more energy and didn't want to leave the dance floor. She looked at Chelsea as she danced and she seemed to have even more energy than Evie did, dancing harder and faster than Evie had seen in a long time. She had taken a whole tablet, so maybe that was the difference. And there was a wide smile plastered across her face. Anyone that came near them became Chelsea's best friend. As much fun as she was having, a voice in the back of her head kept saying they needed to stop and have some water, but she couldn't get Chelsea off the dance floor. Evie gave up asking and went to get some water for herself. She'd only been gone a minute when she heard a commotion. She pushed through the crowd to find that Chelsea had collapsed and was lying on the floor. She was shaking and muttering incoherently.

"Chelsea, what's wrong? Chelsea, talk to me."

"There's an ambulance on its way."

Evie turned and saw one of the security guards kneeling next to her. The other security guard was ushering people out the door. The music had stopped, and when the lights came on, Evie could see Chelsea's face. She was pale, sweat dripping off her, and her eyes were unfocused.

"Chelsea, come on, speak to me. What's happening?"

She mumbled something Evie couldn't make out, so she leaned in closer and asked again. She could only make out one word of the reply. Speed. Evie stood back and watched as the ambos rushed in and worked on Chelsea. One of them turned to her and asked if she knew what Chelsea had taken. Evie didn't say anything. She was asked three times before getting the word out of her mouth. Speed. She watched them put Chelsea on a stretcher, wheel her out and straight into the ambulance and then she heard the sirens as the ambulance screamed out of the car park. She knew now why she'd had more energy and why she'd been so happy, and she could feel her stomach twisting itself into knots. Before coming out, she'd been worried about taking a prescription drug. That would have been so much better than what she'd actually taken. How could Chelsea do that, especially after all the things Evie had said? She'd put Evie in danger. What if Evie collapsed? There was no one to look after her and get her to the hospital if something terrible happened. All she could think about was going home. She'd be alone, but she'd feel safe in her own house, and there was no way she'd go to the hospital right now because someone would notice that Chelsea wasn't the only one who had taken something. Evie didn't want to lose her job, or worse, get arrested for taking drugs. She picked up Chelsea's bag and coat and hurried toward the door.

She was still inside when she started to feel like she wasn't in control anymore. The room started spinning, she started sweating. When she looked around, people seemed to be moving faster, talking louder and standing closer to her. She felt like the walls were closing in and started to feel overwhelmed. After a minute of feeling like that, she couldn't stand it anymore and ran outside. As soon as she reached the alley behind the club, she started vomiting. Instead of feeling hot like she had when she'd been inside, she was now freezing and the colder she got, the more she shook. There was no one around. She was entirely on her own. It was half an hour before she could get up off the ground and all she wanted to do was go home, so she found a taxi and left.

Two hours later, she still felt really sick and scared about what she had done and what could happen. She couldn't call anyone, so she got in the car, even though it was probably not the best idea, and drove to the hospital. She sat in the waiting room for over an hour, but it was so busy at that time of night that no one even came over to her. The longer she sat there, the better she started to feel, so she decided to leave. On her way back to her car, she thought how lucky she'd been. One that nothing terrible had happened and two, that she hadn't seen a doctor because she'd have to be truthful about what she'd taken, even though it hadn't been her choice. She also thought about seeing Chelsea while there, but she was still too angry to speak to her. She decided to come back in a few hours and visit Chelsea when she'd calmed down.

Chelsea lay on the bed, tubes attached to various monitors.

"How are you?" Evie asked.

"Better than I was last night. I don't remember anything. They had me in intensive care for a few hours until I was stable. Must have been boring for you to wait."

Evie didn't say anything. In the cold morning light, she felt ashamed that she hadn't stayed at the hospital or even checked on Chelsea, no matter how angry she'd been.

"It's a good thing the ambulance turned up when it did."

"I hope they didn't recognise me. I'd be in a lot of trouble if they did."

"Neither of them showed any signs that they did."

"That's good. I haven't recognised any of the doctors or nurses that have been in to treat me, so I think I'm safe. I wonder when I can get out of here."

"Why are you in such a hurry? You had a drug overdose."

"It was only one tablet."

"One tablet you lied about. And lied to me about it. How could you do that? I could have ended up in here as well."

"I didn't think you'd mind. You've done it before."

"Not for fifteen years."

"But you enjoyed it. Why did you stop?"

"Because you were the only person I knew who could get any. And because it was dangerous. If I'd known what the tablet was, I never would have taken it. You should have told me."

"It's not a big deal. You're all right today."

"That's not the point. You gave me an illegal drug and didn't tell me what it was."

"I don't understand what the problem is. It's not the first time, and it's not that different to the Dexedrine."

Evie couldn't believe what she was hearing. There was a massive difference between the two. As she looked at Chelsea lying in the hospital bed she realised she would never admit she'd done the wrong thing. And as soon as she was better, she'd probably want to go out again. Evie realised she needed to stay away from Chelsea before she ended up doing something that would put her in hospital.

In the lounge room at Mt Tamborine, Evie sat back from the edge of her chair where she'd been perched the whole time and sat comfortably for the first time since she'd started speaking. It was done, and she couldn't take any of it back.

"The experience that night when Chelsea was in hospital was enough to make me realise how stupid I'd been to be dicing with my health like that. I'm not proud of what I did, especially when I was younger. But it was a long time ago, and I haven't touched anything illegal since. I have no plans to ever touch anything illegal again."

Evie looked at their faces. She was waiting for one of them to say something. Even with the rules, what she'd said would have shocked them. She could see by the look on Gaby's face that she was trying very hard not to open her mouth and let what she was thinking out. Evie would hear it at some point, but she was grateful that Gaby was keeping those thoughts to herself at the moment. No matter how much she'd shocked them, she didn't feel like a group discussion. Out of the three of them, Anna looked the most upset. Laura just stared at her for a moment and then looked away. Evie sat back and had a sip of her wine to try and calm down. She'd never done anything that hard before, and she also felt guilty about not being one hundred per cent honest. Asking for help with what she was doing now had been the main reason she'd talked herself into taking part. And it was that part of her story, the third part, that she'd left out. Although by the look on Gaby's face, Evie wondered if she'd figured it out.

Chapter 15

Evie had spent the past few hours staring at the unfamiliar ceiling in the bedroom that was hers while they were at Mt Tamborine. The things she'd heard last night kept playing over and over in her mind like a song she didn't want to listen to, but she couldn't find the switch to turn it off.

So much had happened in the past six hours. Once they had all shared their secrets, no one knew quite how to act, so they'd gone to bed, preferring the safety of silence and darkness. For the first time in twenty-five years, they hadn't known what to say to each other. Even now, several hours later, she was still trying to get her head around the fact that there was so much they didn't know. Realistically, she never expected to remember every detail of everything they'd done together or every word they'd spoken to each other. But the things that were said were significant events in the lives of the people they were all supposed to know very well. How had these events slipped by with no one noticing? Or had they seen the clues and ignored them? The story that upset her the most was

Gaby's. She was her best friend and had been since grade eight. All this time, she didn't know that Daisy wasn't Oliver's daughter.

She would never be able to count the hours she'd spent with Gaby, Oliver and Daisy, yet she hadn't picked up on anything. Surely there would have been some clues, something that would have indicated that Daisy had a different father. But nothing stood out. She didn't know whether that was because Gaby had gone to great lengths to hide even the slightest clue or whether Evie just hadn't noticed because she'd always been too wrapped up in what was going on in her own life.

And then her thoughts turned to the one thing that was bothering her the most—how would her friends react when they saw her? She couldn't lie in this bed forever. And there was still the one detail she hadn't told them.

The only good thing that came from last night's stories was that they had given her hope, especially Laura's story. Hers was the closest experience to what Evie was dealing with. If the others had been brave enough to face their problems, then she should be able to face hers. Pushing aside the thoughts of the situation with Nick, she instead thought about Gaby and the inevitable conversation that would occur sooner rather than later. In fact, she'd been surprised that Gaby hadn't knocked on her door at some point during the night and said she wanted to talk. Although when the conversation happened, it would be going both ways. Gaby couldn't expect to just lecture Evie about what she'd done when she'd been lying to Evie for the past eighteen years. After listening to what Gaby had said last night, she could understand why she did it when it came to other people, but not her. The thought of anyone making comparisons between Gaby and her mum had bothered her for as long as Evie had known her. But Daisy was her goddaughter, and she was angrier with Gaby than she wanted to admit.

As she lay in bed, the covers tucked under her chin, Evie turned her thoughts to the part of her story she hadn't shared. If Gaby was angry with her now, she'd be even angrier if she found out.

When she'd come back from the hospital, she'd realised that she'd taken Chelsea's handbag with her but not her jacket. It was still hanging over the back of the dining room chair. If Chelsea wants it, she'll have to come and get it, Evie had thought at the time. After the conversation she'd had with Chelsea before leaving the hospital, there was no way she was going back there. She hadn't even wanted to call her because she hadn't wanted to give Chelsea another opportunity to try and justify what she'd done.

She'd looked at the jacket for a while before deciding to hang it up in the cupboard in the spare room. When she'd gone to hang it up, the coat hanger had hit something hard. Feeling around inside the jacket, Evie had found a hidden pocket. When she'd unzipped it, she'd found what must have been two packets worth of Dexedrine. It had been hard to tell exactly because the boxes were gone and some of the tablets were missing, but it had been close to that much. She'd been furious when she found them. There had been no reason to give Evie the speed, but she'd done it anyway. She hadn't known where Chelsea had got them from, someone at the club she'd assumed. As she'd looked down at the tablets in her hand, she'd decided to keep them and confront Chelsea with them if she ever came to get her jacket. And then she'd make Chelsea watch as she crushed them all into dust, then throw them out. Then she'd throw Chelsea out of her house and never see her again. In the meantime, she'd needed to find a better hiding place so Nick wouldn't accidentally discover them.

Looking up to the highest shelf in the wardrobe, she'd seen her pink, fluffy winter slippers tucked away at the very back. Nick hated those slippers, so she knew he'd never touch them. Evie had divided up the packets and tucked some in each slipper. And they'd sat there for a while until she realised one day that she wasn't going to hear from Chelsea again. The same day she'd had another fight with Nick. That was the day she'd first taken down one of the slippers and had reached inside for the contents. And now, there was only one packet left.

Down the hall, Laura was also lying awake in the pre-dawn light. She'd taken two painkillers, but her headache was still there. As was the now-empty wine bottle hidden in her bag that she'd packed at the last minute. The whole time she was packing she kept telling herself that she didn't need it, that she should leave the bottle at home. Even as she'd unpacked her bag yesterday, she was still thinking how disappointed she was with herself for not leaving the bottle behind.

She'd gone so long without having a drink. She hadn't even thought of having one. Not until that day five weeks ago when Sebastian had come over early to pick up Max and said he wanted to talk to her. While Max played in the yard, Sebastian had told her his girlfriend was pregnant. His girlfriend, the one she saw him with at 'their' restaurant the day she drove home drunk and could have killed someone.

For the next few days, she'd walked around without really focusing on anything. She went to work, did her job robotically and then came home and cried. The gallery had held an exhibition on the fourth day after he'd told her. She hadn't wanted to stay for it, but her boss wanted her there, and she knew that Max was with Sebastian so she had no excuse. As the night wore on, she began to feel more and more upset. It was too hard to stand there and smile at the customers and make small talk. The artist was even worse. So self-important that Laura wanted to slap him. She'd been talking to him for a couple of minutes when the waiter came over with a tray of champagne. Laura shook her head, but the artist got her a glass anyway. "One won't hurt," he'd said. The way she was feeling, maybe one, just one, would help. So she drank it. And then she had another one. Then a third. She stopped after that because she didn't want her boss to say anything, even though she was already on her fifth glass, so she wasn't in a position to say anything anyway. As Laura sat on the train on the way home, she'd felt happy. The three glasses of champagne had washed away her pain. And the bottle shop was on her walk home from the train station.

The next day she'd felt awful. Not only with the headache but also because she'd given in. She was proud of having her drinking under control. After work that day, she took the long way home so that she wouldn't walk by the bottle shop. Instead of sitting down drinking, she cleaned the house. Max would be home tomorrow, so all she had to do was keep herself occupied for the night. Everything would be better when he came home, and they would spend the whole weekend together.

It had been 3pm when Sebastian rang. His family had organised a last-minute weekend at the beach, and he wanted to take Max so he could spend time with his grandparents. With no one there to stop her, she'd spent most of the weekend sitting around the house crying and drinking. As soon as Max had come home, she'd stopped. Until last night. And the night before. Laura rolled over and looked at the clock. It was only 6.00am, and she didn't feel like getting up, especially as she heard the front door open, knowing that meant Gaby was up and heading out on her morning run. Laura didn't feel up to seeing anyone yet.

Evie also heard the front door open. She was too restless to stay in bed any longer. She waited a few minutes to give Gaby time to leave, then she got up, pulled a blanket off the bed, wrapped it around her and went outside to watch the sunrise. But Gaby was still there, sitting on the steps, tying her shoelaces.

Gaby looked up. "Morning."

Evie wrapped the blanket tighter around herself. "Off for your run?"

"I was going to, but now I think I'll stay here with you. I know you're still taking something."

Evie looked at Gaby as she sat down next to her on the chair on the verandah. If Gaby got angry, she'd have to deal with it. She was tired of lying.

"How did you know?

"The way you were acting yesterday, being fidgety, and not being able to sit still. I've seen it enough in my students to know the signs. Why don't I go and make us a coffee and we can talk about it."

"I'm not the only one who has something to talk about."

"I know, but I think your issue is a lot more pressing than mine.

"I wouldn't agree with that."

As Gaby walked off into the kitchen, Evie thought about what she would say when she came back. She wanted to talk about it now, and she knew that Gaby was the best one to talk to, although after what she'd heard last night, she wasn't as sure as she would have been yesterday.

"There you go," Gaby said as she handed Evie a cup of coffee.

"Thanks."

"You need to stop taking those tablets."

"Not wasting any time, are you?"

Gaby shook her head. "What you're doing is dangerous. It has to stop."

"I know."

Evie took a sip of her coffee and looked out at the view. That wasn't the only thing she had to do, and the other was going to be much harder.

"You should have told us last night. I was honest when I spoke, and I'm certain that Anna and Laura were too. But you kept something back, even after you heard what we had to say and saw how hard it was for us to speak."

Evie turned to look at Gaby. "I know. I've been awake half the night thinking about it. I wanted to be completely honest, but I just couldn't say everything I knew I should."

"Why?"

"Because my story is worse than all the others and I thought if you all found out that I might lose my friendships."

313

"Firstly, your story is no worse than anyone else's. And secondly, you should have more faith in your friends. You need to tell Anna and Laura the rest of the story."

Evie knew Gaby was right, and she felt even worse than she had last night. She shouldn't have lied to them. She'd known them too long and owed them more than what she had given them.

"I'll tell them."

"When?"

"When I'm ready. Don't push me. I feel bad enough as it is."

"All right. But I'll keep asking until you do."

Evie sighed. Gaby would do exactly that. But it wasn't up to her to decide when it would be the right time to tell Anna and Laura.

"So, where did you get them from, and why haven't you stopped taking them?"

Evie told her about what she found in the hidden pocket of Chelsea's jacket.

"And she still gave you speed that night? You must have been furious."

Evie nodded and told her about her plan for when Chelsea came to get them and how that hadn't happened.

"You should have thrown them out then."

"I know I should have, but I didn't. Anyway, I don't take one very often."

"That's no excuse."

"Maybe not, but it's the truth."

"Is it really the truth?"

"After what I heard last night, maybe I should be asking you that."

Gaby looked at her. "What do you mean?"

"If you lied to me about Daisy, what else have you lied about?"

"I told you last night why I didn't say anything. You should understand my reasons better than anyone."

"Just like you should understand my reasons instead of sitting here lecturing me."

"I'm not lecturing you. I'm trying to get you to see sense."

Evie put down her coffee cup. "I think that's enough talking for now."

She got off the love seat and walked to the edge of the yard, and looked out at the view. The longer she stood there, the calmer she felt. She didn't have to turn around to know that Gaby was still sitting on the verandah and would be until Evie came back. Instead of going back, she walked a bit further away. Gaby would have to wait. To her surprise, Gaby eventually got up and walked over to where she was standing.

"It's a lovely view."

Evie nodded.

"So why are you still taking them? Is it because of Nick?"

Evie nodded again. "I know he's bad for me, and I don't know why I stay. All my life I've had to live with my parents' disappointment, and the past nine years, I've been living with Nick's as well."

When Evie thought back over her relationship with Nick, she couldn't ignore that it had been an equal measure of happiness and sadness, at least from her point of view. Nick always said things were fine, and she was making it up. But she knew she wasn't. How could you make up how you feel?

"I kept thinking last night that if I'd been in the position you found yourself in when you fell pregnant with Daisy, Nick would have walked out straight away. You're lucky Oliver didn't."

"I am, but I don't want everyone thinking it's been easy because it hasn't."

"Your relationship with Oliver is still better than the one I have with Nick. Or the one I had with Matthew."

"Neither of them were good for you."

Evie didn't say anything. She knew how similar they both were and that she had a pattern when it came to men, but she had enough racing through her mind already. She didn't want to add that to the mix as well.

"Are you afraid to be on your own?"

"Sometimes."

Somewhere nearby, Evie heard a kookaburra. She turned around to look for it but couldn't see it. But she did see the curtain in

Laura's room close suddenly and wondered how long she'd been watching them.

"You've never liked Nick have you?"

"Not really."

Evie remembered when she and Gaby had met up for a drink after work one Friday. They'd chosen a bar, and when they got there, they saw Nick. Evie didn't know he would be there. He hadn't mentioned anything about going for a drink after work, and he seemed annoyed that she was there. Gaby said hello to him, he said hello to her, but then turned his back and ignored them. Gaby, being the sort of person she was, said straight away and out loud how rude that was. Evie thought it was too and was embarrassed by how Nick had treated them. Unfortunately, she was getting used to that sort of behaviour, but the fact that Gaby had seen it made her very uncomfortable.

"I know I need to leave but it's scary. My whole life would change."

"Yes, but you deserve to be happy, and not artificial happiness either."

Evie nodded. "I know if I get myself out of the relationship, it will go a long way to giving up the tablets. One led to me taking up the other again. Once the cause is gone, the reaction will hopefully be gone as well. It is only occasionally and only after a bad fight with Nick, so I'm not doing it all the time. Still, I need to stop altogether. Do you think anyone else has realised?"

Gaby shook her head. "I don't think so."

And Evie was glad of that. She knew the coming weeks would be hard, and she would need her friends. After last night, she was less scared to ask them for help. Hopefully, they wouldn't be too angry with her when they found out she hadn't been completely honest with them.

"Can we talk about Daisy now and what you said last night?"

"Ok. Can we go and sit back down first. As lovely as the view is, it's colder here than on the verandah."

As they walked back, Evie saw movement in Anna's room. She must have seen them too. Neither Anna nor Laura came outside though. Evie felt like another coffee, but she wasn't ready to face the others yet, so just sat down next to Gaby.

"I was hoping you wouldn't be angry that I didn't tell you about Oliver not being her father."

"Well, I am. And upset and shocked. Daisy is my goddaughter and what you said last night wasn't very easy to hear. I've known you for so long, and I know how much you never want to be compared to your mum. You could have told me."

"I know, but I had to do what I thought was best and not telling anyone, including you, was the right thing to do. At least it was at the time. As the years have gone by I've realised it probably wasn't."

"How could you ever think that lying to Daisy and everyone else all these years could be what's best for her?"

Gaby sighed. "I honestly don't know. I can't change what I did so there's no point talking about it."

"Yes, there is. I've known Daisy her whole life. You know how close we are. Did it ever occur to you how I'd feel when I found out? Even if we hadn't done what we did last night, it would have come out at some point."

"I thought about it a lot actually. I hate that I've upset you, but as I said, I thought I was doing what's best for Daisy."

As angry and upset as Evie was, she couldn't help but feel sorry for Gaby. While Evie's secret affected only her, Gaby's affected her whole family. Daisy would be devastated when she learned the truth. She'd always been a daddy's girl, always doing something with Oliver. Now she was about to find out that the man she'd thought of as her dad wasn't her father at all.

"When are you going to tell Daisy?"

"I think I should do it when I get home. It's been going on too long now and I don't want to keep it a secret anymore. I've told my best friends but not my daughter. She needs to know, no matter how hard it will be to tell her and how hard it will be for her to come to terms with it. I'm worried about what it might do to my family as well."

Evie reached over and squeezed Gaby's hand. Neither of them said anything. They just stared at the view, the sun coming up over the ocean in the distance, and the trees on the mountain swaying gently in the early morning breeze. For a moment, Evie thought how wonderful it would be if they could stay right where they were and not go back to their everyday lives and deal with what was ahead.

After a few minutes, Gaby turned to look through the window. "I think I hear movement inside. Are you ready to go back in?"

Evie nodded. "It's going to be different, isn't it?"

"Probably, but we've been friends for a long time, and I think we'll be ok. Are you going to tell Anna and Laura the truth before we go home?"

"I'll try."

Evie wanted to say yes, and she knew Gaby was disappointed that she hadn't, but she didn't know if she was strong enough at that moment to tell them.

They walked back inside and found Laura and Anna in the kitchen making coffee. No one spoke and it was the most uncomfortable silence Evie had ever experienced. They just stood there and looked at each other. It was Gaby who finally broke the silence.

"There's no point trying to pretend last night didn't happen, so we may as well talk about it. How are you feeling this morning?"

Laura shook her head. "I'm not ready to talk about it."

Anna looked at Laura and then at Evie and Gaby. "I'm not ready yet either, but I can say last night really affected me, much more than I thought it would."

Evie nodded. "Me too. I guess I shouldn't be surprised considering what we spoke about."

Laura turned to look at Evie. "I said I didn't want to talk about it."

"I'm not. I haven't mentioned anything that anyone said."

Laura turned back to the coffee machine. "And let's leave it that way."

Evie stared at Laura but didn't say anything. Instead, she walked over to the fridge to see what there was for breakfast, but she stared at the food in there then shut the door. She wasn't hungry, and she didn't think anyone else would be either. When the coffee was made, they all went out to the verandah. They drank in silence. After a while, Evie couldn't stand it anymore, so she suggested they go for a walk.

"We can't spend the rest of the day not speaking. It might be easier to talk to one another if we're walking and not just sitting still and staring."

Gaby nodded. "Good idea. What do you think, Anna and Laura?"

"It's ok with me," Anna said. "As long as we stick to last night's rules. I don't want to talk about what I said."

Laura just nodded. They already knew how she felt about sticking to the rules.

"We could just walk and talk about other things," Evie said. "We should probably get our coats."

Standing on the driveway, it occurred to Evie that if she hadn't been completely truthful, did that mean that someone else hadn't been either? She looked at Gaby and Anna, shivering in the cold, waiting for Laura to come out. She couldn't imagine Anna not being truthful. As much as last night had been hard for her, Anna wasn't one to lie.

Evie was sure that what Anna had said was all there was to the story. And Gaby hadn't hesitated in talking to Evie earlier, so she was confident that Gaby had told them everything last night as well. That just left Laura. Evie didn't doubt anything that Laura had said, but there was something in the way she told her secret that hadn't seemed right to Evie. Something was different from the way Gaby and Laura had spoken. It was only then, in the early morning light, that she realised there was a similarity between the way Laura had told her secret and the way Evie had told her own.

"About time," Anna said. "It's cold, and we want to go."

Laura had one arm in her jacket and the other hand was holding her beanie. "Let's go then. I'll put the rest on while we walk."

Laura set off down the driveway first, leaving the others to almost run to catch up. Anna was walking the slowest, almost dawdling, and she was getting left behind. Gaby took in the surroundings as if it was yesterday, pointing out things like the tall fig tree with roots that stretched three metres in every direction. And the cruise ship that was just a speck in the ocean from their position

325

high up on the mountain. Evie listened to what Gaby was saying, but she was also looking at her three friends out of the corner of her eye. And she could tell the others were doing the same. They kept walking until they came to a lookout. Gaby marched right over to the edge to get the best view, and the others followed, but they stood further apart than they normally would. For a few minutes, they stood in silence until Gaby spoke.

"It's beautiful up here. The view is even better in the morning light."

Gaby was right. Yesterday, in the afternoon, the light had made everything look softer. Today the light was brighter and made everything look sharper and clearer. The ocean looked bluer, the sun brighter, the trees on the mountain greener, and the mountain itself looked steeper. They were much higher up than they'd first thought. A long way from where they'd been yesterday morning.

Gaby turned to Laura. "It's a shame you didn't bring your camera."

"Didn't think to bring it. I've got other things on my mind."

Evie looked at her friends. "Do you think we've damaged our friendship by what we did last night?"

She knew things would change because of what they'd said the night before. There was no way it couldn't. But what would change, and by how much she didn't know.

Gaby shook her head. "No, I don't think we have. Once the shock has gone away, we'll be ok. We've been friends for too long to let something like this end our friendship."

No one said anything. They just looked at the view, hoping that Gaby was right. Again, after a few minutes, it was Gaby who broke the silence.

"Do you want to keep walking or go back?"

"Go back," Laura said.

The others nodded, but they heard a loud bang as they started to walk away from the edge.

"What was that?" Anna said.

They ran back to the edge of the lookout and scanned the area below.

"Down there," Evie said, pointing to a spot about three-quarters of the way up the mountain.

"Oh my god," Anna said. "It's a car accident and a bad one."

They could see the two cars that had crashed head on, one of which must have veered onto the wrong side of the road. Both vehicles were crumpled, and even from where they were standing, they could see there was no movement in either car. Gaby grabbed her phone out of her pocket and rang triple zero. It seemed like forever before they heard the sirens. No one took their eyes off the two cars. By now, other cars had reached the same spot. The drivers and passengers got out to help, but there was nothing they could do, and as soon as the ambulance and fire truck arrived, they quickly moved out of the way. None of them spoke as they watched the firefighters start to cut their way into both cars to free the occupants, the ambos right behind them with their stretchers. Anna looked over at the others, needing to take her eyes off the scene below. She looked at Laura and saw she had tears in her eyes.

"Are you all right?" Anna said, putting her arm around Laura.

"That could have been me."

Gaby turned to look at Laura as well. "But it wasn't."

Laura quickly wiped the tears from her eyes. "Forget I said that."

"We can't," Evie said. "And as much as you don't want to talk about last night, we have to at some stage. We can't go on acting like this around each other for the rest of our lives. And from my point of view, what we're seeing now makes any concerns I have about how you feel about what I told you are minor compared to what's happening down below."

Anna nodded. "I was upset last night when I went to bed. I lay awake for hours, worrying about the same thing. But those people down there, they might not have a chance to fix anything again."

They all looked back down and saw that the firefighters had freed one of the drivers. As quickly as they could, the ambos got him on the stretcher and into the back of the ambulance. The sirens and lights were on before they even started moving, and then it was gone, racing down the mountain to the hospital.

"I don't think it's that easy," Laura said.

"It could be if you want it to be," Gaby said. "The reality is we all kept secrets when it would have been better to be honest, but that doesn't mean we make the same mistake now. There's no reason we can't talk more about what happened in our lives when we're ready and help each other if we need it."

Laura didn't say anything. She still didn't look convinced. Just when it looked like she was about to say something, they all heard a loud noise. They looked down and saw a section of the car roof being peeled back and the other driver being lifted onto a stretcher and into the back of the second ambulance. It seemed like only a minute before it was racing down the mountain too.

"I can't stop thinking that could have been me," Laura said. "Let me think about what you've all said on the way back. I could use another coffee."

As they sat outside on the verandah, sipping their coffee, Evie felt uneasy. It was ok to say that after what they'd seen, they should be able to deal with any fallout from last night, but she hadn't been entirely honest, and at some point, she would have to confess. She got up and walked over to the railing and leant against it, her back to where her friends were sitting, just in case the unease showed on her face. She stood there drinking her coffee until her thoughts were interrupted when Gaby called her name.

"What…sorry. I didn't hear what you said."

"I just asked if anyone wanted to talk."

Laura shook her head so Gaby looked at Anna.

"Not about what I said, but there is one thing I wanted to say. Last night is really bothering me. I mean it's us. We've known each other for years. I should have been able to tell you what was going on. Even if I couldn't say it back then, I should have told you in the years since."

"You obviously weren't ready to say anything sooner," Gaby said. "I wasn't either. Last night was the right time. I can't put off telling Daisy any longer."

Evie still wasn't sure it had been the right time, but it was out there now, and there was nothing she could do to take it back. She looked over at Laura, who was staring out at the view as if she wasn't listening, and wondered again if Laura had told them everything.

Anna also noticed that Laura was staring at the view. "Is our conversation boring you?"

"Of course not. I'm just tired. And I'm hungry. It must be time for breakfast."

"Maybe you could forget your stomach for once and concentrate on what we're saying."

Laura stared at Anna for a moment before replying. "You're right. I know this is important, and I know I've been acting like a child this morning. But I meant it when I said I'm not ready and I'd appreciate it if no one pushed me."

"We won't," Gaby said. "Maybe we should have some breakfast and talk more later."

The others nodded and followed Gaby into the kitchen, Evie being the last one. She needed the few extra moments to decide whether or not to tell them the rest of her secret before they went home.

Chapter 16

No one lingered over breakfast, and soon they were packing up. Even after everything that had happened, Evie was still sad to leave. Strangely, the weekend had been pleasant and she felt better than she had in a long time. Last night may have been challenging and this morning uncomfortable, but it had helped her see clearly what she needed to do when she got home. While she was packing, Anna wandered into the room.

"Do you have any tissues? The box in the lounge room is empty, and I forgot to pack some."

"I think so. I'll check my bag."

As Evie undid the zip, she remembered what was in the side pocket. "Actually, I don't have any. I used the last one yesterday afternoon."

"That's all right. Gaby's probably got some. I'll ask her."

Evie sat down on the bed after Anna had gone.

There was no way she could explain if Anna had seen the tablets in her bag, and before she knew it, Anna would have them all in the room wanting an explanation. And Evie would have enough to deal with later that day when she spoke to Nick. Between that and what happened last night and that morning, she didn't need any more drama.

"Evie, where are you?" Gaby called out.

"Just finishing packing. Be there in a minute."

She pulled the package out, put it in her pocket and then walked down the hallway to the toilet, shutting and locking the door behind her. Taking the package out of her pocket, she unwrapped it and looked at the contents. She hesitated for a moment, then, before she could change her mind, lifted the toilet lid and flushed all the tablets she'd brought with her. Her hands were shaking as she did it. She was under no illusion that by flushing the ones she'd brought with her that everything would be ok now, and she'd never feel like taking another one. When she got home, she needed to flush the ones that were still hidden in her slippers.

When Evie had finished packing, she walked back into the lounge room where Laura was standing, holding the picture she'd drawn the previous night.

"That's amazing, Laura. It's just beautiful."

Anna leaned in over Evie's shoulder. "Let me see. Wow, that is good. I can't wait for mine."

"Thank you, Laura," Evie said. "I'm going to get it framed and hang it in my lounge room."

Each one of them looked beautiful and so natural. Laura had captured them as they were at that moment, sitting in a lounge room in a house on top of a mountain, together and in the last moments before things changed in a way that could never be changed back.

Laura smiled, the first one they'd seen since yesterday. "Thanks. Are we stopping for lunch on the way home?" Laura asked.

"We only had breakfast two hours ago," Anna said.

"It's a long drive home, and it's already 11.00am," Laura said.

Evie didn't want to just leave the house, get in their cars and drive off. It would be too abrupt to end the weekend like that, so she said she wouldn't mind going back into the village for another look around and some lunch.

"Ok with me," Gaby said.

Anna nodded in agreement.

Laura turned and headed out of the room. "I want to get some photos before we go, so I'll see you outside."

As Laura focused her camera, Evie looked at the view for the last time. In the distance, the water was sparkling and inviting. Evie thought it would be nice to have a swim and wash away all her cares, but it was too cold. The beach would be packed with tourists who had travelled a long way to be there, and they wouldn't go home without going to the beach at least once. A holiday was exactly what Evie felt like, and if she went through with what she knew she had to do, then she'd probably need one. And maybe it was time to think of something longer than a holiday. She didn't want her dream of living overseas to stay a dream forever.

Gaby opened the driver's side door of her car. "Come on. It's time to go. Has anyone checked the house to make sure we haven't left anything?"

"I have," Anna said. "It's a shame to leave such a beautiful house behind."

Laura kept taking photos, but she turned her attention to the house and the rose garden in the front yard where Anna sat on the love seat. Evie took her shoes off to feel the softness of the grass one more time and to take the last few breaths of the clear mountain air. After Laura had taken her last photo, they all climbed into the cars and headed back towards the town. In the car, Gaby had asked Evie if she would tell Anna and Laura the truth before they left, and Evie had replied the same way she had earlier.

"Same place as yesterday or somewhere else?" Anna asked after they'd parked the cars.

"Let's try somewhere else," Evie said.

They chose a cafe that was almost full, partly for the noise and partly because if it was crowded that meant the food would be good. As they sat, Evie noticed a group of four older women, all with grey hair.

Evie leaned across the table and whispered, "Do you think we'll still be friends when we're that old?"

"I hope so," Anna said. "And I hope we still come away for weekends."

Laura smiled. "When we're old, we might go away for bowling weekends."

"I refuse to play lawn bowls," Gaby said. "Even when we're older. Let's order."

Towards the end of their meal, Gaby put down her knife and fork, had a sip of water and then looked at each of them in turn.

"If everyone is still ok with talking about some options of how to tell Daisy, it would be great if we could do it now before we go. I don't want to put off telling her for much longer."

"Ok with me," Laura said.

Anna nodded. "Me too. And I thought you didn't want to talk, Laura."

"Not about me, I don't. I'm happy to talk about what Gaby needs to."

Evie looked at Gaby before replying. She hadn't been able to shake the feelings she'd been experiencing since Gaby's revelation. But she looked so stressed about the conversation she needed to have with Daisy that Evie put her feelings aside for the moment. "Happy to talk about it now as well."

"So, what do you think I should do?" Gaby asked.

"You need to tell her as soon as you get home," Evie said. "She's so much like you that if you walk in the house looking like you do now, she'll know something is wrong, something more than just the fight you had before you left."

"I agree with Evie," Anna said. "The longer you leave it, the more it's going to upset you, and that will make the situation worse."

Gaby looked across the table at her friends. "How do I say it though? It's not like I'm telling her she has a long lost second cousin. It's about her father."

"Just tell her what happened," Laura said. "And let her know you made the best decision you could with what you knew at the time. Doing anything else but sticking to the facts is too risky. We can't tell how she's going to react."

Gaby closed her eyes for a moment and rested her head in her hands. As Evie looked over at her friend, more of her own anger slipped away, and she reached across the table and took her hand.

Anna also reached across the table and took her other hand. "Whatever happens, it won't stay that way forever. She loves Oliver too much, and eventually, that feeling will be stronger than any hurt or anger."

Evie hoped Anna was right. Daisy had a strong personality and could easily decide not to forgive Gaby or Oliver. She may even want to track Chris down, which she had every right to do, but that would break Gaby's heart. And Oliver's too. That wasn't something she thought should be said aloud right now, so she said something else instead.

"I think you should include Oliver in the conversation. She needs to see that this doesn't change how Oliver feels about her."

Gaby nodded. "Yes, we both need to sit down. And make sure she knows that Oliver loves her. Always has, and always will."

Laura nodded. "It's essential that she knows that."

Gaby picked up her water glass and took a few sips. "Thank you all for your advice. It's been a great help. And I want to repeat what I said last night. Just because I needed to talk things through doesn't mean any of you have to. The rules still apply if you want them to."

Evie could feel Gaby looking at her, waiting for her to say the things she'd left out last night, but she wasn't ready. They ate the rest of their lunch in silence. As they stood up, ready to go, Gaby looked at her again.

"Didn't you want to say something before we go, Evie?"

Evie shook her head. "It doesn't matter now."

They'd only been in the car a minute when Gaby said what Evie knew she was going to. "You should have told them."

"I thought you wanted to focus on your situation and what you need to tell Daisy."

"You're still upset with me, aren't you?"

Evie didn't say anything, and they drove in silence for a while until Gaby spoke.

"What are you going to do when you get home?"

"I need to talk to Nick and tell him I'm not happy, that I haven't been for a long time and that I don't want to be with him anymore."

"Are you sure? You know I think it's the right thing to do, but you have to be one hundred per cent sure yourself."

For the first time, she was sure. Even though she'd had the same thoughts many times before, she'd always heard Nick's voice in her mind telling her she never knew what was best for her or that she wasn't capable of making the right decision. But she knew this was the right choice for her, and she wanted that voice to be silenced.

"Yes, I'm sure. I should have done it a long time ago."

"So we'll both be having difficult conversations when we get home."

As they pulled into Evie's driveway, she went over the words she wanted to say in her head for the last time. She hopped out of the car, grabbed her bag and shut the boot. Gaby came to stand beside her.

"Do you want me to stay for a while?"

"No, I'll be ok on my own. It's time I took responsibility for my situation and did something about it. How about you? Are you going to talk to Daisy as soon as you get home?"

"I'll talk to Oliver first, then if he's ok to do that, yes, we'll talk to her tonight."

They hugged goodbye, told each other to call if they needed to, then Evie watched as Gaby drove away. She'd felt much braver in the car than she did now, standing alone on the driveway in the fading light. It was a few minutes before she could put the key in the lock and open the door. In those few minutes, she forgot everything she wanted to say, so she just said the first thing that popped into her head. She had to do it right then, or she'd lose her nerve.

"Nick, I need to talk to you."

"I'm watching the football. We can talk when it's over."

"I need to talk now."

"What's so important that it can't wait?"

"I don't want to be married anymore."

"What are you going on about? Why would you say something stupid like that?"

"It's not stupid. It's how I feel. I'm not happy and haven't been for a long time."

"Is this some sort of joke?"

Evie shook her head. "Nothing I do is good enough for you. You want to change everything about me, and you criticise me all the time. I don't want to be in a relationship anymore with someone who won't accept me as I am."

"Have those friends of yours talked you into this?"

"No, they haven't. This is my idea."

"Well, in that case, why don't we talk about it tomorrow when you've come to your senses."

"I'm not changing my mind."

"I've had enough of this. You're just being stupid now. Sometimes, Evie, you act like such a child. Now I don't want to talk about this anymore."

Nick got up from the lounge chair, walked into the kitchen, picked up the phone and rang his brother. Evie heard him organising a fishing trip for the following weekend. Just listening to him made her angry. She'd been scared up until that point, but the fact that he wasn't even willing to listen to her about something so important took the fear away and replaced it with anger. She waited until he finished his phone call because she didn't want Stewart hearing anything she wanted to say.

"You may not want to talk about it, but I do. The way you walked away from me when I was talking reinforces that I'm doing the right thing. No matter what you think, I know what's best for me, and I want to be with someone who cares about me, supports me, and wants me to succeed in whatever I choose to do. And that person isn't you."

"You don't know what you want. It would be easy to care about you if you acted like a normal adult. And if you actually wanted to stop being lazy and achieve something, then I could support you, but that's not who you are. You'll never succeed at anything because you're not good enough."

"Actually, I am good enough. It's you who holds me back and puts me down, and I'm not putting up with it anymore. I've had years of being put down by my parents, only to be followed by years of being put down by you. You're just like them, and maybe that's why I stayed with you or even picked you in the first place, but I'm not doing this anymore. I want out of this marriage."

"I'm not having this discussion with you anymore. I'm going to stay at Stewart's tonight. There's no point being here while you're acting crazy."

He walked into the bedroom and locked the door so Evie couldn't get in. No matter how many times she knocked or called out, he wouldn't let her in.

"Open the door, Nick. Talk to me." Evie leant against the door, frustrated at his childishness.

Eventually, the door opened. Evie stepped aside as Nick strode past with his bag in hand and without a glance her in direction. Evie stood there, stunned. Then as Nick closed the front door behind him, she started to cry. She wanted this done. Now she'd have to start again the next time she saw him, whenever that would be. And if the next time wasn't enough, then she'd keep going until she finally got what she knew was the best thing for her. Unlike her relationship with Matthew, where she hadn't found the courage to leave, this time, she would be the one to walk away because it was what she needed to do. It took her almost forty minutes after Nick left before she calmed down enough to start unpacking. In the background, she could hear the phone and picked it up and heard her father's voice.

"No, Dad, I can't come tonight. I've just got back from a weekend away with the girls."

"No, I'm not coming."

"Dad, listen to me. I don't like Mexican food, and I don't want to watch that movie."

"Mum won't be disappointed. I really am too tired."

"Dad, I'm not coming."

"Dad."

But he wouldn't listen, so she hung up. She would pay for that later, but she didn't care. She finished unpacking her bag, put the washing machine on, then took Laura's picture and stuck it to the lounge room wall. Nick would never let her put the picture up, but she needed it up. It was a reminder of what they had gone through over the past two days and how she'd finally found the courage to do what she should have done a long time ago.

Chapter 17

Evie woke when she heard the front door slam. It had been two days since she'd told Nick she didn't want to be married anymore. Two days when she expected him to come back at any minute and tell her again that she didn't know what she was doing. She should have known he'd drag it out as long as he had. When she thought back to the fight, she realised that not once had he said he wanted to stay married or that he loved her. And he'd left very quickly after Evie had said that she didn't want to be married anymore. She knew Nick could be spiteful, but if he wanted to stay married, he would have stayed and talked to her or contacted her before now.

Evie thought about staying in bed and pretending he wasn't there, but that wouldn't solve anything. She got up and headed for the kitchen, stopping in the ensuite first to check that he wouldn't be able to tell she'd spent the past two days crying. She hadn't left the house either, calling in sick for the first time ever when she wasn't physically sick. Nick didn't need to know that though. He was in the kitchen making a coffee as if nothing had happened. He didn't offer to make her one as she walked in.

"Have you stopped being stupid yet?" he said.

"If you mean have I changed my mind about wanting to separate, no, I haven't."

"I thought if I gave you some time on your own, you'd realise how stupid you're being. You can't survive on your own."

"I've done ok these past two days."

And she had. There'd been times when she'd questioned what she was doing and a few times when she thought how easy it would be to take a tablet and make everything ok. She still hadn't thrown out the last of the tablets she'd found in Chelsea's jacket.

"I can't imagine that being true. I called in to get my suit jacket for work, and then I'm going. I'll be back tonight. This is my house, and I'm not leaving. And this marriage isn't over unless I say it is. And Stewart agrees with me in thinking that you're being stupid."

It's my house too, Evie thought as she watched him go. And there's two of us in this marriage. She knew this was going to be hard, but it was worse than she anticipated. She didn't believe him either when he said Stewart thought she was being stupid. Out of Nick's whole family, he was the only one who'd taken any time to get to know her, and he was the one who spoke to her the most when they had a family gathering. And after a few too many wines, it was Stewart who had told Evie that Nick hadn't ended his previous relationship before he started seeing her. For the first few months they were together, he was seeing Evie and the other woman. Evie had been shocked, and when she asked Nick about it, he said because they hadn't been in a serious relationship yet, only dating, it didn't matter. And he had ended the previous relationship, but only saw her occasionally for a while. Evie took that to mean they still had sex now and then. She'd been upset by that revelation, but Nick told her she was being silly and there was nothing to be upset about. Stewart had apologised later and said he shouldn't have said anything and that he hoped he hadn't upset her too much. Thinking about it now, she realised that was the first time she had doubts about whether Nick was the right person for her.

Nick returned that night and moved into the spare room. Over the next four weeks, a pattern emerged. He mostly ignored her. Occasionally, he got angry at her, telling her she didn't have the right to make a decision that impacted him like this. That he should have been the one to say they should get divorced. Again, not once did he say he wanted to stay together. She learned to ignore his comments as best she could and didn't let him see her tears. Every time she bumped into him in the house, she wished she wasn't there, but he'd use it to his advantage if she went somewhere else.

Eventually, Nick stopped talking to her altogether and they only communicated through their solicitors. The first night he walked straight by her as he headed out the door without even looking at her. She stood for a moment, trying to reign in her emotions. Yes, she wanted the marriage to be over, but what she was going through ached more she thought it would.

When she'd composed herself, she ran a bath to try and relax. She opened the lid of the bath salts, and tucked down the side was a tiny alfoil package. She'd forgotten that she'd once used the bath salts as a hiding place. It was safe because Nick had never had a bath in the time she'd known him, and he thought most of the things she had in the bathroom were useless, so he never touched any of them. She turned the alfoil package over and over in her fingers. One wouldn't hurt, she thought. She'd been so good not giving in so maybe she deserved a treat. Evie opened the alfoil and held the Dexedrine tablet in her hand. It still looked alright, so she filled up the glass by the basin with water. Everything will be better in a minute. In the background, she heard her phone ring but ignored it. Almost as soon as it stopped ringing, it started again. She put the glass and tablet down and went to check. It was her dad, but she didn't answer. The call before had been from Gaby. The message she left said her plans for that night had changed, and she could meet if Evie still wanted to. She thought about how disappointed Gaby would be if she took the tablet. Instead, she went back to the bathroom, flushed it down the toilet, then rang Gaby. After they'd hung up, Evie went into the spare room, pulled the slippers out from the wardrobe, tipped the remaining tablets into the toilet and flushed them as well.

"You look tired," Gaby said as Evie arrived at her place an hour later.

"I haven't been sleeping well lately. The situation with Nick has been awful. Some days I wonder how I'm going to get through it."

"You will. And you know I'm here for you if you need anything. What you don't need is any artificial help."

"I've thought about it a few times. I found a tablet in the bathroom tonight and I almost gave in, but I flushed it down the toilet instead."

"I'm glad. You know it's not an answer to anything."

Evie nodded. She didn't mention that she'd also thrown out the other ones. As far as Gaby was concerned, they had been thrown out when they returned from their weekend away. She hadn't asked Evie directly if she had thrown them out, so technically, it wasn't lying. They were gone, and that was all that mattered.

"Has it got any better, both being in the same house?"

Evie sighed and then gave Gaby an update on what had happened since they'd spoken a few days ago.

"I can't think of another option other than staying in the house for now, at least until we agree on a settlement. Nick has said several times that he won't move out and will only pay his half of the mortgage and nothing more. I can't afford money for my half plus rent."

"Then you need to finalise the paperwork sooner rather than later."

Gaby was right. Getting that paperwork done was what she needed to focus on right now. Once that was done, she would have some certainty about the future.

"Have you told Anna and Laura the part of your story you left out?"

Evie shook her head.

"You need to tell them. They deserve the truth."

Evie knew Gaby was right, but with all that was happening, she wasn't sure she'd cope with adding anything else to the mix. She'd spoken to Anna and Laura separately a few times since the weekend away but only about the situation with Nick. Each time she spoke to them, the thought was always in the back of her mind that she was supposed to have organised a catch up for the four of them, but she hadn't got around to doing it. There was too much going on right now, and she knew if the four of them got together, the subject of the weekend would come up. Instead of addressing what Gaby had said, she asked how things were with Daisy.

Gaby and Oliver had sat down with Daisy on the Sunday night after Gaby got home.

Gaby sighed. "There are good moments and bad. Sometimes she seems ok with it, and other times she's angry at us both. I don't know how long it's going to continue for."

"As long as she needs, I guess. How are you?"

"It's been hard, and I'm tired. Oliver and I have had a few arguments, but they didn't last long. We're both really concerned about Daisy."

Evie smiled. "She'll be fine. She's a lot like her mother, and her mother can get through anything."

Gaby squeezed Evie's hand. "Thanks. It helps to be able to talk about it."

"Did she ever tell you why she's been acting out lately?"

A short, bitter laugh escaped from Gaby's mouth. "She didn't feel like part of the family. She thinks she's different from the rest of us and doesn't quite fit in. She said she'd been feeling like that for a while."

"Was that before or after you told her?"

"While we were telling her. It was one of the things she threw back in our faces. She said we must have been treating her differently and that we didn't love her as much as Grace and Lucas. And then she said, maybe she should track down her real father because he would love her."

"Have you ever heard from him?"

"I haven't seen or heard from him since I dropped him off at Anna's the next morning. I wasn't expecting to though. I can't even remember his last name."

Evie couldn't remember it either, although she hadn't spoken to him a lot that night. It had been clear that he was interested in Gaby and that she had been interested in him. At the time, she'd thought it was good for Gaby to have some fun, and all Evie had been interested in was finding out all the details afterwards.

It had never occurred to her that one night would change Gaby's life forever.

"Anna might remember it, or if not, her mum would know."

Evie couldn't imagine the thoughts that would be going through Daisy's mind right now. The family she'd taken for granted all her life was not what she thought it was. And Oliver must be struggling too. Not only with doing everything he could to let Daisy know how much he loved her but also with knowing that the girl he'd raised as his daughter wanted to find her real father.

"How are Grace and Lucas taking it?"

"They seem fine, but I'm not sure they fully understand what it means. They're only ten."

Evie reached across the table and took hold of Gaby's hand. "I'm here if you need anything. You've been there for me. It's my turn to return the favour."

Evie thought again about how upset she'd been when she'd heard Gaby tell her secret but again, she bit her tongue. It was not the right time to raise it with Gaby. It would have to wait for another time, if she even raised it at all. Maybe it was better to just let it go.

"Have you got any good news to talk about," Gaby said. "I think we could both use the distraction."

"Sort of. I've been thinking a lot lately about maybe moving overseas."

"Wow, that's big."

Evie nodded. "I haven't thought about it in a lot of detail. There are too many other things going on. But this could be my chance."

"Have you thought about where?"

"I think I'd go to London. Right now though, I have to focus on moving on from Nick. Once things are sorted out, I'll start thinking about it seriously."

They talked for a while longer about Evie possibly moving to London. The more they talked about it, the more Evie thought that maybe it could finally turn from a dream into a reality.

The following week, Evie organised a catch up with Anna and Laura, and Gaby said she would be there for moral support. She made a booking at a local restaurant. Even though it wouldn't be as private as she would have liked, it was better than inviting them to her house in case Nick walked in and interrupted them. She knew he would have used the opportunity to say something to her friends, to blame them for what was happening, even though she'd told him it was her decision and hers alone. She managed to book a table in the corner away from other people, so at least they would have a little bit of privacy.

"The last time we were all together, we were sitting at a table similar to this," Laura said.

"The circumstances are different now," Anna said.

"Are they?" Laura said.

Evie looked over at Laura. When she'd rung Laura to organise the dinner, she said she'd be happy to come and was looking forward to seeing them, that she didn't want the secrets getting in the way of their friendship. So what she'd just said seemed odd.

"Yes, they are," Gaby said. "You wouldn't be here if you didn't value your friendships enough to deal with whatever fallout there is from all our revelations."

"Of course I value our friendship," Laura said. "It's just different now, and I don't know how to act."

Evie wasn't sure how to act either. They'd gone out for dinners hundreds of times, and they had always been full of laughter and non-stop talking. Now no one seemed to be in a hurry to speak, and with what she had to tell her friends, there would definitely be no laughing.

"We're still the same people who've known each other for twenty-five years," Gaby said. "We just found out we all had a secret. It shouldn't change anything if we don't want it to."

"You're right," Laura said. "I'm just still not ready to talk about anything."

"The rules still apply," Gaby said. "If you want to talk about it at some stage, you can, but otherwise you never have to mention it again."

Laura smiled. "Thanks. I appreciate it. There is one thing I want to talk about though. Sebastian's girlfriend is pregnant."

"What!" Gaby said.

"Yeah, I found out just before we went away but I couldn't deal with it at the time, so I pushed it to the back of my mind. He's well and truly moved on and having another child with someone else."

"I thought he didn't want to be part of a family," Evie said.

"Apparently, he does. Just not the one that has Max and me in it."

Anna reached over and held Laura's hand. "It's got nothing to do with you or Max. He's changed. That's all."

"Even if that's what it is, it still means we'll never be a family again."

"Are you going to be ok with that?" Evie asked.

"I don't have a choice. I have to be."

Evie looked at her and remembered when she'd let slip during one of their phone conversations that she wished she, Sebastian and Max could be a family again. When Evie asked her if she thought that was possible, Laura said she was just being silly and changed the subject. Evie couldn't imagine how upset Laura must be right now. Especially since Sebastian seemed to be in more of a hurry to create a family with his new partner than he ever had been in creating a family with Laura.

"So that's my news. What about you Evie?" Laura asked.

"I've probably had the most changes since we last saw each other."

Evie spent the next twenty minutes updating them about the situation with Nick. She didn't go into all the details. She just gave Laura and Anna the highlights of what had happened since they last spoke. What amazed her the most when she finished was not that they reiterated their earlier offers of help and support. But, for the first time, they both said they were happy that she was ending her marriage. Neither of them liked Nick. They didn't like the way she changed when she was around him or how he treated her. No one had ever said anything like that to her before, although saying you didn't like someone's husband wasn't something that even close friends usually said.

"Anything you need," Laura said. "We're all here to help."

Anna nodded. "Absolutely. And I know we said we wouldn't talk about anything we said at Mt Tamborine unless the person wanted to, but the most important thing is that you don't take one of those tablets because you think it will help during this stressful time."

Evie could feel Gaby staring at her. This was the perfect time to be honest, but it was harder to start than she thought. How could she admit she hadn't been truthful? She took a few sips of water.

"About that."

By the time she'd finished telling them the truth, her stomach had twisted into knots. Even though they tried to hide it, the looks on Anna and Laura's faces were ones of disappointment. Without meaning to, she'd hurt her friends, the only people who were on her side at the moment.

"I know it must have taken a lot to tell us that," Anna said. "But it's hard not to feel upset by it when we were all truthful when we told our stories."

Evie looked at Laura and Anna. "I'm sorry. I know I should have been truthful, especially after you were all brave enough to be honest. I just thought my story was so much worse than yours and that you might not want to be friends anymore if you knew the whole truth."

"That's not giving us much credit," Anna said. "It would take a lot more than that to stop us being friends."

Anna was right. She should have trusted them more, and now she didn't know how to fix it. Even though Anna and Laura said they forgave her, she knew they were more upset with her than they let on.

Gaby rang later that night. "How are you?"

"I feel worse than I did before dinner. They both looked so disappointed in me."

"You did the right thing by telling them. They'll be ok. Talk to them one on one and sort things out."

It took her two days to ring Anna. She organised to meet her at the nursery on Saturday morning. It wasn't the ideal location for a conversation, but Anna had to work all weekend, and Evie didn't want to put off seeing her any longer. If things went ok, she would psych herself up to call Laura.

"Thanks for making time," Evie said. "I know you're busy."

"Of course. Evie, you're one of my best friends. I was disappointed when I found out you weren't completely honest, especially when I was, but you've told us now instead of continuing to keep it a secret."

"I know, and I'm really sorry about that. As I said the other night, I just thought that if you knew the truth, you might not want to be around me anymore."

"You were taking drugs. It's not as if you murdered someone. You're not the first person to do what you did, and you won't be the last. You've told me the truth now, and you came down here this morning to talk to me. So as far as I'm concerned, you and I are fine."

Their conversation was interrupted by a delivery driver who'd turned up with a ute full of plants. Evie followed Anna outside to help her unload them.

"How are things with Nick?"

Evie told her about the letters going back and forth between their solicitors. He was trying everything he could to get more than his share.

"You're not going to let him are you?"

"No. I've gone through too much to give in. All I want is my half, and I'll keep going until I get it."

"Good. If you need a hand with anything, let me know, ok. And don't be tempted to take any drugs."

"I won't. Now, what about you? I know we said we wouldn't talk about what we said but are you ok? Do you still have problems with eating?"

"Not as much as I used to, but I still struggle with it sometimes."

As they carried the plants from the ute into the nursery, Anna told Evie about that first visit to her doctor and then the psychologist. How those sessions had helped her make progress, slow at first, but the more sessions she went to, the easier it became. She told Evie that it had taken a long time before she stopped thinking about every single bite she took but gradually, it stopped.

"The thoughts are still in the back of my mind. Not as much as they were, but they're still there. I'm not sure if I'll ever stop thinking about it completely. I still see my psychologist occasionally if the thoughts get really bad, and that always helps."

"Does Ethan know?"

"He actually brought up the subject. He was telling me about his family one night over dinner. He and his sister went to their parents' house one weekend for lunch, and he watched his sister push her food around her plate but not eat very much. He noticed I was doing the same thing at dinner."

Evie put her arm around Anna's shoulders and squeezed lightly.

"I didn't go into a lot of details. I just said I had an eating disorder back in high school, and sometimes I still struggled with it. Turns out his sister is the same."

"I'm glad he knows and that it's all ok. Speaking of things being ok, how are things with Laura?"

"It took a couple of conversations after our weekend away, but things are good."

They picked up the last two plants from the back of the ute, and Evie listened to Anna as she told her about her talks with Laura as they carried them inside. The first time they talked, Laura had been hurt that Anna hadn't confided in her, especially when she had been correct back in high school. When Anna pointed out that Laura hadn't confided in her about what she was doing, the conversation didn't continue for much longer. The second time they talked for longer, and the third time Anna told her how she was doing now and about the conversations she'd had with her mum.

"They were hard conversations," Anna said. "She blamed herself because she wasn't there to look after me. It took a while before she understood that it would have happened whether she was there or not. It was dad's death that triggered it. The need to be in control of something because I couldn't control my grief."

"Do you still miss him?"

"We both do, all the time. The pain and grief have gone, but the wish that I could see him again is still there."

"I'm glad you talked with your mum."

"Me too. It was a big help. I left out the part about her jeans though. I thought that would upset her too much. But, on a different subject, I've been speaking with Gaby about Chris."

"She told me last night when we spoke."

The phone call the night before had lasted forty minutes, which for Gaby was a record. Anna had found out that Chris had died in a car accident in India eleven years ago. Even though it had been eighteen years since she'd seen Chris, Gaby said she still felt sad that he'd died so young. What concerned her most was how she was going to tell Daisy.

"I don't envy her," Anna said.

Evie nodded. "Daisy has only just found that the man she thought was her dad isn't, and now she's about to find out that the man who is her dad died several years ago, and she'll never get to meet him."

"It's sad, and it will be hard for Daisy to deal with on top of everything else. I wonder if she'll think about meeting Chris' mum."

"If she does, I hope it's a long time from now. Gaby and Oliver already have enough to deal with."

As they walked, Evie looked around and felt so proud of Anna and everything she achieved. It was such a beautiful nursery, always busy, but every customer was treated like they were the only customer. This had been Anna's dream, and she'd achieved it. Evie had been thinking about her own dream and had decided the previous day to go for it. So in the middle of Anna's nursery, Evie told her she was going to move overseas.

Anna threw her arms around Evie. "I'm so excited for you. You're finally doing it. Tell me everything."

"There's not much to tell at the moment. I've only just made the decision. But as soon as I figure out exactly what I'm doing and when I'm doing it, I'll let you know."

They were interrupted again by a bus pulling up outside.

"Local gardening group," Anna said. "They come in once a month, and this month they're early. Sorry, but I'm going to have to go."

"That's ok. And thanks for saying that everything is ok between us. I hope I can soon say that about Laura."

Easier said than done, Evie thought a few days later. She'd rung Laura three times before she answered. Laura was polite enough when Evie finally got hold of her, but that didn't last long.

"You should have trusted us," she said.

"I know I should have. But it's easier to say that now than it was then."

"Not really. I was there, remember."

"My story is worse than yours."

"How? I drove while I was drunk and could have killed someone. Or myself and left Max without a mother."

Evie paused for a moment. Laura was right. She'd only thought about Laura drinking too much and not about her driving while drunk.

"I hadn't thought of that."

"I guessed as much. And doing that is much worse than what you did. Your actions only affected you. Mine could have had terrible consequences for Max and me."

"That must have been an awful feeling the next day."

"Worst I've ever felt. And I still feel bad about it now."

Evie realised she wasn't the only one on the phone who was struggling with the after-effects of what they'd done.

"I guess we both have things we're still dealing with."

"Yes, we do. Don't think that means I will let you off the hook though. You still should have trusted us. It really hurt finding out that you'd lied to us, especially considering how hard that night was for each of us."

Evie sighed to herself after she'd hung up. It was going to take a while to sort things out with Laura. She just hoped it would be before she went overseas, whenever that turned out to be.

Chapter 18

A week later, she rang Laura again and it was a short, awkward conversation. After Evie hung up, she realised that Laura had meant it when she said she wouldn't let her off the hook so easily.

"She'll come around," Gaby said. "You know Laura holds on to things longer than the rest of us."

Evie sighed down the phone line. "I was hoping we could sort things out by now. I've started planning for my move overseas, and I don't want to go without everything being ok between us."

"I'm delighted the plans are coming together, but I'm going to miss you. When are you going?"

"I'm hoping to be ready in three months."

"Are you sure you want to go so soon? What about the divorce? And the tablets?"

"If I don't go as soon as possible, I'll chicken out. I already have enough reasons running through my mind for not going, and if I leave it any longer, I'll end up listening to those reasons. As far as the divorce goes, it's all paperwork now, so I can do that anywhere and just scan and email or post what I need to. I don't actually have to be here for the divorce to go through. And I haven't thought about the tablets at all since I threw them out. Now, what am I going to do about Laura?"

"You can't force it. You'll sort things out with Laura. But it might take longer than you want it to."

"I know what Laura is like when she holds a grudge. I'd like a few months of us being good friends again before I leave. I guess I'll just have to keep trying and be patient."

"Have you heard from Nick?"

"Not for the past few weeks."

Evie had agreed to sell her half of the house to him, but not until just before she left. And she held her ground and wouldn't move out until it was time for her to go. She'd need every cent she could save before she went, and covering her half of the mortgage was cheaper than paying rent. Finally, after weeks of arguing about it, he'd moved in with Stewart. She hadn't expected him to do that and she was surprised when he did. That was until he told her that he wouldn't be paying half of any bills or any maintenance costs during that time.

The only thing he said he would pay was his half of the mortgage so he wouldn't be disadvantaged when the house became his.

"Why doesn't that surprise me," Gaby said. "But things will sort themselves out, and things with Laura will be ok too. Just give it time."

Time was something she didn't have a lot of. Maybe it would be best to ask for Anna's advice. She was closer to Laura than anyone else.

"I spoke to Laura again," Evie said on the phone later that day.

"How did it go?" Anna asked.

"Not as well as I'd hoped. Any advice on how to fix things?"

"Laura doesn't hold a grudge without a good reason. I know she's upset because you weren't completely honest. I think it's more than that though. Something else is bothering her, and I don't know what it is. She hasn't said anything to me."

"I wonder if she'll tell me if I ask?"

"Only one way to find out."

The next day she went to Laura's house. She had been thinking about what Anna had said on the phone, and the more she thought about it, the more she thought Anna was right. There was something else, and she needed to find out what it was. She thought back to the Sunday morning on Mt Tamborine when she wondered if anyone else had held anything back and how Laura was the only possibility. Could that be it?

"Come in," Laura said after she opened the front door.

Evie followed her down the hall and into the kitchen. She didn't say anything except to ask Evie if she wanted a coffee. It was clearly going to be up to Evie to start the conversation.

"You know I'm planning on going overseas soon, and I don't want to go until we sort things out."

"Then you shouldn't have lied."

"It wasn't really a lie. I just left some of the story out."

"If that's the way you want to look at it."

"There's something else though. I think there's another reason you're still angry with me."

"What makes you say that?

"I've known you long enough to know there is something else you're not telling me."

"You didn't know me well enough to know I was drinking."

"That's because you hid that and didn't want anyone to know. Just like I did. You're not hiding this."

Laura turned away to boil the jug. She didn't say anything as she made them a coffee and took the cups outside. Max's bike was lying in the yard, waiting for the training wheels in the box next to it to be put on.

"Is Max with Sebastian?"

"Yes, he's spending the whole week there."

"That's a change."

"I think Sebastian is more comfortable being alone with him now. He's realised he's not going to break him. I guess he's also getting in some practice before the baby arrives."

"Are you feeling any better about that?"

"Not really, but there's nothing I can do, so I've just got to get over it. We're not talking about that though. We're talking about you and me."

"Yes, we are. I understand you're upset because you were completely honest, and I wasn't, and you think it was because I didn't trust you. I've told you it wasn't that. It was because I was scared of how you'd react. As I said before, though, I think there is another reason, and I was hoping you'd tell me what it is."

Laura sipped on her coffee and waited a few minutes before speaking.

"You're right. There is something else, and when I said I was upset because I'd been honest and you hadn't, that wasn't the reason. Even though I told you all I had my problem under control, there have been a couple of times since I told you I'd stopped drinking excessively that I've slipped."

Evie was speechless. So she had been right. Laura had left some of her story out too. She'd let Evie and the others believe that she had her problem under control. The thought that Laura had stopped her destructive behaviour had given her strength at times when she wanted to give in and take a tablet. And all this time, it was a lie.

"So you let me think you were angry because I didn't tell you the whole truth, and yet you didn't tell me the whole truth. I've spent the past few weeks feeling terrible because of how much I thought I'd hurt your feelings, and then during that time, you've been lying to me."

"I knew before I said anything that you'd be angry with me, and you have every right to be. I didn't say anything because I've only slipped a few times, one of those being the night before we went away when I caught up with Meg. When I said we'd had a few glasses of wine together, that was true. But what I didn't say was, after she left, I finished off the bottle. And the other bottle that was in the fridge. It also happened when Sebastian rang and told me his girlfriend was pregnant."

Evie didn't know what to say. She was so angry at Laura, but she felt like she couldn't get mad at her because of what was happening in Sebastian's life and its impact on Laura. The thought of upsetting her even more than she already was didn't sit well with Evie. It felt like when she found out about Gaby's secret all over again.

"Have you seen Sebastian much since he told you?"

"Only a couple of times. He usually picks Max up from child care."

"Max doesn't have long to go at child care."

"No, he's off to prep soon. These years are going so fast. The faster, the better though at the moment so I can get to a place where it doesn't hurt."

"You'll get there. But drinking won't help."

"I know. Mostly I've been ok. It's just been a few times. But I've been thinking about what you said at dinner when you told us the rest of your story, and I started getting angry with myself because I should have said something too."

Evie started to think about what she'd gone through the night she told them. How she'd been feeling since, thinking that Laura was angry with her, the earlier thoughts of not wanting to upset Laura further started to fade.

"Instead, you just let me sit there and feel like the worst person for upsetting you. You could have said something too. It would have helped me so much."

"I know. And now it's my turn to apologise to you."

"Does that mean it's my turn to not let you off the hook so easily?"

"I guess it does."

"Good. Because it's going to take a lot more than an apology."

That night, Anna rang to see how things had gone with Laura.

"Not as well as I'd hoped," Evie told her. "We talked, but things still aren't ok."

By the time she'd left Laura's, she'd been furious. She couldn't believe Laura had done that. Evie had enough going on without wasting time worrying about something that wasn't what she'd thought it had been.

"I still don't understand why she's so angry. I've asked her, and she wouldn't tell me."

Evie didn't say anything. It wasn't up to her to tell Anna that Laura hadn't been truthful. That was up to Laura.

"How are the plans for moving to London coming along? You must be excited."

Before she knew it, thirty minutes had passed and she'd told Anna about the enquiries she'd made and what she'd found out about the things she'd need to do before she could go.

The next three months went faster than Evie could have believed, and she was amazed at how quickly everything had come together. When she first started seriously thinking of moving overseas, she thought it would take a long time to get things organised, but things just fell into place. When she told a friend at work that she was planning on going, he said his sister was living in London and had mentioned a social worker vacancy where she worked. Evie had sent off her resume, had an interview via Skype, and was offered the job two days later. She'd also found a place to stay, thanks to the sister. From there, it was organising flights and work visas and finishing up packing her belongings, which to her surprise, her parents had offered to store in their spare garage. It hadn't stopped them from using the opportunity to question her decision again though. She also worked things out with Laura, although she was disappointed that Laura hadn't told Gaby and Anna that she'd left out part of her story too. That was her choice though, and Evie couldn't make her say anything. Laura would do it when she was ready.

A week before she was due to leave, her parents came over to try and talk her out of going one last time.

"I don't understand why you want to move to the other side of the world," her mum said. "What's wrong with staying here?"

Evie sighed. The conversation had been going on for too long now.

"There's nothing wrong with staying here. I love Brisbane. But I want to try living somewhere else just once in my life, and this is my opportunity."

"It wouldn't be an opportunity if you hadn't left Nick," her dad said. "I still think you made the wrong decision."

"You're entitled to your opinion, Dad, but it was my decision, and it was the best one for me. I wasn't happy with Nick, and I hadn't been for a long time."

"Maybe you should have tried harder," her dad said.

"I did try, as much as I could. But there were two of us in the relationship, and if one person doesn't want to try, then it doesn't matter what the other one does. Nick didn't want to try. Can we change the subject now? I've made my decision about Nick, and I've made my decision about moving to London. I'll be gone in a week and it will be a while before we see each other again. I don't want to spend this time arguing with you. It's my life, and I will do what I think is best for me. I'd appreciate it if you'd be happy for me."

Her parents looked at her, and for the first time ever, they were speechless. There was no further criticism of her decision, no mention of her not being the best judge when it came to what was right for her. After everything she'd gone through in the past few months with Nick, standing up to her parents had been easier than she thought. She wished she'd done it a long time ago. She knew, though, that without the weekend at Mt Tamborine, she wouldn't have done it. Nor would she be moving to London, and she wouldn't have left Nick. She owed a lot to that weekend, and even though her friendships had changed since then, she couldn't help but think that maybe they were in a better place than they were before.

"I've always wanted to see London," her mum said. "Maybe we could visit sometime."

"That would be nice," Evie said.

She knew them well enough to know they wouldn't change and that there would still be criticism in the future, but at least their relationship was finally heading in a direction she was comfortable with.

Evie looked at the suitcase lying open on the bed. It was the last one. Deciding what to take with her and what to leave in storage had been hard. Not as hard as the fights with Nick over what she could take from their house, but still hard. Even though she had dreamt of doing this for such a long time, she felt nervous now that the reality was here. It was a big change, moving to the other side of the world where she didn't know anyone and where she would be on her own for the first time in her adult life. She still thought about Nick a lot, and she was still sad that things hadn't worked out, that it hadn't been the marriage she'd wanted it to be. But as each day went by, any doubts she'd had about her decision became less and less. The way he'd reacted when they were both still living in the house had erased the last ten per cent of doubt about going through with the divorce. The way he behaved had shocked her, even though she was used to his tantrums. He'd been so angry, and when she thought about it later, he'd been angrier at the fact that she was the one ending their relationship, not that it was ending. "You don't leave me," he'd yelled during one of their arguments. But she'd stood her ground for the first time in a long time. She hadn't yelled. She hadn't traded insults or banged her fists on the table. She'd waited until he'd finished and told him she'd made her decision. He'd started again, telling her she wouldn't cope without him, that she wasn't capable of making the right decision for herself. She'd come crawling back before too long, but when she did, he would say no. There were a few moments when she'd wondered if he was right, but she dismissed those thoughts. She deserved better, and now she wanted better. All her life, she'd wanted to be in a truly loving relationship and from now on, she wasn't going to settle for anything less, no matter how long it took to find it.

On her last night in Brisbane, Gaby organised a farewell dinner.

"I can't believe you're actually going," Anna said. "It's going to be so exciting."

"And scary," Evie said. "I'm going to the other side of the world by myself. I've wanted to do this for so long, and it's finally happening."

"That's because you made it happen," Gaby said. "You've turned your life around in the past few months and you've done it yourself."

"With help and encouragement from you all. If we hadn't gone away that weekend and shared our secrets like we did, I don't know if I'd be doing this. That gave me the courage to take those first steps."

And all the steps that followed. There had been so many changes in her life over the past few months that Evie sometimes had to stop and say to herself that it really was her life.

Evie looked around the table at her friends. "I need to know something before I go. Is everything ok between us all? I know a lot has happened since our weekend away, and we've all spoken and seen each other a lot, but I just want to make absolutely sure before I go. After tomorrow I can't just drop in and see any of you for a coffee or catch up for dinner."

"As far as I'm concerned, we are," Anna said.

Gaby nodded. "That goes for me too."

Evie looked at Laura and waited for her to speak. She'd been confident that things were ok with Gaby and Anna, but she wasn't as sure about Laura.

"I assume you both know that Evie and I haven't sorted things out the way you both have. That's actually my fault. It's not because I'm still angry with her. It's because I'm angry at myself."

Gaby and Anna looked at each other and then at Laura.

"Why would you be angry with yourself?" Anna asked.

"Because I wasn't completely honest either, and it's very hypocritical of me to be angry at Evie when I did exactly the same thing."

"So you left out part of your story as well?" Gaby asked.

Laura nodded.

"And what part would that be?" Gaby asked.

"There have been a couple of times where I've had more to drink than I should have. More, like what I used to have."

"I wondered why you weren't drinking tonight," Anna said. "I assume that's the reason?"

Laura nodded and then filled Anna and Gaby in on what she'd told Evie, and as hard as Anna tried, she couldn't hide the shock on her face. "Why didn't you tell me?"

"I was ashamed about what I was doing and that I didn't have the willpower to stop. And I kept thinking every time it happened, it was the last time, so I didn't need to say anything because I wouldn't do it again."

"If you'd told us, we could have helped," Gaby said. "In case you've forgotten, my mother's had a drinking problem her whole life. I'm the last person to be shocked about that."

"Yes, I remember, but I still didn't say anything. There is nothing I can do about it now. Evie did offer to help after she found out, but I kept pushing her away."

Evie looked over at Laura and saw how upset she was and reached over and held Laura's hand. "As far as I'm concerned, Laura and I are ok. I understand why she left part of the story out because I felt the same way. I was ashamed of what I was doing, and I didn't want anyone to know. If you need to take longer to be ok with Laura leaving out part of her story, then that's what you need to do. I'm leaving tomorrow, and I want everything to be ok between the three of you and me before I go."

"Things are ok between you and us," Gaby said. "I don't think anyone would disagree with that. Am I right?"

Laura and Anna nodded their heads.

"And everything will be fine between Laura and us too. We'll sort things out and help Laura if she wants us to. In the meantime, tonight is about you."

Anna nodded. "We can't spend our last dinner with you for who knows how long dwelling on things we can't change. But

Laura, that doesn't mean I'm not upset about the fact that you still lied. We've had a lot of conversations since that weekend and I've told you so many things. I can't believe you kept something back and haven't been as open with me as I have been with you."

"I'm sorry Anna. I didn't mean to upset you, and you're right. It isn't fair that you've shared a lot more with me than I have with you. I promise I won't do that anymore, and I'll tell you everything."

"That's a start," Anna said. "For now, let's focus on Evie."

So they spent Evie's last night in Brisbane talking about the new life she was about to embark on.

"It's such a long way from home," Evie said. "And I won't know anyone except the sister of the person from work."

"You'll be fine," Gaby said. "You'll meet people soon enough. And remember, we're only at the other end of the phone if you need us."

"Or the computer," Laura said. "This opportunity may never come again."

Evie knew they were right. She'd just waited so long to do this, and it was the first time she'd done something so big on her own. It made her a little nervous.

The next morning Evie looked at her friends standing there with her in the crowded airport. Barely a moment went by when one of them wasn't hugging her. Or crying. Or both. Evie wasn't sure what people around them must have thought, but she didn't care.

"I know I said it last night, but I still can't believe you're going," Anna said, finally letting Evie go after a hug that seemed to last forever.

"But even though we're sad you're leaving, we're also glad you're following your dream," Gaby said.

Laura nodded. "And you know we'll come and visit. As often as we can."

Evie smiled. "I'd love that. I don't know what I'm going to do without all of you."

"We're here anytime you need us," Gaby said. "We're just a bit further away."

Evie laughed. "I don't think the distance I'm travelling could be called a bit further away."

Gaby laughed too. "Ok, a twenty-three-hour flight then."

"One which even I will do," Anna said, her fear of flying well known.

Evie hugged her again. "Thank you."

She hadn't invited anyone else to the airport. There was no one else she wanted to spend these last moments with before she headed off.

She'd had breakfast with her parents that morning, and even on the last day she would see them for a while, they still had some questions about her decision and her plans. Not as many as they previously had though. She couldn't hope for a miracle, but at least there were moments when it seemed they were coming around to being ok with her decisions. She'd asked them not to come to the airport. She'd told them it was because she would find it too upsetting, and that was true. They thought it was because she didn't want to say goodbye to them there, and she let them believe that. In reality, she didn't want to give them one last chance to say something negative. Just because they were improving didn't mean they had changed so much that they wouldn't take the opportunity to say something in person before she left.

She hadn't heard from Nick for a long time, and she wasn't expecting to hear from him that morning. He knew she was leaving, but even after the years they'd spent together, he couldn't put aside his anger to wish her well. She wasn't surprised. He just wasn't that type of person. He was the type who had texted her every second day when he'd first moved to his brother's to tell her, over and over again, how she'd fail and that she wasn't capable of doing anything on her own. She responded the first few times but then stopped and deleted all the messages. And as each new message appeared on her phone, she deleted those too. Eventually, she stopped receiving them. She'd already heard from mutual friends that he was telling everyone it was all her fault and that she must be having some sort of mid-life crisis. It was typical of him to blame her rather than admit it had anything to do with him. But the people who knew her, and were important to her, didn't believe his words. That was all that mattered. That and the fact she was finally standing at the airport. What she had dreamt of for so long was finally happening. The changes she'd made since that weekend had made it possible. She'd thought about that weekend a lot, along with the things that had happened after. Even though they'd all had secrets to share that had made a significant impact in their lives, they'd all come through ok for the most part, and so had she. She hadn't been tempted to take a tablet for a while, and she hoped it would stay that way even with the big life change she was about to embark on. If she ever needed support, it would be there at the other end of the phone. If she could take anything with her, it was the fact that her friends were standing there, wishing her the best and feeling genuinely happy for her. That was worth more than any chemically induced happiness.

The time at the airport went quickly, and before she knew it, she had gone through customs and was hearing the boarding call for her flight. Her phone beeped. There was a message saying turn around. She looked up and saw Gaby, Anna and Laura holding a sign that said *We'll miss you!* Evie took a photo and waved before turning away and walking toward her departure gate. There was one spare space in the picture frame that she'd packed, and that was where the photo would go. Right between the photo Laura had taken and the drawing she'd done of the four of them on their weekend in Mt Tamborine.

Shelley Banks is a passionate writer who enjoys creating a story that will entertain readers. She is the author of two full length novels - One Weekend and The Diary and the Green Dress.

She is also the author of three fiction and non-fiction short reads - Short, Sweet and September, Short, Sweet and September – The Second One and Short, Sweet and September - The Third One.

Shelley is also the author of September Sprouts a monthly fiction and non-fiction blog that encourages you to read something you might not normally read. Who knows – you might find yourself smiling, laughing or being reminded about something good in your life.

She has a Bachelor of Arts (Communications), majoring in creative writing.

Shelley lives in Brisbane, Queensland, Australia.

You can contact Shelley via:

Facebook https://www.facebook.com/writershellb/

Instagram https://www.instagram.com/writershellb/

Made in the USA
Middletown, DE
24 October 2023

41353719R00223